Melanie

CANDLELIGHT REGENCY SPECIAL

CANDLELIGHT ROMANCES

THE
CAPTIVE BRIDE

Lucy Phillips Stewart

A CANDLELIGHT REGENCY SPECIAL

Published by
Dell Publishing Co., Inc.
1 Dag Hammarskjold Plaza
New York, New York 10017

Dell ® TM 681510, Dell Publishing Co., Inc.
ISBN: 0-440-17768-5
Printed in the United States of America
First printing—March 1978

CHAPTER ONE

The sound of horses traveling fast drew the attention of the passengers to a curricle-and-four sweeping around the ponderous accommodation coach. Miss Redding, unfailingly curious, and unable to restrain the impulse, craned her head from the window to gaze in admiration at the magnificently matched chestnuts thundering by. The gentleman in the curricle, quite heedless of the narrowness of the road, and easily controlling his horses, checked their breakneck speed and swung to the in, effectively blocking the highway before the coach. The dragsman, forced to haul his team to a plunging standstill, could only shake his fist at the smart equipage drawn up across the road.

Miss Redding had time to observe the gentleman as he leisurely descended from the curricle. From his beaver hat set at a jaunty angle to his gleaming Hessian boots, he was the epitome of fashion. The cut of his coat, the arrangement of his cravat, indeed his whole aspect, proclaimed him the dandy. But one could not be misled. He had the look of a man, strong and masculine. Annette had to own him handsome, quite the handsomest creature she had ever seen.

He was very soon beside the coach, his cold eyes raking her face. Their expression made her aware of her unladylike posture; she withdrew her head in some confusion. His disdainful glance, indeed his whole bearing, put her sadly out of countenance—she found no difficulty in taking exception to his person. Her chagrin found expression: she turned her head away and affected indifference.

He pulled open the door, his steely gaze sweeping the passengers. "Is Miss Redding among your number?"

Annette shrank against the faded squabs. With a lowering presentiment, the certainty of his identity took possession of her brain: he was the Earl of Ardley, Papa's relative whose largess she had refused. Her slight movement drawing his attention, his eyes fastened on her face. "I would presume you are she?"

"W-who are you?" Annette managed to stammer, aware of the shabby appearance her cloak and plain cambric gown must present to this fastidious dandy.

"Ardley," came his prompt reply. Stepping back a pace, he held out one elegantly gloved hand. "Come," he said abruptly.

Annette was annoyed. Not accustomed to being addressed in such a manner, the indignity of the situation did nothing to improve her temper. "I do not in the least understand why I should," she snapped.

"Miss Redding, you will oblige me in this."

Raising her brows, she prepared to do battle. "Is that a command?"

"I have avoided giving it the appearance of one."

Annette unaccountably became interested in a contemplation of the scenery beyond his shoulder. "Thank you, my lord, but I will remain where I am."

His lips set firmly, he surveyed her from under weary lids. "You are mistaken in that, Miss Redding."

Meeting his eyes with a look of withering contempt, she was perfectly certain he would exert force if necessary to attain his purpose. The Earl looked at her meditatively but merely raised his brows. He said, "You will notice that I am waiting."

Annette bit back the retort rising to her lips. There was nothing conciliating in his manner, nothing relenting in his devastating glance. Beneath his air of negligent languor dwelt a strength quite beyond her ability to overcome.

She allowed him to assist her to the ground, and, contriving to present an icy countenance, swept before him to the curricle. His hand beneath her elbow elicited from her an angry speech: "I don't need your help," she said fiercely, then gasped as her waist was encircled in an iron grip and she found herself tossed up and onto the seat. Quivering with anger, she sat rigidly erect; to give vent to her thoughts would be undignified, to speak with civility was impossible.

The chestnuts, skillfully turned, were soon trotting back along the way they had come. Annette remained silent and tried to ignore the masculine presence so close to her shoulder, but she found herself admiring his curling black hair and well-chiseled features.

He allowed several miles to flash by before remarking, "You are perhaps admiring my cattle."

Flushing slightly, she could not easily reorder her thoughts. "They are beautifully mouthed," she finally said, for seldom had she been privileged to ride behind such outstanding horseflesh.

He turned his head to glance at her in surprise. "You appear to have an understanding uncommon in a female."

"Not all females are without intelligence!"

He regarded her quizzically for several minutes. "Miss Redding, since our association appears inevitable, we may as well be civil." When she chose to ignore this overture, he lazily continued: "You may perhaps prefer to be moving in the opposite direction."

Annette's cold blue eyes met his cool gray ones for a moment in a look that would have quelled many gentlemen. His lordship was not impressed.

But she could not remain mute indefinitely. She said with a proper resignation, "Please have the goodness to tell me our destination."

"We are en route to London."

"London! But I have no lodgings in London."

"You will lodge with me." Glancing briefly at her incredulous face, he added, "I trust you find that to your liking."

"I may be an ignorant country girl, my lord, and unacquainted with city ways, but I will inform you—"

"My great-aunt is residing at Ardley House, Miss Redding. You will find her chaperonage adequate."

She bit her lip. The man was insufferable.

He regarded her momentarily, then said kindly, "I am aware of your desire for independence—indeed, I applaud your sentiments—but you will appreciate my position. You are my relative, Miss Redding, however distant. As head of our house, it would be unthinkable for me to permit you to become a governess."

Annette searched her mind for a suitable retort. None came. She could only remark, "It is an odd thing that one's duty should invariably be so disagreeable."

A flicker of a smile twitched at the corners of his lips. "I am not going to make your life unbearable, Miss Redding. Indeed, I shall contrive to make myself pleasant."

"I am beginning to think you delight in casting aside my wishes."

"I cannot admit that to be true. I am not at all delighted."

Annette allowed the remark to pass. It was evident that objections to his high-handed behavior would fall on deaf ears, and she had to admit life as a governess was scarcely alluring. If she must cease her objections, she would salvage her pride. Accordingly, she said, "We will come to an agreement, my lord."

"By all means," he promptly acquiesced.

"I will accept your largess, however unhappily, but I will earn my way. Having cared for my father's establishment since an early age, I am able to assure you of my accomplishments in the household arts."

"You are no doubt efficient," he murmured helpfully.

"Thank you, my lord. I think you will not be disappointed, for I am able to inform you that I am a passable cook. Also I—"

"You are extremely obliging, Miss Redding, but I engage a staff of servants to see to the housekeeping." His smile gleamed. "There are, however, other duties at your disposal. Aunt has on occasion graced my table as hostess, but you will fill this office in a more decorative manner."

Blushing furiously, she dropped her eyes. Ardley studied her at his leisure, his gaze lingering on the whiteness of her skin contrasting with the blackness of her hair. God, what a beauty, he thought, as long and curling lashes trembled against her cheeks.

"Shall we consider the matter settled?" he suggested gently.

"Yes," she whispered. "I will consider myself honored to act as your hostess."

"Good. Now may we enjoy the drive?"

The chestnuts had been steadily maintaining their

speed without visibly tiring. Annette thrilled to their surge of power as the Earl dropped his hands, giving them their heads. It seemed to her they fairly flew over the ground. Had she been looking, she would have surprised a strange expression in his eyes as he gazed down at her.

The outskirts of the metropolis came into sight; Annette fairly bounced on her seat at the strange sights and sounds assailing her senses. It seemed to her that all too soon the curricle drew up before an imposing edifice. She had time only to glance in wonder before the groom was at the wheel-horses' heads and the Earl was assisting her to alight.

"Bring in the trunk, Watkins," he instructed the butler hurrying down the steps. Glancing up, he stiffened as he stared across the street. Sensing his tension, Annette followed the direction of his eyes and saw a fashionably dressed dandy bowing as he strolled along the walk. Ardley returned the courtesy, then turned and escorted her up the steps and through the door.

As she walked into the marble hall, Annette felt a moment of panic. She could not feel it seemly to comment before the servants and so contented herself with gazing around. Never had she seen such luxury.

"You must be tired," the Earl spoke at her elbow. "You will perhaps wish dinner in your rooms?"

"It has been a longish day."

Turning to the butler, he said, "Miss Redding will occupy the yellow suite, Watkins. And will you be so good as to inform Mrs. Williams she is to attend me immediately."

"Very good, m'lord." Watkins bowed. "Will your lordship desire refreshment brought to the library?"

The Earl looked at Annette with a questioning

look in his eyes. "Would you care for a cup of tea, Miss Redding?"

Declining this offer, she allowed herself to be escorted to the library, and, settling into a leather chair, folded her hands carefully. Without a very clear notion of what a wealthy man's residence would be, she had never imagined anything even remotely approaching the reality of the Earl's home. From what she had seen of it thus far, which admittedly was not much, the habitation most certainly must be quite large, though why a single gentleman should need a mansion she did not in the least know.

"Ah, yes, Mrs. Williams. Come in," the Earl spoke in his lazy way. "Miss Redding will be lodging with us. Her trunk has been taken to the yellow suite. You will assist her in settling in and assign a maid to her personal service."

"I'm—we're related, you see," Annette said in a rush, acutely aware of the housekeeper's thinking. "Actually, I had engaged to become—" Seeing the expression in the Earl's eyes, she stopped short.

"Miss Redding will now retire, Mrs. Williams. She will dine in her rooms."

CHAPTER TWO

It was past noon of the following day before Annette approached the library in the wake of a footman. The events of the past twenty-four hours had left her brain in a whirl, and, to cap all, the luxury of her rooms took her breath away. She was impressed by the size of her sitting room and could only feel awed by the noble proportions of her bedroom. The furnishings were to her taste, the pictures and art objects scattered about admirable in every respect. Having partaken of luncheon, she had received the information that his lordship sent his compliments and waited the pleasure of her company.

She was always to remember that interview, of crossing the threshold, her steps faltering to a halt as the Earl rose from his desk and stood looking at her with what she could only suppose to be an unusual sternness. This reception not being what she expected, she made no move to cross to his side, but stood waiting for him to speak. He knew only too well that what he had to say was of an extreme delicacy and had been wondering how it could be handled to spare her as much humiliation as possible. Finally raising his eyes to her face, he was surprised to hear himself inquiring if she had spent a restful night. Having disposed of this inane civility, he further surprised himself by inquiring if she had enjoyed her luncheon.

It was Annette who took the initiative. She inquired, "Did you wish to see me on a matter of importance, my lord?"

"I did." He spoke firmly, knowing he could not longer delay his disclosure. "You will remember I informed you my aunt was in residence to act as chaperone? It seems I was mistaken, Miss Redding. I cannot express to you my regret at finding this to be untrue." Pausing, he glanced at her, then hastily averted his eyes from the shock he read in her face.

"But—I d-don't understand," Annette stammered.

"My aunt is not just now in the house. I have been away and did not know her intention."

"Her intention?" she whispered, feeling suffocated. Must I continue to stupidly parrot his words? she wondered somewhat hysterically. Feeling her legs would not support her, she sank onto a chair.

"She is away visiting an elderly friend. This puts us in an awkward position." Holding her eyes with the steel of his gaze, he added, "I have a solution to put to you."

"Perhaps the position of governess will be—"

"Disabuse your mind of that notion. I will never agree to such a scheme."

"I do not need your permission."

He gave no sign of having heard. Instead, he paced to the window to stand with his back to the room. At any other time Annette would have enjoyed the sight of his close-fitting coat of superfine beautifully molding broad shoulders. She might even have admired the tight pantaloons hugging his muscular thighs. And she surely would have noticed the shining Hessians with their little golden tassels bouncing merrily with each movement he made. As it was, she sat rooted to the spot and felt her mind to be reeling.

Abruptly he crossed to seat himself facing her. "In

bringing you to my establishment, I sought to secure your financial situation. By having you remain here overnight, in circumstances of which I was unaware, I have jeopardized your reputation. I have taken steps to set this right."

An angry flush rose in her cheeks. "I will take my own steps, my lord. I will contrive to leave immediately—"

Ignoring this outburst, he continued imperturbably: "I have procured a special license, Miss Redding. We will be married immediately."

Annette stared at him, dumbfounded. "You cannot have said—surely you cannot imagine that I—"

His glance swept her face. "Our arrival last evening was witnessed by Lord Bodkin."

"What can he possibly have to do—"

"Lord Bodkin has been most accurately described as England's foremost gossip."

"Oh!" she groaned, tears starting to her eyes. "There is some mistake! There must be some mistake!"

"Possibly. But it was not of our making."

Her fierce glance met his in a look that spoke volumes. "I refuse to marry you," she declared in a shaking voice.

"We will consider that remark unsaid. I have this morning made arrangements for the ceremony to take place at two o'clock this afternoon."

"Will you listen—"

"I would be pleased to do so indefinitely if I thought something was to be gained by it." He added in a kindly tone, "You will not find me difficult, Miss Redding. I trust I will not find myself obliged to interfere overmuch in your life."

"Thank you," she said witheringly.

"The story the world will hear is this: Having conceived a mutual regard, we became betrothed, but due to your father's illness, postponed publishing the banns until such time as he should recover. But as events unhappily transpired, we have been quietly married, thereby fulfilling our promise made to your father shortly before his death. We have now removed to London to live quietly while observing the customary period of mourning."

Annette, with a haughtiness that concealed an inner trembling, said tartly, "Are you quite sure you have not left something out? Or have you not thought to consider my sensibilities."

"When you know me better, you will realize I forget nothing." He studied her meditatively, then drew a gold, enameled snuffbox from his pocket. Flicking it open, he took a pinch between finger and thumb. "It is my intention to remain your husband in name only, Miss Redding."

There was nothing left for Annette to do but blush. Which she did. Profusely.

"I felt it inadvisable to send to the dressmaker for a wedding gown, our nuptials having already taken place," he added without a trace of emotion in his level voice.

Under the circumstances it was scarcely surprising that she felt she was being bullocked, though she was honest enough to concede he was doubtless acting in her best interests. This admission brought another thought to mind—his lordship had fallen willy-nilly into the same troubled waters in which she found herself. He had no more wish to marry than she.

Her first impulse was to cry off; she could swoon, or become ill of some dreadful and quite incurable disease. She could take to her bed and remain there, the hapless victim of a veritable parade of aches and pains, their exact identity as yet unformed. An overworked ploy, yes, and, on reflection, she was forced to admit it would not serve.

Watkins entered the room and approached the Earl. "A box has just been delivered from the greenhouses, m'lord. If I may say so, I felt your lordship would wish it placed in your hands without delay."

If the butler hoped for further information of the coming nuptials, he was doomed to disappointment. The Earl merely said, "Thank you, Watkins," leaving him no choice but to leave the room sedately.

He left silence behind him, broken only by the rustling of floral tissue. "Will you carry these?" the Earl said quietly to Annette, holding out a bouquet of white orchids.

"They are beautiful," she murmured, bending over the blossoms to hide her confusion. "Thank you," she added softly, her cheeks pink as she placed her fingers on his arm and walked beside him from the house.

She was surprised by the coach drawn up before the door. A hired conveyance pulled by weary horses, there was nothing to distinguish it from the many of its kind seen about the poorer sections of the city. Sitting beside the Earl, she knew his eyes were on her face, but felt self-conscious and shy and could think of nothing to say.

"I thought it wise to travel as inconspicuously as possible," he offered by way of explanation. "The ceremony will be performed in the vicar's private chapel."

Annette felt her pulses race. She wanted to reply but try as she would she could not put words to her tongue. It seemed to her that time stood still until they drew up before the church. Convulsively clutching her bouquet, she prepared to descend.

"Miss Redding," his voice halted her slight movement. "May I inquire your name?" he asked as her eyes flew to his face. "The vicar will need to know."

"Annette Elizabeth," she whispered rather breathlessly.

Without further comment, he assisted her to alight and led her through a side door where the priest awaited their arrival. Her hands felt icy but she was scarcely aware of it as she moved by his side up the aisle of the small sanctuary. Kneeling beside him, her mind in a whirl, she heard his name for the first time as he repeated his vows: "I, Drake Edward, take thee, Annette Elizabeth—"

Upon their return to Ardley House, they found the servants lined up in the hall. Watkins, ramrod stiff, his dignity unassailable, pompously intoned in his most salubrious voice: "On behalf of the staff, may I offer your lordship our most happy congratulations and extend to her ladyship our heartfelt good wishes."

The Earl thanked them with a few appropriate words and led Annette down the line, introducing her and chatting a moment with each retainer, Annette aware the whole time of his eyes on her.

Refreshments awaited them in the library. The doors were closed and he was handing her a glass of sherry before she became acutely aware of how alone they were. Holding her eyes over the rim of his glass, he toasted her: "To you, my dear." Startled, she flushed and hastily averted her eyes. She hadn't expected the endearment.

After a long moment of silence he spoke again. "I regret ours was not the wedding of your dreams."

There was something in the way he said the words that brought her eyes back to his face. "We should discuss our plans," he continued quietly. "Will you care to remain here, or is there another place you would prefer?"

Turning her head away, she said in a stifled voice, "It doesn't signify."

"But of course it does."

"You have done enough as it is, my lord. You have m-married me. The least I can do in return is to—"

"You are talking nonsense."

"I am trying to be fair, my lord."

"My name is Drake. You should now use it."

"My lord—"

Amusement gleamed in his eyes. "You have a short time ago promised to obey me."

"Oh!" she stormed. "I cannot be in your company above a minute but that you become provoking."

If anything this speech had the effect of deepening his amusement. "Let me assure you, my dear, there is not the least need for my absurdities to distress you."

"It is your self-consequence I find distressing!"

"You are forgetting my other somewhat reprehensible shortcomings. I am obstinate and self-centered, and shockingly overbearing."

"Are you laughing at me?" Annette shot at him, a martial gleam in her eye.

"No, not at all," he murmured, still with his slight smile. "I thought to assist you."

"This conversation may amuse you, my lord, but I am constrained to tell you I find it in excessively bad taste."

"To tell the truth, my dear, you were beginning to paint me the knight in shining armor. I assure you the comparison does not fit."

Annette controlled her tongue with a visible effort. "As it happens, my lord, I was attempting to express my gratitude."

The Earl fished his snuffbox from a pocket and took a pinch, studying her from between narrowed lids. "It is not your gratitude I wish," he murmured somewhat enigmatically.

She could not trust herself to speak. She briefly considered sweeping from the room, but the door was closed and she could place no dependence on its opening smoothly to permit her graceful exit. He was coolly watching her, and she suspected he would enjoy the spectacle she would present should she resort to missish posturings. She further had a decidedly uncomfortable premonition that he could read her thoughts.

"Shall we declare a truce?" he asked after a long moment. "As a rule married couples use the other's name."

It was on the tip of her tongue to comment, but she caught the gleam in his eye and remained silent.

"You will address me as Drake and I will name you Annette," he continued in his quiet way. "You are my wife and will accept what I can offer you with a good grace. Neither of us is experienced in matrimony, but we are intelligent people and should manage to deal well enough together. And now, Annette, we will speak no more about it. We will, instead, discuss our plans. I asked you before if you wished to remain here or would prefer to go elsewhere."

"Have you a preference?" she asked in a very small voice.

"I leave it entirely up to you, my dear. Would you perhaps enjoy to travel?"

"N-no. Not while in mourning."

"The country, then. We will depart for Monks-haven immediately your trousseau is ordered."

"Monkshaven?"

"My estate in Kent. This is not the best season for it, but, as you say, we are in mourning and will pass a time of quiet."

"Won't you find that dull?" she asked curiously.

His smile flashed. "Boredom may never again plague me."

Annette had fully intended to object if he again alluded to the ordering of a trousseau. But she soon found herself powerless to decline his polite insistence. It began the following morning when her maid brought the chocolate. "His lordship sends his compliments, my lady, and will be pleased to speak with you at your ladyship's convenience."

Annette was thoughtful as she descended the stairs. She wondered briefly what he wished to speak to her about, but put it from her mind as she paused before the library door. Should she knock before entering, or should she walk right in. Undecided, she finally rapped and stood waiting until his deep voice bade her enter.

"You are not a servant, my dear, to await admittance," he said after an uncomfortable pause. Raising his eyeglass, he watched her cross the floor, inspecting her carefully. "I thought I could not have been mistaken," he then said judiciously.

"I beg your pardon?"

"You will permit me to inform you that you pass muster most adequately."

Annette's eyes flashed. "How very odd of you!" she snapped.

"I will remind you, my dear, you will be the subject of a rude and reprehensible scrutiny wherever you go. It is my intention to assist you in becoming accustomed."

"It was my intention to greet you in a civil manner, my lord, but if you will have none of it, I am sure I do not in the least care. You have put me in the horridest position imaginable by forcing me to marry you, and now you send for me when in a disagreeable mood." She paused and took a deep breath. "No!" she said firmly. "I refuse to lose my temper."

"Beauty in distress," he murmured with perfect composure.

It was too absurd. Her smile quivered as she considered his methods. Laughing in appreciation, she said, "You are become most odious, my lord."

"Drake," he corrected with a marked politeness in his tone. "My dear, a decided air of consequence will win you a distinguishing notice. You will never display any emotion whatsoever." His smile gleamed. "You may save that treat for when we are alone."

"I had no idea marriage could produce such unnerving results. The cross must be more than you can bear."

"I can bear it," he said with gravity, lifting his brows a little. "I perceive that it is you who may find my authority irksome."

"Then you plan to use me abominably, my lord?"

"Drake." Eyes alight with laughter, he commented, "You may find it no great task to put your tongue around my name. It only requires the effort."

Annette picked up the gauntlet. "Drake," she said with perfect calm. "As you say, my lord, it is no great task."

A light tapping sounded on the door, it promptly opened, and a little lady came tripping in, crying a greeting in a chirping voice as she advanced across the room. Annette stared at the newcomer, quite struck with the vision she presented. Her gown of jaconet muslin was of a most peculiar shade of green, ruffled to the throat and buttoned beneath her chin. A pink bonnet perched atop improbably yellow hair, and framing the fuzz of curls peeping from beneath its straw, was tied beneath her chin with long, trailing ribands. High-heeled kid boots and a long-handled parasol completed the ensemble.

"My dear Ardley," she cried. "I am returned home."

"So I perceive," he returned dryly, bending perfunctorily over her hand. "I trust you are well?"

"Yes, dear boy, and excessively glad I am to be back. I cannot but think it odd, this preoccupation with one's constitution, for all it is becoming the fashion. How do you do, my dear," she said, noticing Annette. "Have we met?"

"Permit me the opportunity and I will perform that office," the Earl said with perfect honesty. "I am honored to make known to you my wife, the Countess of Ardley. Annette, this is my Aunt Agatha, Lady Hartford."

Annette curtsied as a pair of surprisingly bright eyes swept her slim form and moved again to the Earl in utter astonishment. "Good God!" Agatha said blankly.

"Thank you," the Earl murmured, showing no surprise.

"Ardley, have you gone mad? You cannot be married. Not above a week ago, you weren't."

"I am now."

Casting up her eyes, Agatha sank into a chair. "You are becoming more like your father every day. He could never make the least sense."

"Annette and I are married. Is that so difficult to grasp?"

Agatha's eyes moved to Annette. "Is this true?" she demanded. At Annette's timid nod, her gaze swung back to his face. "Well, if you wish to know what I think, there is something smoky about this, Ardley. Though I haven't the smallest doubt that you don't."

"You are not being courteous to Annette." He spoke quietly but an edge could be detected in his voice.

"I had no idea to infer any disparagement, I'm sure. She is lovely. But I must have the dressing of her." Turning to Annette, she continued: "Not that you do not present a pleasing aspect, my dear, for you do. It is just that you cannot appear in society until we have you the talk of fashion."

Annette's mind was in a whirl. She did not wish to appear impolite, but she could not believe it would rebound to her credit to appear in public duplicating the very odd appearance Aunt Agatha presented. Apparently the Earl was of a like mind, for he bowed to his relative and politely declined her services, stating his intention of himself leading Annette through the byways of the fashion world. It did no good to protest, she soon discovered, for he bore her off and guided her from dressmaker to dressmaker, and to the bootmaker's, the milliner's, and to every sort of warehouse catering to the garbing of a lady. She stood patiently still through the ordeal of the measuring, allowed one gown after another to be whisked over her head, and paraded before his inspection, like a prize boar at the county fair, she thought with some humor.

When they returned home to Grosvenor Square, they found Aunt Agatha eagerly awaiting their arrival and demanding in her impetuous fashion to know whom they had seen and where they had gone. Annette was relieved to have the Earl carry the conversation.

"What!" Agatha cried, startling Annette's attention back to what they were saying. "I cannot have heard you correctly!"

"My meaning cannot have been obscure," the Earl replied. "I was under the impression my words were quite precise."

"But you can't run off now. What will people think?"

"They will think what we tell them. But we wander from the point. If you wish to accompany Annette and myself, you are of course at leisure to do so. However, I must add that we will not press you, if such is not your pleasure."

"You cannot be suggesting that I set foot in that dreadful pile, Ardley. For you know very well that I will not."

"In that case—"

"Have you told Annette?"

He lifted one well-manicured hand to gaze at a finger. "There is nothing to tell. You have allowed your imagination to get the better of you."

CHAPTER THREE

Annette had finished dressing and was gazing at her reflection in the long mirror. Never had she expected to possess so becoming a gown. The yellow muslin transformed her, molding her slender form in the most fetching way imaginable.

"His lordship has sent jewelry, my lady," her maid said, holding out a velvet box.

Annette stared in astonishment at the jewels glittering in the light. Lifting out a necklace, she stroked the topaz stones, then bent her head for Marie to fasten the golden chain. Clasping a bracelet about her wrist, she slipped a ring on her finger and leaned back to study the effect.

A tap on the door drawing their attention, Marie crossed to open it and admit Mrs. Williams. "Lady Hartford sends word that Lord Bodkin has come to call, my lady. They await your ladyship in the drawing room."

"Oh, dear," Annette murmured faintly. "Is it not early to be receiving callers?"

"I believe Lord Bodkin has informed her ladyship that he could not wait to make your ladyship's acquaintance."

"Very well, Mrs. Williams. I will be down shortly." Turning back to the mirror, Annette slowly removed the necklace and bracelet, but left the ring on her hand. Lord Bodkin! I will ask Drake, she thought. She knew his rooms were just beyond her own. Crossing to the connecting door, she tapped lightly and hurried through. "Drake," she began, then stopped short, mortified to find herself, not in his sitting room as she had expected, but in his bedroom.

He was seated in a chair, a square of linen covering his shoulders, his face partially lathered. His valet stood beside him, the razor suspended in midair, as both men stared in surprise.

"Oh," Annette gasped. "I—d-didn't mean to—"

"Please be seated, my dear," he said calmly. "I will be with you in a moment."

Fisher moved a chair forward for her and she sank into it, only too conscious of the large, canopied bed and wishing herself anywhere but where she was.

His duties finished, the valet discreetly bowed himself out. After glancing at her averted face, Drake strolled across to take a seat and leaned back at ease. "And now, my dear, how may I serve you?" he asked pleasantly in a voice designed to put her at ease.

Her embarrassed gaze flitted to his face. "I am s-sorry—"

"Nonsense. You have every right to enter my rooms. May I say you are looking lovely this morning?"

"Thank you for the jewelry," she said, his matter-of-fact attitude putting her more at ease. Holding out her hand, she gazed with delight at the ring. "Oh, Drake, it is so beautiful. I've never had any jewelry before," she added honestly.

"I'm glad you are pleased. Was this what you wished to discuss?"

"I came to tell you Lord Bodkin has come to call."

He stared at her a moment, then smiled encouragingly. "We will go down together."

"Why has he come?"

"To pry, of course. He will leave with nothing to

report, other than the state of our conjugal bliss." His smile flashed. "Aunt Agatha will enjoy helping us face him down."

"Drake, why does she not wish to visit Monkshaven?"

"Though there is not the slightest reason, she believes it to be haunted, by whom she is not quite certain. Some local superstition, I should suppose."

"Then you do not think—"

"It would surprise me very much. I have no scruple in agreeing that a part of Monkshaven is ancient and would seem a likely habitation for alien spirits, at least to the extent that anyone is inclined to believe in such things. I, myself, am not so inclined."

"I daresay you are right." Annette began to fidget, wondering how long they would remain in his bedroom.

Sensing her discomfort, he said, "We will join our guest at eleven o'clock. If he chooses to call at a very early hour, he must await our pleasure. We will not be annoyed with further callers, Annette. I will instruct Watkins we are not at home. And that reminds me. We will depart for Monkshaven in three days' time, if this meets with your approval."

"That sounds entirely reasonable."

"A groom will follow with your additional wardrobe when it is delivered from the dressmaker."

"That puts me in mind of what I have been intending to say to you, Drake. I am sensible of your kindness in bestowing on me such lovely clothing, and now the jewelry, and—"

"Don't mention it, pray."

"But I must. I want to thank you—"

"My dear, a husband customarily supplies his wife's needs."

"Yes, I know that. But our marriage—" Annette faltered to a halt. She was about to be indelicate.

The Earl glanced at her with amusement in his eyes and seemed on the verge of making some remark. Thinking better of it, he stood to remove his dressing gown and toss it on the bed. Taking his coat from a hanger, he shrugged into it, and studied his reflection in the long mirror. Satisfied, he smiled at her. "Shall we proceed downstairs?" he asked, crossing to the door and standing back for her to go first.

"It is eleven?" she murmured, reluctant to face Lord Bodkin, before walking with a purposeful stride to precede him from the room.

He sauntered in his leisurely fashion down the stairs, his hand comfortingly beneath her elbow. As they neared the hall, her step unconsciously slowed as she thought of the coming ordeal.

"Faint heart?" he murmured provocatively, then chuckled at her instant glare. "Much better," he approved, leading her forward into the salon.

As they moved down the carpet, Annette was obliged to raise her eyes; she could scarcely forbear to laugh, for surely there could be no stranger sight. He could not appear more ridiculous, this exquisite leaning toward Agatha with so much affectation. The points of a monstrous neckcloth rose so high on his cheeks as to render unlikely the turning of his head more than an inch or two to either side. He could not be better, Annette thought, enjoying the largest buttons she had ever seen on any coat.

She scarcely took in Drake's courteous introduction from experiencing a moment's fear at the relish written all over Lord Bodkin's face. "So," he purred. "The little bride."

"I am pleased, my lord," she managed with a confidence she was far from feeling. "It has been some time now since I have been described as little."

"And a good thing that is, with Ardley so tall," Agatha broke in, much to Annette's relief. Glancing at her, Annette liked what she saw. Agatha was smiling pleasantly but her eyes rested on Lord Bodkin with what one could only suppose to be disdain, certainly a credential in Annette's rising opinion of Drake's relative.

The Earl's gray eyes were steadily on Lord Bodkin in a way his lordship could not read. He wondered if he had gone too far. You could never tell with Ardley; he baffled one with his air of easygoing indifference that could turn to steel when least expected. The man betrayed nothing but could withdraw behind an icy contempt as incalculable as it was damaging. It would be pleasant to whisper in Polite Circles, to bring low the haughty Earl. But Ardley had an uncanny way of turning the tables which Lord Bodkin suddenly felt disinclined to challenge. He would need to be careful; he had no wish to alienate so powerful a man.

But the habits of a lifetime are not so easily quelled. He quickly forgot the wisdom of his musings of scant moments before. "I had no idea you were about to enter the married state, Ardley," he intemperately remarked.

The Earl raised his brows. "Is there any reason why you should?"

"Well, no, now you mention it." Lord Bodkin plunged heedlessly on. "It is a romance, then?"

"Really, sir," Agatha broke in, "what can you be thinking of, to talk like this? Of course it is a romance. How could you imagine else. Annette and Ardley had been secretly betrothed."

"Secretly?" Lord Bodkin whispered, a world of insinuation in his tone.

"How could it have been otherwise with Annette's father grievously ill?" the Earl said flatly.

"Well, I am sure that is very interesting, but I would have expected some announcement to appear," Lord Bodkin sniggered.

"Not at all," the Earl returned levelly. "Lord Redding's illness unhappily terminated in his death."

Lord Bodkin had the grace to extend his sympathy to Annette, his eyes lingering for a moment on her face. He then turned his attention back to the Earl. "May I inquire, my lord, when you found time to marry?"

Annette and Agatha marveled at his control as Drake answered with outward calm. "To ease Lord Redding's passing, we informed him of our attachment and promised to wed immediately following the interment. It will forever rebound to Annette's credit that she followed her father's wishes."

"Secretly married, you say?"

The Earl's tone was suddenly cold. "No, I did not say we were secretly married. I said we were quietly married. You may find it in your interest, Bodkin, to choose your words with care."

"I feel confident he will wish to do so," Agatha said sweetly. "As you know, Lord Bodkin, Lady Jersey is a particular friend of mine. While some may find her frightening, she can be charming to those whom she considers socially acceptable."

It was a threat and Lord Bodkin knew it. Holding the town enthralled, agog and hanging on his every word, was a dream to be abandoned with the greatest reluctance. "I am sure one must be delighted with Lady Jersey's condescension," he simpered.

The Earl's lip curled imperceptibly as his glance flicked over Bodkin's face. "What a fool you are," he said in tones of exquisite boredom.

"Pray, my lord, how am I to take that?" Lord Bodkin demanded.

"I was not aware of being enigmatic," the Earl replied acidly.

Bodkin seemed to shrink against his chair. One might almost suppose Ardley bent on forcing a quarrel. The thought sent a quiver of fear through him. "I—really, my lord, I protest I do not un-understand."

A humorless smile touched the Earl's lips. "Do not take alarm," he drawled in a deceptively quiet voice. "I do not plan to call you out—yet. But you will be wise to consider the results should you continue your unwelcome interest in my affairs."

"No. No, of course not. I assure you—" Lord Bodkin ran the tip of his tongue over suddenly parched lips. "Do not take offense, I beg you. I shan't discuss your affairs—"

The Earl gave a wry smile. "I am glad to hear it. I'm done with you, Bodkin, so long as you quell your poisonous tongue."

This speech had a powerful effect on Lord Bodkin. He beat a hasty retreat; indeed, he got himself from the room in record time, and in a very brief span of minutes his carriage could be heard moving away from the house at a speed considered excessive for city streets.

"He is the most detestable creature I have ever met," Annette declared with feeling.

"Yes, love," Agatha agreed, patting Annette's hand. "I'd scarce noticed before, I must admit. But then he is not in the common way of being present at most assemblies. I declare I now see why."

Agatha was not, as a general rule, loath of plain speaking, but in this instance she found herself lacking the courage to pursue the subject of her nephew's marriage. While she had in the past enjoyed a fair deal of Ardley's confidence, she felt he might now deliver a most unpleasant snub should she trespass on forbidden ground. With this in mind, she settled down to discuss the latest fashions until he bore Annette off in search of breakfast.

Alone in the salon, Agatha sorted out her thoughts. She had urged him to marry, and while she could not flatter herself that her influence was such as to precipitate his compliance with her wishes, she had pointed out on several occasions, though discreetly, that he would require a wife to produce an heir. What she had not ventured to say was that a wife's influence could be all to the good. While he did not conduct himself with quite the abandon exhibited by many of his contemporaries, still she was well aware of his relation with certain "bits of muslin" and knew also of his involvements with other ladies, though it was to his credit that these women were invariably married and certainly knew what they were about.

So now what could be the matter with the man, she wondered, for she was well aware of the state of affairs. She had always known what was going on in the house; it was not to be wondered that she would. Returning home to find him married had been a surprise, for all he had never discussed his amorous adventures, but this had been nothing to compare with the astonishment in store. Establishing a girl in the house—how the servants must have twittered, she thought, momentarily diverted—he had departed for his club, not returning until the dawn. Upon then learning of her own absence from the house, he had stormed about slamming doors. Agatha chuckled, wishing she could have witnessed the scene. Even more amusing would have been the sight of him en route to his wedding in a hired coach, a dilapidated conveyance, from all accounts.

But beyond these musings, Agatha was of another frame of mind. If her information was correct, and she had no reason to suppose it wasn't, he had spent his wedding night apart from his bride. She couldn't credit it. To leave a charming wife untouched—it did not answer the purpose near so well as Annette herself apparently did. Lord! grinned her ladyship. What a dance he had in store.

That these musings so delightful to his aunt never entered the Earl's head was not surprising. The fairer sex had fawned and preened, had in fact vied for his attention, since before he was down from Oxford, and had ever since received him eagerly, whether in the drawing room or boudoir. That one could close the door in his face had never occurred to him, nor would it have made any difference if one had. He quite simply accepted what a lady was willing to give, as she accepted what he cared to offer, and there the matter ended. That the Earl could foresee the unquiet future predicted by his aunt would seem improbable—that he would have an inkling of its certainty was not long in coming.

It started as they were about to depart for an entertainment he deemed suitable to their state of mourning. Having accepted with equanimity the suggestion they attend Lady Bingham's musicale, he had presented himself in the drawing room promptly on the stroke of two. By two-fifteen he had drunk a glass of wine, paced several times the length of the salon, and glanced often at the clock relentlessly ticking the minutes away. By two-thirty the state of good humor in which he had entered the room was rapidly evaporating.

Agatha had been surreptitiously watching his perambulations with growing amusement. That he had agreed to the expedition was a wonder, for not in the usual way would he have lent his person to the prospect before him. She had, in fact, been astounded to learn that he had. The chit must mean more to him than she had supposed, she thought with some surprise.

"What can be keeping her?" he suddenly demanded.

"I do wish you would stop fidgeting, Ardley. It won't do the least good, you know."

"Much longer and we shan't go."

"Don't be a fool," she returned somewhat stringently. "Though I make not the slightest doubt you won't listen."

He stopped his pacing to glare, opened his mouth to retort, then closed it again as Annette's step was heard in the hall. Hurrying into the room, she spoke unwisely. "Oh!" she said. "You are waiting."

"Yes," he shot back grimly. "We are."

"I had to change my gown."

"Naturally," he replied tartly. "May I inquire how many times you found yourself obliged to do so?"

Annette defiantly raised her chin. "I will tell you, my lord, you are making me cross."

"Drake," he corrected automatically.

Her back stiffened. "If you are intending to spoil our outing, I won't c-call you that."

There was an uncomfortable pause. The anger died out of his eyes, to be replaced by a tenderness he quite forgot to mask. "Will you permit me to say the gown you selected is most becoming," he said in a voice that had gentled considerably. "You will forgive me, will you not?"

"It wasn't entirely your fault," she admitted honestly. "And I am sorry to be late."

"Perhaps we should depart for Lady Bingham's. To be the last arrival may be much in the mode, but I have never found it effective."

"No, and neither have I," she agreed as he crossed to hold open the door into the hall.

Upon entering Lady Bingham's drawing room, and Drake leading her around the salon, names and faces soon became a blur in Annette's mind. She couldn't help noticing the flattering complaisance with which the ladies greeted Drake and tried to hold his attention. When finally he guided her to a settee and sat down beside her, she commented on the scarcity of gentlemen present and received the reply that few males cared for the entertainment provided.

"Perhaps you will wish to converse with them," she said earnestly. "You need not stay by me if you do."

"The prospect is not very encouraging," he replied, the gleam in his eye making her strongly suspect he did not, as a rule, find himself in their company, or desire to do so now.

"What will the entertainment be?" she asked curiously.

He was amused. "The melancholy truth will soon present itself."

A gentleman standing nearby had been looking at Annette in a calculating way. "Please present me, sir," he begged, coming forward and smiling ingratiatingly. "I was tempted to seek an introduction when I first saw you enter, but deemed it suitable to wait and avoid the crush."

Good manners forced the Earl to his feet, though a tightening around the lips warned Annette he was not pleased. "Lord Morely, my wife, the Countess of Ardley," he said briefly.

"Wife, eh? Well, no matter. I will still sit and chat."

"The place is taken," his lordship said shortly.

"'Tis a pity you've lost it," Lord Morely blithefully brushed aside his objection. "I am persuaded you will find some lady to entertain. They are certainly present in plenty."

What the Earl would have replied to this was forever lost by the approach of their hostess. She bore down on him to relentlessly pursue her intent: his lordship must indulge the company by lending his service in turning the music while dear Miss Appleby favored them with a few select numbers on the pianoforte. Brushing aside his attempts at refusal, Lady Bingham led him in triumph across the room, stationed him beside Miss Appleby, and regaled the assembled company with a lengthy recitation of the honor accorded them by the presence in their midst of so distinguished a personage as the Earl.

Annette, anxiously watching, paid scant heed to the conversation of Lord Morely. Beyond bestowing one cursory glance on him, Drake seemed to pay him even less attention, but Annette had caught the expression in his eyes and wondered how, without appearing rude, she could persuade Lord Morely to engage some other lady in conversation. To her relief he rose and bowed his withdrawal upon the completion of Miss Appleby's number, but another dandy immediately took the vacated seat during the scattered applause and further rendition that followed Miss Appleby's blushing little show of reluctance to play again. The second piece being at an end, and Miss Appleby properly applauded, Drake sauntered with his habitual languor to Annette's side.

"Sir," he drawled to the exquisite seated beside her, "surely I am not mistaken in thinking you have my seat?"

This gentleman, being less audacious than Lord Morely, immediately rose and beat a stammering retreat.

"It is an odd thing the way you welcome the overtures of these jackanapes," Drake sneered as he sat down. "I have no notion of turning my head while your carry on your little flirtations."

"Don't be absurd."

"I can safely promise you I won't," he muttered as a harp was brought into the room. The harpist was followed by a vocalist, the vocalist by a string quartet. Through it all Drake sat silent beside Annette, outwardly relaxed but seething inside.

His temper had not abated when the gathering adjourned and he escorted her to their coach. Seated facing Annette and Agatha, he continued his stony silence until the coach deposited them on their doorstep. In the hall, he said tersely, "You will excuse us, Aunt. I wish to speak with Annette." Waving the footman aside, he grasped her arm none too gently, stalked beside her to the library, hustled her into the room, and closed the door.

Yes, thought Annette, he definitely slammed it. He was determined on a quarrel. She felt at a disadvantage and was annoyed to feel the color rush into her cheeks; his very attitude put her in the wrong. She had done nothing to deserve his censure and would not act as if she had. Crossing to a chair, she folded her hands and waited.

He paced the length of the carpet and back, glowered at her (Annette felt her pulses race), and finally said in a very level voice, "We leave for Monkshaven tomorrow."

"Of course," she answered in just as level a tone.

"Is that all you have to say?" he demanded unreasonably.

Annette stared at him, then lowered her gaze to her hands. She hadn't meant to give in, but found herself saying, "I did not mean to disturb you, but I didn't know what to do."

"You could have discouraged their advances!"

"I did! You have no right to think that I—" She stopped, stung, but aware of a surprising desire to gain his approbation.

"You are leaping to conclusions. I am not accusing you of improper thoughts. Rather, it was your tolerance of their presence I object to."

Annette raised her eyes to his face and studied him with deliberation. What was there about him that she found so compelling, so disturbing? Why did she feel a powerful attraction to him? He stared back at her, a slight flush rising in his cheeks. Some new knowledge flickered in his eyes before he glanced away.

"Drake," she said softly. "The other day you suggested a truce. May I do so now?"

"I'll play fair, Annette, and beg your pardon. It was my damnable pride and seeing those simpering— no man would wish his wife receiving the addresses— I'm doing this badly."

A giggle which she tried to stifle escaped her. "I'll lay a monkey apologies rarely rise to your lips."

"Wherever did you learn such language?" he demanded, taken aback.

"I've been poorly brought up, I'm afraid."

"Your father's grooms?"

"I would hear them talking in the stables."

"You should never have been in the stables. But we stray from the point. You haven't much experience of men, have you? No, I thought not. You must learn to deliver a proper setdown on occasion."

"I will imitate you, my lord," she teased.

"A very adequate example to follow," he gravely assured her, a smile now lurking in his eyes.

"Do we go to Monkshaven tomorrow?"

"If you agree."

"Good gracious, Drake. I have no objections."

"It is the sequel you may find annoying. You see, my dear, it will be necessary for you to precede me to the first night's lodging. I will join you in time for dinner."

"Well, don't go off in a twitter, Drake, for I haven't the smallest notion of going off into a spasm."

CHAPTER FOUR

"And then Cribb got in a good jab with his right, followed by a left, then a doubler to the body. He fought like a tiger, let me tell you. He has a tremendous punch and bores right in, dancing around the ring and closing when he chooses. Well, as I was saying, he was having all the best of it, putting some straight hits to the throat, then a half arm to the eye, and fibbed for a time. Cribb didn't let up a minute but got in some flush hits, then a full arm hit, and it was over. A first-class mill, ma'am."

"Oh!" breathed Annette. "I do wish I could have seen it."

And then a voice spoke from behind them, a slow drawl cutting the air, vibrating around the room. "I should have thought not, my dear," it said with deceptive quiet.

Four pairs of eyes turned to stare at the gentleman on the threshold, booted and spurred and wearing a heavy surcoat.

"Drake!" Annette gasped.

"Just so," he said lazily, advancing into the room. "Will you not introduce me to your—friends?"

Somehow Annette stumbled through the task, forgetting names and needing assistance from the red-faced youths now on their feet and bowing sheepishly. "We're honored, my lord," one of them mumbled. "Your wife has been most kind."

"My wife is always kind," his lordship agreed. "Please be seated, gentlemen. May I offer wine?"

And so they sat. The Earl conversed pleasantly and treated them as equals, not talking down to them as their elder brothers were wont to do, nor thinking them callow as their fathers did, and after a quarter of an hour in his company, they thought him the best of good fellows.

Annette was sorry to see them go, for she well knew what was in the Earl's mind. She was not misled. "What am I to do with you?" he said wearily. "I send you here to await my coming. Such a simple request, or so one would be led to suppose. But I arrive to find my wife entertaining strange men, the door on the latch, and discussing the unladylike pursuit of prizefighting."

Annette would have given all she possessed to be able to go back and relive the past hours over again. But she could not. She could only raise her chin in the air and attempt to stare him down. "Be pleased to listen to me, Drake. I meant no harm."

"That—or something very like it—I have heard before."

Her cheeks reddened but she stood her ground. "They were friendly boys, only being nice to me."

"You are quite out of the way, you know. I am forever finding you tête-à-tête with 'nice boys,' and all you can find to say is that I shouldn't fault your conduct."

Annette's eyes flashed. "You are being horrid!" she cried.

"On the contrary, I am being excessively polite."

"I wish I hadn't married you!"

"I do not doubt it, my dear. But you did, you see. I am only wondering what explanation you will produce on this occasion. For I will require one, you know."

She looked him straight in the eye. "I expected you would," she said bitterly. "You will refuse to believe me."

"Certainly not," he answered imperturbably. "I am quite intending to accept whatever you feel inclined to tell me. I have never questioned your truthfulness, Annette. It is your judgment that causes me concern."

Her cheeks flamed. The worst of it was she knew he was in the right. "I have—offered provocation."

There seemed to be a bit of lint on his lordship's sleeve. He carefully removed it.

"I know I have b-been a nuisance. But they were so gay."

His eyes were on her face in a way that was hard to read. "There hasn't been much gaiety in your life to date," he finally murmured thoughtfully.

"I was happy with Papa," she said coldly. "He taught me himself. I have an understanding of the classics unusual in a female, and my knowledge of languages—"

"Did you have acquaintances of your own age?"

"That did not signify, let me inform you. Papa provided all the companionship I could desire."

Leaning back negligently, he took out his snuffbox and flicked it open. "Annette, I am pleased you cherish your father's memory. I would not have it otherwise. But you will forgive me if I lecture. Ladies are not to be found in male company in a public house, unless in the presence of a husband."

"Will any husband do?" Annette's eyes twinkled.

His lordship sighed. "Levity is misplaced at this present."

"You could find something to admire in me, I should think," she stated with some asperity.

"You are making that rather difficult," came his deliberate reply.

In the uncomfortable pause that followed, Annette flushed painfully. "I have behaved outrageously," she admitted in a whisper.

"Do you think you can refrain from actions of which you know I will disapprove?"

"I will try. I really will, Drake."

"That is all I ask," he said, getting to his feet. Moving around the table, he took her hands in his and pulled her to her feet. Lifting her chin with his fingers, he stood looking down at her. "We will sheathe our swords. And I have found much to admire in you," he added softly. Annette stood statue-still, her eyes staring into his, as he lightly pressed his lips to hers.

She found it almost impossible to breathe, she was so shocked by the warmth of his mouth lingering sensually against her own. Jerking her head away, she averted her eyes.

The Earl, visibly shaken, stood regarding her, unwilling to accept her reaction, yet unable to deny it. She had just given an excellent imitation of a young lady about to be overcome by a fit of revulsion, brought on, apparently, by himself.

Annette slipped from the room and fairly flew up the stairs, her senses reeling. She hadn't until now known how deep-seated was her long-standing fear of personal intimacy. She had half a dozen times backed off from a friendship that was rumored on the brink of marriage, not because she found her partners ill-favored, but because she could not face the closeness of the relationship that came with marriage. Only Drake's stated intention not to press his husbandly prerogatives had induced her to enter into this contract. But surely they could be friends? She could not visualize living in such close proximity to another without friendship.

The Earl, meanwhile, was thinking his own thoughts. The fright he had read in her eyes at the lightest of intimacies had been a shock and was certainly a force to be reckoned with. For an enchanting female made for love to shun his veriest touch—the prospect was not very encouraging. It would require all the tact and gentleness he could muster to overcome her fears. It was altogether too bad. To say the truth, if their marriage was not to be a disappointment to both of them, he would need to put fate to the touch.

No hint of their collective inner strife was apparent on the surface when they met for dinner. Covers were laid and the room was bright with candlelight. The Earl escorted Annette to the table, seated her on his right, and signaled to a liveried servant as she unfolded her napkin. Annette tasted her soup and looked up in surprise. "My own chef is in the kitchens," he explained. "I can do without my man but not without my cook."

Throughout dinner he talked on a number of subjects, entertaining her with amusing anecdotes and more seriously discussing topics he thought would interest her. She was glad her knowledge was sufficient to allow her to make an intelligent contribution to the conversation. By the time the cheese and sweetmeats were on the table, he was watching her with delight.

Stretching out a hand, he lifted the decanter and refilled their glasses. Smiling at her over the rim of his, he said, "I am able to inform you with a clear conscience that dinner in the company of an alluring companion is most pleasing."

"I daresay I will become conceited if you compliment me with any regularity."

"It is not in my usual way to utter statements I do not mean. When I am not pleased with you, I shall coerce you."

Startled, Annette glanced at him, then chuckled at the laughter gleaming in his eyes. "I wonder if you would," she murmured, her head cocked to one side.

"You may not wish to test me," he blandly returned. "And I would certainly regret the necessity of calling out an overly zealous admirer."

"You mean a duel?" Annette cried in delight. "Oh, I do wish you would, Drake. I'd so like to witness another one."

"Another one!"

"I don't know that you could rightly term it a duel," she continued judiciously. "At least I am not quite certain, in the circumstance of my not having seen one previously. And I must admit my view was somewhat restricted, there not being any closer shrubbery, you see."

"Shrubbery!"

"Well, it was fought in a copse, and the ground around had been plowed. That would account for the lack of cover, I should imagine. But I do think they could have found a likelier spot."

His lordship, bereft of speech, could only stare.

"But of course," she blithefully continued, "they could not have thought, I'm sure, not knowing a great deal about it themselves. I forget for the moment what it was about—" Annette paused to ponder, then shrugged. "Well," she went on, oblivious to the thunderstruck expression on his face, "no matter.

Where was I? Oh, yes. I remember it was cold, being right upon the dawn, and I thought they might have changed their minds when I heard them coming. I crouched as low as ever I could and they didn't see me. They were riding their fathers' horses and argued for a time before someone produced some swords. Or at least they looked like swords, but it was hard to tell, I being so far away. I really must say they didn't know the first thing about swordfighting."

"And you would know?" he interjected dryly.

"But of course. And you may believe me, they most certainly did not. It was so funny, Drake. They flailed away with the loudest noise, becoming madder all the while. And finally—oh, Drake," she gurgled, "they threw down the swords and went at it with their fists."

Her tale ended, she became aware of the look on his face and flushed to the roots of her hair. Her hands clenched. "I only thought you w-would be interested."

"Interested," he repeated with hard-fought calm. "I am surprised, though why I should be, I cannot imagine."

There came a pause during which she tried to decide what to say next. But with his eyes on her, her mind drew a blank.

"Yes, Annette, you read me correctly," he said grimly. "I hesitate to remind you of my jurisdiction, but if you are cherishing dreams of a like conduct in future, banish them. I will never permit it. Nor will I allow you further recitations of past escapades. You will bear in mind, I trust, that I am perfectly capable of forcing my will over you."

"Please do not address threats to me, Drake."

"Do you not realize I set the same rigid standards

for myself? I plan to take steps for providing entertainment, Annette. Duels and prizefighting, however, cannot be said to head the list of pastimes I will find acceptable."

"I wouldn't have told anyone but you."

"I may have bungled this," he said in a tone completely devoid of censure. "But you see, my dear, I haven't had much experience along this line. I have known many women, but what they did, or did not do, was ever before of the least interest to me."

"What women have you known?" she could not stop herself from asking.

He sat perfectly still, his eyes never wavering from her face.

"Well," she finally murmured, "you will admit it was tempting."

Suddenly he got up from his chair and stood looking down at her. Taking her fingers in his, he pulled her up into his arms. "There's no help for it," he said. "I must kiss you."

Annette hadn't time to gasp before his lips swooped on hers. I should struggle, she thought dizzily. But, surprisingly, she had no wish to struggle.

He knew he had won a small victory and chose his words with care. "We've known each other a very brief time, Annette. Less than a week, in all truth. I will not rush you into an intimacy you might despise. For you might, you know. And I couldn't bear that. I want your love."

Her eyes involuntarily flew to his. "Oh," she said. "Do you love me?"

"I fell in love with a girl who went uncomplaining to her wedding in an unfashionable gown. You couldn't have been more beautiful had you been robed in gold."

"Oh," was all she seemed to find to say.

He abruptly changed the subject. "We have a long day before us tomorrow. You will need your rest. I trust you found your chamber comfortable?"

"I was never used to be surrounded by luxury, Drake. I felt quite grand to find my valise unpacked and a fire burning on the hearth. I am deeply grateful for your kindness."

"My good girl, such a thought never entered my head. I am much afraid you must accept the luxury so necessary to my comfort."

Accompanying her up the stairs and down the hall to her room, he murmured, "I will escort you to breakfast," and moved on to his own chamber.

Annette woke refreshed the following morning, remembering his words of the night before. Having by now acquired a fair knowledge of his character, she would bet a monkey he was not much in the habit of giving thought to the vicissitudes of the feminine sex. Well, sir, she thought, you will soon find a frailty of purpose on the part of the female you have espoused to be completely lacking. Though she must admit she hadn't minded his kiss—not really—not all that much.

A quick step sounded in the passage, and Drake stood on the threshold. His angry gaze swept the room as he strode in—and stopped dead in his tracks. Annette, startled, had come to a sitting position in the center of the bed, the transparency of her night rail concealing little from his view. His breath catching in his throat, he stood stock-still, his eyes fastened on her breasts, held spellbound by the beauty of the gently cupping mounds. Tearing his gaze away, he mumbled an apology and backed stumbling through the door. It was some minutes before Annette gathered her scattered wits and swung her legs over the side of the bed.

A full hour later she had not left her chamber. Still in her morning wrapper, she was unable to decide which gown she would wear when a footman relayed a message through Marie. My lord sent his compliments and awaited her arrival below. "Tell his lordship's man I will be down soon." She dreaded facing Drake but knew it could not be avoided.

The lackey's footsteps clattered back down the stairs, to be replaced almost immediately by the Earl's firm step coming up them. Without bothering to knock, he strode into the room and stood looking grimly at her. "What is causing this delay?" he demanded.

"I am making all possible haste. You cannot expect me to—"

"I have little doubt that females have scant regard for time, but I should think the smallest intellect could understand so simple a thing."

"As soon as I decide which gown—"

"Is that all!" Grabbing the first one that came to hand, he thrust it at her.

Annette cast him one look and motioned to Marie. Between them they got her into the dress—why must the one selected have so many tiny buttons? she inwardly groaned as they struggled with the fastenings, their fingers trembling. "I'm ready," she said breathlessly.

Grasping her arm, he tossed, "Get this mess cleared and pack," at the flustered maid, and marched Annette from the room.

"You have acquired a most unpleasant tendency to come bursting through my door," she said indignantly.

He shot her a fulminating look. "I shall shake you if you push me," he growled with ill-concealed impatience.

"You are forever quarreling. Well, sir, I will not be bullied."

"Bullied!" he snorted. "Let me inform you, my girl, I will not tolerate missish behavior."

"You are odious and hateful, and I wish you will go away and leave me alone." But there was a break in her voice, which he caught, and which held him silent.

Annette sipped her coffee. She could not rid herself of the conviction that she was again in the wrong. She knew she had spent an unconscionable time in dressing, and this admission brought a crease between her brows. Seeing this, the Earl's scowl deepened, setting her nerves off course. To begin with, she had found facing him a task almost beyond her powers, and to cap it off, she had lost her temper, a thing she had determined not to do.

"Coffee alone will not sustain you," he remarked with more calm than she had any reason to expect. "Eat your breakfast."

"I am quite fine, sir."

"Don't be foolish, Annette. We will not be stopping until luncheon."

She looked at him a moment, and, after a slight hesitation, picked up her fork. Tears stung her eyelids but she forced a few bites down her throat. "Good girl," came his comment when she had at last finished and lay down her napkin.

Both were silent as they set forth on their journey. Annette reflected sadly on the ruin she had made of the morning. She should have known better—Papa had always been in a taking when forced to wait. She

wondered how Drake had passed the time. Had he sat
and scowled? Or had he paced about, gnashing his
teeth, perhaps crossing to peer up the stairs? Her
lively sense of humor got the better of her and she
chuckled.

"You are amused?" he asked, slightly disconcerted.

Her gaze met his unwaveringly. "I have been posing as a wronged and ill-used creature, haven't I,
Drake? You are treating me with more consideration
than perhaps I deserve."

"Acquit me," he said softly. Not endowed with feminine intuition, he could not hope to fathom her
feeling. He only knew he had hurt her and she had
fought back. Reflecting on his damnable temper, he
told himself he would not allow it to overset his conduct again. Love had come swiftly to him, but of Annette's sentiments he could only wonder. The mere
thought that she would not love him was not to be
borne.

"Then your regard has reanimated toward me?"
her soft voice asked.

"Reanimated?" he repeated, startled. "My dear, I
was afraid, with my temper, you had taken a disgust
of me."

"If you had more experience of women, you would
not contemplate such a piece of foolishness."

What he thought of this remark he kept to himself,
though admittedly with an effort.

CHAPTER FIVE

Dark had fallen before they pulled up before the door of Monkshaven, so Annette had no real idea of what the house was like. But an impression of the enormity of the structure proved correct when she crossed the threshold to find herself in a commodious hall. It was just what she had come to expect a possession of the Earl would be, with its air of quiet elegance and handsome appointments.

"My God!" he suddenly groaned beneath his breath, his eyes staring in disbelief at the lovely creature coming forward to greet them. "Lady Ellen. Had I sent you here?"

"Yes, you did," she answered with her charming smile. "Six months, it is now."

"Paul and Harriette?"

"We do appreciate your kindness, Cousin Ardley. I don't know what would have become of us otherwise."

The Earl seemed embarrassed by this statement and hurried Annette through the introduction and up the stairs. "You are wondering about Lady Ellen," he began, then shook his head when she would have interrupted. "Do not drown me in an excess of good manners, my dear. One must draw the line somewhere and you are entitled to an explanation."

"More of your burdensome relations?" she impishly inquired.

"I am no saint, as you have probably discovered for yourself," he answered with a hint of a smile. "No sacrifice on my part was involved. I do not as a rule spend an excess of time at Monkshaven."

"I see," was all she could find to say.

"In that case, I can only conclude you possess extraordinary powers, my dear. For I am quite confident you do not in the least see. You had rather demand an explanation for arriving at your home to find strangers in residence."

"But I have no right to demand anything."

"And why not?" he exploded, furious. "You are the mistress of this establishment. Kindly get that through your head!"

"Drake!" Annette gasped, shocked. When they had entered Monkshaven he had been quite in charity with her, as he had been during the day's journey, laughing with her in happy spirits and entertaining her with easy talk. But upon their entrance into this place a cloud had settled over him.

He drew a deep breath. "I beg your pardon," he said briefly.

Her color mounted. "I do not know what possessed me to say anything so thoughtless. It was foolish of me, but I am not really your wife."

This unfortunate remark further inflamed his anger. "That can be easily remedied," he said deliberately. "It is as well to establish the relationship here and now."

"Don't come any nearer," she said in a low voice.

Again her words proved a poor choice. His face hardened. "And who will stop me?" he gritted. "You have not the strength and I think you will find screaming will gain you nothing."

A dawning anger chased the fright from her eyes. "You would resort to force, my lord? I should think your pride would prevent your coercing an unwilling female."

"Your virgin state has gone to your head. You are not the only female I have kissed. The difference in my other conquests is that I have married you."

"What have I done that you should insult me?"

"You are hardly the one to speak of insults, for mine can't compare with yours. I have honored your person in leaving you untouched, while you trampled on my manhood without the least regard for it."

"You are insufferable," she shot at him, her breasts heaving. "I am glad you have left me untouched."

"Such protestations arouse in me nothing more than a desire to make you regret them. And that, my dear, is precisely what I intend to do."

"Your behavior—" Annette paused. This was not the way out of her difficulty. "Drake," she began again, "I admit to a want of proper deportment in the past, but I had thought here at Monkshaven to become the kind of wife you wish."

"You are about to do just that."

"At Monkshaven?" she asked inspired. "Do you really want—" She couldn't complete the thought. "At Monkshaven?" she repeated.

With one hand reaching for her, he paused. Annette stood perfectly still while the battle raged within him. She knew full well she had angered him past control with her fearful response to him as a man.

"No," he said at last. "Not at Monkshaven. Forget your alarm. My behavior has become exemplary and I will apologize."

"Drake, could we sit and talk? We haven't spoken much of Monkshaven. I would know its history."

"There is not a great deal to tell. As the name implies, it was formerly a monastery, though on a small scale from all accounts. At least it did not particularly thrive. It was a haven for boys orphaned and left homeless by the wars and pestilence of the times. They gave it its name."

"Why did it not thrive? Most monasteries did."

"I don't know how else to say it, but scandal did arise—it was probably women from the village. Our oldest records do not indicate an affiliation with the church. It is thought the monks were not of a religious order."

"But if they established a monastery—"

"My God, Annette!" he exclaimed, exasperated. "All men are alike under their clothing. The difference lies in the mind."

"I don't quite understand what you mean, Drake," she said uncertainly. "How do you feel about Monkshaven?"

"I hate it."

She was silenced and sat looking questioningly at him.

"I daresay that may seem a strange thing for me to admit, but my memories of the years I spent here are not pleasant ones. You see, Annette, my mother died when I was very young. My father removed to London and remained there until his death; in all truth I seldom saw him. My welfare was left to the discretion of a tutor, a cruel and abusive man. It is a part of my life I wish to forget. I thought in bringing you here to find a happiness that would alter my dislike for the place. Monkshaven has been the seat of my family for generations and I would prefer to feel an affinity for it."

"I will help you to be happy here, Drake."

Pushing his shoulder away from the mantel where he had crossed to lean, he straightened up and smiled at her. "Come here, my dear."

She walked slowly across to stand before him, and greatly to her surprise, he bent and gently touched her lips with his. "I have one more thing to say before we forget this conversation. I have told you what you mean to me. When you feel you can be—happy here, will you let me know?"

"Yes, of course, Drake."

"You will wish to rest now. Dinner is served at eight."

Annette dressed for the evening with care. She told herself it was to present a pleasing aspect before Drake's family. Almost she convinced herself that that was the reason. Almost, but not quite.

Entering the drawing room later in the wake of a footman, she found him waiting her arrival in the company of Lady Ellen and a girl she knew must be Lady Ellen's daughter. A child of seventeen, Harriette was small for her age, with enormous green eyes and a mass of curling, auburn hair. Drake came forward to take her hand and lead her to the sofa. He was supremely elegant in evening dress, his superbly cut coat of blue satin and his white knee breeches fitting him flawlessly and emphasizing the muscular perfection of his body. Sapphires gleamed from the folds of a spotless white cravat and glittered on his fingers. Annette, much aware of his presence by her side, turned away in some confusion to engage Lady Ellen in conversation.

"In the drawing room, are they?" a voice demanded. "Now, never mind. I can get myself through the door."

A slight young man came hurrying in and crossed

to grip the Earl's hand in his. "My dear Ardley, it's famous to see you again. How's London, and when am I to leave this backwater for the city?"

"When your ears are dry," the Earl answered in some amusement. "But you must meet my wife. Annette, little though you may desire the introduction, this graceless scamp is my cousin, Paul."

Paul, Lord Wrexly, stared at Annette in disbelief, an expression of admiration mingled with incredulity in his eyes. "Is it really possible?" he exclaimed. "A beauty in this benighted place!"

Annette was unable to withstand this outrageous remark, going off on a peal of laughter.

"If you continue in this manner, she will think you to let in your attic," the Earl remarked.

"Ardley, my good fellow, you've kept her hidden. Hardly sporting, I'd say," Lord Wrexly proclaimed in mock anger.

"No, it isn't, is it?" his lordship agreed.

"I've a good notion to charm her myself. You'd best have a care. Unless, of course," he continued, grinning, "you prefer to send me away. London, for instance."

His lordship raised his eyeglass and leisurely surveyed Paul from his head to his heels. "I think not," he commented dryly. "The metropolis is hardly ready for that rig-out."

All eyes settled on Lord Wrexly, for that dashing young blade was indeed startling in his choice of raiment. The inordinately high points of his cravat were rivaled only by the height of his coat collar, that garment having shoulders padded to an extraordinary width, nipped in tightly at the waist, and adorned with numerous and quite useless brass buttons. The carefully loose sweep of his waving red hair was equaled only by the equally loose hang of his very full trousers.

"This, my dear Ardley, is the highest crack of fashion," Paul declared, striding to the center of the room to strut about that they might view him the better.

The Earl shuddered. "Don't tell us your arbiter of fashion, I beg you."

"Oh, I don't mind," said my Lord Wrexly generously, while thrusting out a foot to gaze in admiration at his trousers. "Dickie Beauchamp's brother has gone to London and wrote Dickie all about it. Big of him, won't you agree?"

"No, I can't agree to that piece of impertinence. You might mention to your friend that following the mode of every loose screw on the town will gain him less than a polite condescension."

"Oh, come now, Ardley," Paul grinned, nonplussed. "Ask our Annette. She likes my new togs."

The Earl said with amusement, "I trust you are not intending to dine in such glory?"

"But, sir, this is my best rig," Paul replied impishly, going forward to offer Annette his arm. "You have restored my faith in miracles, ma'am. I grant you the privilege of entering on my escort."

"The vulgarity of your dress rivals only your conceit," the Earl remarked, coming along in their wake with Lady Ellen and Harriette.

Annette had been dreading the ordeal of dinner, visualizing the conversation somewhat strained in the face of the newness of their acquaintance. The advent of Lord Wrexly on the scene, however, banished any feeling of trepidation she might have been experiencing, for a more charming rattlebox she had yet to meet. His gaiety left little room for those tedious lapses into silence that could spell the ruin of the most carefully organized gathering, and his manner of address so infectious as to entertain them all. He paid unblushing compliments to Annette, drew sallies of surprising wit from a child of Harriette's age, and found much to amuse Lady Ellen. The conclusion of dinner found the family greatly in accord.

Annette spoke of this to the Earl when, after an enjoyable evening, they dispersed for bed, Drake having escorted her to her rooms. "Paul is blessed with a happy nature, don't you agree? And he infects others with his high spirits."

"He seemed to find an admiring regard for you."

"I am sure he is charming to every woman who chances to cross his path."

Drake chuckled. "Had you ever seen such a Banbury rig?"

"No," Annette laughed. "I must confess I hadn't. You will need to show him how to go on."

"Very shortly into our acquaintance I seem to have told you I would not likely experience boredom. I appear to have been prophetic." Crossing to a table, he poured out two glasses of champagne. Handing her one, he said, "I had it sent up earlier. You are remarkable, my dear, but I cannot expect you to languish here without entertainment."

"I promise you that Monkshaven itself will offer an endless variety of pastimes. Do not think me an object of pity."

"My thoughts of you have nothing to do with compassion."

"Oh," she stammered, wondering if she correctly interpreted his meaning. She did.

His eyes twinkled. "When I became an April gentleman, I did not intend remaining a December husband. Your first lesson in the gentle art of wooing will take place tomorrow morning."

Annette debated and determined to make light of the matter. "Oh, dear," she groaned in mock dismay, "as if I weren't in bad enough loaf already."

"You may as well stand buff, my girl," he said, rising. "Wear a habit. I have a mare I think will do."

The scene that met her eyes when they walked through the front doors the following morning bore eloquent testimony to his opinion of a mount suitable for her. Standing docilely, the mare rolled her eyes at their approach but evinced no further reaction to the humans gathering around. His lordship's mount was another matter. Tossing his head and pawing the gravel, the huge stallion danced around, then jerked at the reins, making every effort to pull free of the restraining hands of the grooms. Annette allowed Drake to mount her, then watched while he brought the stallion under control. Thus it was with no great anticipation that she rode beside him as they moved off down the drive. Not many minutes passed before she brought the mare to a standstill. "I cannot believe I am to ride this slug," she said with a great deal of indignation.

Drake looked a little startled. "She's a gentle goer—"

"You may as well know I am used to spirit in my mounts. Surely you have better animals in your stables?"

"Naturally, but—"

Annette wheeled the mare, if the slow turning accomplished could be so termed, and returned along the way they had come. Sliding to the ground, she tossed the reins to a surprised groom. "Be so good as to saddle a horse with mettle." Seeing the Earl's imperceptible nod, the boy hurried to obey.

Annette could not fault the next mare led out for her inspection. The filly was tossing her head and frisking about, eager for exercise. Drake watched for a moment and seemed satisfied with his wife's ability, though a grimness could be seen about his mouth as she urged the mare into a gallop. Sending his stallion thundering after, he soon drew abreast and reached for the mare's bridle.

"Pooh!" she said airily. "Do you take me for a timid fireside rider?"

"You're wasting your breath, my dear," he replied, inexorably slowing her progress. "A brisk trot is all I will allow you."

"I don't know what you hope to achieve by mouthing such fustian rubbish, for I don't propose to make a sedate progress. I am used to being said to have a reasonably good seat."

"Up to every move on the board, aren't you?" he asked in amusement. "Our progress will be 'sedate,' as you put it." Grinning broadly, he added, "I much prefer you all of a piece. And you do have a good seat."

"If that is a compliment intended to flummox me, my lord, I must inform you I am used to riding at my pleasure and in a manner I find pleasing. Moreover, my papa never raised the least objection."

"If you think to compare us, let me remind you that I am not your papa. I know you consider me a gudgeon, my dear, but you will permit me to say you are the slyest thing in nature?"

"Perhaps I am the gudgeon," Annette mused reflectively. "For I note we are moving at a sedate pace."

Chuckling, he said no more, letting his silence

speak in his stead. They spent a pleasant morning riding over the estate. The weather was fine, the scenery exemplary, and if they did ride at a walk, and an occasional trot, Annette generally held the excursion to be an agreeable one. She therefore was in a frame of mind to feel that his suggestion that they ride each morning a commendable idea altogether.

They returned to Monkshaven quite happy with each other. Indeed, Annette was beginning to think she was reasonably safe from further strictures, pleasant or otherwise, and she was most certainly sure to be free of teasing remarks designed to overset her composure. She was quickly led to a realization of the error in such thinking.

Drake was climbing the front steps behind her; his sudden burst of laughter caused her to turn her head to look back at him. His gaze moved upward from her rounded bottom; his eyes glinted into hers; his words were impertinent: "May I repeat my remark about your good seat?"

Turning red to the roots of her hair, Annette vanished through the door.

She hardly knew what to expect at luncheon. She understood that gentlemen were on occasion prone to indelicate remarks and did not guard their tongues before their wives. She need not have worried. He maintained a proper conduct before the family.

The conclusion of the meal found Annette and Paul alone in the salon, Drake having ridden out to visit a tenant, with Lady Ellen and Harriette off on pursuits of their own.

Casting himself into a chair, Paul smiled at Annette. "What shall we do to entertain ourselves?" he lazily asked.

"I shouldn't keep you from your own amusements."

"I haven't any. And besides, I'd be an insufferable fellow if I couldn't be pleased with your company."

"You certainly are easy with your compliments."

"Now, is that fair?" He grinned irrepressibly. "I'll tell you what. Let's take out the curricle. I've been wanting to, but haven't dared."

"I wouldn't care to do so without Drake's permission."

"Why not, I'd like to know? Are you telling me you're afraid of him?"

"Oh, no. But we might do well to wait."

"He would scarcely blame you, in any event." Paul jumped to his feet. "Hurry and get your bonnet," he urged with an enthusiasm she found irresistible.

Annette hesitated. She was torn between a desire to ride out and the thought that Drake might well be incensed.

"Do make haste," Paul admonished, hurrying from the room.

And so, much against her better judgment, Annette found herself on the front steps when the equipage was brought around. Staring in disbelief, she gasped, "Not the chestnuts!"

"Fainthearted, m'dear?" Paul asked provocatively. Grasping her arm, he hurried her forward. Following her up, he said hopefully, "Shall I drive?"

"I should think not. What we are already doing is quite enough."

Annette set the horses forward under the disapproving eye of the groom. The chestnuts had not been taken out for several days but responded to her commands, giving no trouble as they bowled along the roads. She was soon in charity with her decision to ride out with Paul. He was an amusing and carefree companion, his laughter and easy banter proving contagious. Thus it was she raised no objection to stopping for refreshment. She did hesitate a moment on discovering the inn did not boast a private parlor, then shrugged. The village was off the usual roads (she had not before heard its name) and in any event Drake would never know.

In this she was mistaken.

Sitting with Paul at a table in the public room, she glanced at the local men leaning on the bar and idly looked toward the door—the Earl stood there. "Oh, no!" she groaned. "Drake cannot be here. He simply cannot be."

Paul regarded Ardley quizzically. "It appears he is, m'dear. Well, buck up. Ten to one he'll think nothing of it."

In a moment his lordship had crossed the room to stand surveying them with bitter saturnineness. "I feel confident you will, as usual, have an explanation to put forth."

Annette eyed him doubtfully. "We can explain. You see—"

"Not at all," he interrupted levelly. "May I join you?"

"If you intend being pleasant." Paul grinned, not in the least chastised by Ardley's glare. "You may even buy the next treat. Neither of us has any more money."

"That doesn't surprise me," Drake said, sitting down and motioning to the landlord. "What will you have, Annette?"

"Nothing, thank you."

"My dear," he said, correctly interpreting the train of her thinking. "I do not intend a scene in a public room."

"Oh, come off it, Ardley," Paul said in a pleading voice. "Blame me. It was my idea."

"I see little to discern between the pair of you."

"I could drive Annette back to Monkshaven," Paul hopefully suggested. "Then we could explain."

"You will ride my stallion. I will drive Annette home."

But sitting beside him as the team moved forward, she could only wish that Paul held the reins, for they rode in virtual silence to Monkshaven. Nor did Drake speak as he assisted her from the curricle and into the house. As they climbed the stairs, she glanced at him. "I wish you will forgive me," she said as steadily as she could contrive. He did not reply as they moved along the hall to her rooms. Following her in, he stood by the door looking at her as she nervously removed her bonnet and gloves. Drawing a deep breath, she said, "We should not have taken the chestnuts."

"What I have is yours. I thought you understood that." When there did not seem to be anything she intended to say in reply, he crossed the room to stand before her. "Will you tell me why you saw fit to patronize a public room?"

"There was not a private parlor," she said as if she expected her words to offer all he could desire in the way of explanation. Her curiosity asserted itself. "How did you happen to be there?"

"I had been to discuss business with a tenant and saw the curricle before the inn."

"I seem to be forever in a coil. You must regret marrying me."

"I have no regrets. Have you, Annette?"

"No, Drake. But then, I'm a sad character." She smiled beguilingly. "I seem to display a shocking lack of consequence for your Countess. I wonder you tolerate my excesses."

"Do you think of yourself as my Countess?"

"Drake, I—" Annette paused, her eyes avoiding his. "You never shout at me," she continued unreasonably in a small voice.

"Should I?" he asked with admirable restraint. "Would it do any good?"

"I never know what you are thinking. I would rather you said how you feel."

She found herself in a crushing embrace, too surprised to struggle. It was a bruising kiss. Ardent and demanding, his lips seared her senses in a manner that left her trembling. "Once and for all," he said angrily, "I won't be taken to task for not forcing my attentions on you. But you've about pushed me to the end of my tether, so don't imagine I'll be able to keep my hands off you indefinitely. Good God, woman! What do you expect!"

Annette tried to move away, but his grip tightened. She became intensely aware of the passions she had aroused in him and felt terrified in the face of his desire, for she knew she would be defenseless should he decide to force her.

But she found the courage to meet his eyes. "If you will be p-patient—" she temporized.

"I will make every effort to do so, but I am not by nature a patient man. Do not expect me to wait much longer, Annette. I doubt I am capable of it."

CHAPTER SIX

Annette was arranging flowers in the large vase standing on a table in the main hall. Head cocked to one side, she considered the effect before nodding her satisfaction and handing the last blossoms to Watkins. She was smiling as she turned toward the stairs, for she was happier than she could ever remember having been. As the days passed, her relationship with Drake was very slowly altering, the result of his wooing, as he termed it. As she set her foot on the first step, a ripple of laughter escaped her. It was turning out to be fun to flirt with Drake.

"Annette, dearest," Lady Ellen's voice trilled from the doorway to the blue drawing room. "Do I find you busy?" She was charmingly attired in a gown of lavender silk with a double row of pleating encircling her neck to frame her face, a cap of Brussels lace perched saucily atop fashionably dressed hair. She looked fragile, elegant, absurdly youthful and feminine. Fluttering her hands in the most appealing way imaginable, she implored Annette: "Do come in a moment, my dear. There is someone I desire you to meet."

Somewhat taken aback, for Lady Ellen was blushing like a schoolgirl, Annette followed her into the salon. Standing before the fire warming his backside was a gentleman of a thinness to startle strangers meeting him for the first time.

"Sir Carlton," Lady Ellen smiled brilliantly, "I have someone I especially want you to meet—my dearest cousin, the Countess of Ardley. Annette, may I present Sir Carlton Bellamy."

Coming forward with a quick stride, he said with a twinkle in his eyes, "Lady Ellen has told me of you, ma'am. I am pleased to make my bow to beauty."

"Do you always say such charming things, Sir Carlton?" Annette asked as he raised her fingers to his lips.

"Oh, no," he assured her, adding gallantly, "only to Ellen."

"Upon my word," Lady Ellen exclaimed. "You are a flatterer."

"Nonsense," he returned, beaming fondly at her. "There is no need for that. You don't look a whit less youthful than Lady Annette. You could pass for sisters."

"Indeed we could," Annette smilingly agreed, leading the way to the settee. "Tell me, Sir Carlton, do you reside in these parts?"

"My home is in Sussex. I hastened to call when I learned an unforgettable lady of my youth was in residence here. Naughty girl," he said, glancing at Lady Ellen. "She had neglected to let me know."

"Oh, pooh," Lady Ellen exclaimed, flushing prettily. "I could never have been so forward. You must know that I could not."

"It was always my joy to serve you, Ellen. And well you know it. Couldn't let me know, indeed!"

"Dear Sir Carlton," she murmured, pleased. "You always said the prettiest things. Everyone remarked on it."

"No, I didn't," he objected mildly. "You will recall that I had more rumgumption than to bore the ladies with rhymes."

"Annette, he was ever a tease." Lady Ellen gurgled

entrancingly. "He had only to exhibit the smallest regard for a female to fall victim to his charm."

"Now, now," he protested, pleased.

Watching them together, Annette was delighted, thinking them ideally suited. Lady Ellen's irrepressible laughter, so like Paul's, set a seal on her thoughts.

It was to Drake she expressed them. He had entered her sitting room before retiring for the night, as was now his custom, and was seated in his favorite chair, his long legs stretched out before him. "What is your news, my dear? For I can see you are fairly bursting with it."

"Lady Ellen has a cavalier," she announced in a conspiratorial manner.

"I think you must be mistaken, Annette. I have seen no suitor about the house."

"You would have fallen over him had you been around earlier in the day."

"It's plain as a pikestaff you are bent on teasing. What in the world are you talking about?"

"Lady Ellen and Sir Carlton Bellamy. They were friends when young. He had heard she was residing here and came calling. Oh, Drake, he is the nicest man and quite taken with her—it was as plain as the nose on your face. Isn't it famous? Now, if only they will realize they are suited. But I have the most melancholy conviction they will need a gentle prodding."

"My dear, you are to leave them be."

"You must realize Lady Ellen will not continue living at Monkshaven, Drake. She has in mind retiring to an establishment of her own. She told me so. And you know what a muddle she would make of it. What will serve her best is a husband. Sir Carlton—"

"My dear, I have matters of our own to discuss."

Annette looked apprehensively at him. "Is something wrong?" she asked hesitantly.

He studied her briefly, then answered regretfully: "I find I must go to London on business. It will not require an unconscionable time to transact. I will be away for possibly two weeks."

"Could I not accompany you?"

"No, my dear. It is best I go alone."

With this she had to be content.

It was not many days before she realized she had never before known the meaning of loneliness. One day was much like another. Brooding in her room, she sat looking across the inner courtyard toward the east wing. In the gathering dusk it did look haunted. No breeze stirred the ivy climbing its stone walls toward shuttered windows. She had never given credence to intuition, but she had the strangest feeling of doom approaching, of an aura of evil lurking in the gloom. Shaking off these strange thoughts, she chided herself for thinking a shadow moved.

But she could not rid herself of the notion that it had.

Although she tried to be cheerful before the others, no one was misled. Lady Ellen favored her with a searching glance and embarked on an amiable campaign to keep her beguiled. In this she was joined by Paul and Harriette. Annette appreciated their efforts on her behalf, but she was out of reason discontent—she could not find the heart to respond.

Lady Ellen could not rest easy; a tonic must be found. The problem was not, after all, so insolvable; a party bringing together a group of congenial companions must assuredly answer the purpose. Accordingly, most regretfully, she sent out invitations for a dinner.

But Providence, for all its benevolence, did not see fit to interfere—the fateful evening eventually arrived.

The party was not destined to be ranked among Lady Ellen's growing number of successes, for Lord Bodkin's presence cast a pall over the proceedings. In all truth, the only person who enjoyed the evening was Lady Ellen, who, conscious of little but Sir Carlton's proximity to her own person, sparkled with the brilliance that was her way.

By the time dinner had come to an end, few of the guests were looking forward with any degree of anticipation to the prospect of further entertainment—with the notable exception of Lord Bodkin. The instant the gentlemen finished their port and rejoined the ladies, he made his determined way to Annette's side. Without preamble, he said, "I hardly know how to tell you the present on-dit about the Earl that is going about London." Smiling slightly, he watched Annette's face with a sly look in his eyes—she longed to slap him.

"You are very obliging, I'm sure, but—"

"Tut, tut. Think nothing of it. The fact of the matter is that Ardley has been escorting certain lovelies about the town." Pausing for this to sink in, he added a final barb: "I understand his almost constant companion has been Lady Ada Kinsley."

Annette looked blank.

"Surely you know of his, er, long-standing attachment to that lady?" Bodkin said, much discomposed. He considered the surprising aspect that Annette had obviously never heard of Lady Ada. "By Jupiter," he said, licking his lips, "you are an innocent. Lady Ada, m'dear, has enjoyed Ardley's protection for an unconscionable time."

Annette kept the smile on her lips with an effort.

"You mean to make mischief, Lord Bodkin, but you are wide of the mark."

The remainder of the evening passed in a haze for Annette. Nothing could have prevailed on her to display her despair before his expectant eyes.

If the majority of the guests remained unaware of her misery, Sir Carlton did not. The last guest to take his departure, he lingered to draw her to one side. "I owe you an apology for bringing Bodkin here tonight. I don't know what wheedle he was trying to cut, and you don't need to tell me, it's no affair of mine, but I did see him buttonhole you earlier in the evening and feared he was bent on mischief."

"Please do not refine on it, Sir Carlton."

"I will confess I was surprised when he contacted me for an invitation for tonight. I just regret being a party to any havey-cavey business and hope he hasn't disturbed you to an uneasy degree."

"You are not to think it. We are grateful to you for your support. I am sure Lady Ellen is."

"As to that, you may be aware of the way the wind blows," Sir Carlton said, not mincing words. "As a matter of fact, I have hopes of becoming more than an onlooker to the family." He grinned boyishly. "If Lady Ellen will have me, that is. Do you think she looks on me with favor?"

"I am sure she does," Annette answered truthfully. "How could she not, sir?"

But for all her brave show, only grim determination kept her back straight until she was free to seek the solitude of her rooms.

She had pleaded fatigue when she excused herself at the conclusion of the evening, but it was not long before Lady Ellen was at her door. "Merciful heavens!" she cried, advancing into the room. "Why are you sitting in the dark?"

Annette looked vague and said the fire gave off enough light.

"Nonsense," Lady Ellen replied. "I can scarcely see my hand before my face. Now you just rest, dearest, while I light the candles."

Annette's nerves by now were quite frayed. She reflected that the last thing she desired at the moment was to relive the evening, then resigned herself to the inevitable.

"I'll be bound it was a prodigious pleasant party," Lady Ellen began, and was off. Annette needed only occasionally to murmur in the affirmative, and otherwise let the sound wash over her. Lady Ellen eventually wound down, said she would retire, and rustled to the door.

Annette said quickly: "Ellen, what do you know of a Lady Ada Kinsley?"

"What?" Lady Ellen squeaked. "Nothing, I assure you," she added hastily. "Why do you ask?"

"I heard her name mentioned."

"I declare, I don't know where. A more wicked, deceitful creature—well, never mind. You just put her right out of your thoughts, dearest. As I am sure you will."

Annette gave a short laugh and turned her head on Lady Ellen's somewhat breathless departure. She saw that she was trembling, on the verge of tears. Drake did not scruple to seek his pleasure elsewhere with someone named Lady Kinsley. Lady Ellen's thin denial only put the stamp of truth to this. She, herself, was an apostrophe, unwanted, the understanding growing up between them at an end.

Knowing this, could she remain at Monkshaven?

She ought never to have wavered from her original intent to become a governess; she could not now face caring for another woman's child, though the reason for this she mustn't permit herself to ponder. But if she could not become a governess, she could seek employment as companion to an elderly lady.

Her decision made, she methodically packed a few necessities and crossed to her desk. One hundred pounds! Well, it would have to do; more moneys she did not possess. Choking back her tears, she quietly slipped from the room and departed Monkshaven.

CHAPTER SEVEN

An occasional flambeau shone on the Earl's face as his coach rattled over the cobbled streets on its way to the town house of Sir Andrew Steppen-Andrews. He had journeyed to London without an inkling of the reason for the trip. He particularly regretted leaving Annette behind, but his instructions had been explicit: he was to report immediately, and alone. The communiqué had been couched with the usual diplomatic subtlety, correctly polite and impersonal. But his lordship could not regard the coming evening with anything but a feeling of profound regret. He disliked mysteries of any sort, particularly those which involved himself, and thought it a very odd thing to have received a summons in all the manner of a royal command. His expression did not reveal any sign of agitation when the coach arrived at its destination, and he walked in his leisurely fashion up the steps and passed into the brightly lighted hall.

Bowing lackeys took his cloak and hat and opened the door to the study at the back of the house. "Well, Drake," Lord Collingham said, coming forward to grip his hand. "I understand you have finally been walked up the aisle. Do I know your lady?"

"I think not, Charles. Annette has always lived in the country."

"You must bring her to town."

"As you may have heard, we are in mourning. But you will visit us at Monkshaven, I trust."

"Just say the word. By the by, Bellamy tells me

Lady Wrexly is presently in residence there. She was a particular friend of m'mother, you know."

"She will be charmed to receive you, I'm sure," Drake replied, accepting a glass of burgundy from a footman. "May I inquire if you know the reason for our presence here tonight?"

"You may inquire, old boy, but the fact of the matter is, I can't tell you, for I don't know."

"Well, I trust we will eventually be informed."

"That is correct. But after dinner, dear boy. After dinner." Sir Andrew entered the room, to clasp the Earl's hand in warm welcome. "It's refreshing to see your face, Ardley. You have been too long from town. But then, I understand felicitations are in order, eh? One might have known you were up to something."

The Earl bowed, smiling faintly. "It will be my honor to make my Countess known to you."

"I will look forward to meeting her," Sir Andrew replied, and turned to greet Lord Collingham.

Dinner proved altogether a more interesting affair than the Earl had expected. Their host was unusually urbane, with Charles in excellent spirits. Quite an hour had elapsed before they returned to the study. The butler placed a tray with wine and glasses at Sir Andrew's elbow, inquired if any further service was required, and withdrew.

Their host poured out a glass for his visitors, waited until they had sipped, and sat back at ease. "You are wondering at the reason for this meeting. A tedious business which will, without saying, remain untold to anyone but yourselves. To put it bluntly, gentlemen, there is an intelligence leak at our office. Information has been finding its way into the hands of the French. While nothing vital has been leaked, I know I need not point out the seriousness of the situation."

The Earl leaned forward, his elbows resting on the arms of his chair. "Have you any idea, sir, of the identity of the defector?"

"An idea, Ardley, yes. Or more accurately, rather, a hypothesis of the manner in which it is being accomplished. I am hoping you gentlemen will desire to be of assistance in uncovering the identity of the traitors. Your loyalty is unassailable and, quite frankly, I cannot say the same of my own staff with any degree of certainty. One of them, a minor employee, yes, but still an employee, has been found to be involved."

"Speaking for myself," Collingham said, "I will be of service in any way I can, but I must remind you, sir, that I am not a professional intelligence operator."

"No, neither of you is. And therein lies your strength. Who would suspect you?" Sir Andrew chuckled. "A more unlikely pair of sleuths would be hard to imagine." Sobering, he held their eyes with his. "You have something else in common, my lords. You own important estates in Kent."

"You think this information is leaving England through Kent?" the Earl asked, surprised.

"I am fairly certain of it, Ardley. I just don't know the identity of all those involved, or the details of how it is being accomplished. I am convinced, however, that the position you gentlemen occupy in society would be of inestimable value in getting to the bottom of this unsavory affair."

"Are you saying you believe a member of society is involved?"

"Yes, I am saying just that. Social gatherings, by the way, provide excellent cover for passing information without attracting undue notice. The connivance, or at least the cooperation, of the host assures an invitation to all parties concerned. It is a dangerous business, gentlemen, played by dangerous men. If you agree to undertake the assignment, you will be doing your country a service that will no doubt go unrewarded, and, in addition, your lives may well be forfeit. Before you make your decisions, you will want to know more of the case. Some six months ago a memorandum could not be found. Intelligence was not particularly perturbed since it contained minor and quite unimportant data. I gather a clerk was questioned, but the paper turned up incorrectly filed and the matter was dropped. It was not until history repeated itself that intelligence became alarmed. You can conceive the agitation. You may be sure everyone was questioned; you may be just as sure, no results obtained. And so a trap was baited. False memoranda replaced the originals in the files—and the waiting began. Something more than a fortnight elapsed—I imagine he thought himself secure—in any event, I will not weary you with details. Suffice it to say, the fish was in the net. A minor clerk and a very small fish indeed. We are after larger game." Sir Andrew smiled slightly. "Now enter you gentlemen upon the scene."

"The information was passed to a member of the aristocracy? I find that hard to credit."

"But a despicable member?"

"You interest me," the Earl said sharply.

"Yes, I thought I should."

"Bodkin?"

Sir Andrew nodded. "He has been losing heavily at the tables for some time and is now rusticating in the country. I believe Bodkin Hall is situated not far from Monkshaven. Chance, or fate, I know not which, has dealt you in."

"I will gladly play the hand, Sir Andrew. I dislike villainy in any form."

"A more unpleasant form would be difficult to imagine. I need not dwell on the character of a traitor—I like to think it a weakness in the genes and not a thing that could flourish in any but a few. Is a man consumed with the fires of anarchy and willing to resort to any means to obtain his objective? Or is it merely greed? It could be either, or it could be else. A situation fraught with possibilities, you perceive."

"Well, I can tell you, I'll do my bit. And gladly, sir," Lord Collingham instantly said. "Should be quite a frolic."

Sir Andrew held up one hand. "If you please, gentlemen, strive to bear with me. I am about to the end of my tale. For while I can give you suppositions, I cannot give you proof. Our erstwhile employee did contact Bodkin—did I tell you he remained at large to be followed?—but what passed between them we can only guess. We may surmise that information changed hands, to go in its own good time into the possession of another. And perhaps another? And still another? Suppositions will not do, my lords. We need proof: names, places, dates—the entire array of sordid detail. No fish, large or small, will be allowed to evade discovery. You will understand that while the present emergency is of a minor nature, a future one could be disastrous?"

"We are aware of the ramifications, Sir Andrew."

"Then I need not say more. Gentlemen, your estates lie close to Bodkin's. Social exchange between neighbors will seem natural, and to have him on the scene, as it were, keeps him under surveillance. You will begin with an occasional invitation to dinner. Not often enough to raise questions, though I am sure his conceit would rule this out. He will no doubt return your courtesy. The Earl and Countess of Ardley will be pleased to accept any invitation he may care to extend. The same goes for my Lord Collingham. But do exercise care, my lords. Bodkin's associates may not be so foolish as he."

"Have you any idea whom they might be?"

"None whatever, my boy, but my best operatives have been assigned to the case. If it meets with your approval, Hodges will join the staff at Monkshaven, with Peale going to Collingham Hall. They will remain with me for the present, but will journey together to report to you. They will keep you abreast of the groundwork we will finish before we are ready for you to take a hand. Make them aware of anything you might stumble across, however trivial it may appear. They will keep me informed. After you leave these premises tonight, we will have no further contact whatsoever." Sir Andrew suddenly gave the throaty chuckle that so endeared him to his fellows. "Should we meet, you may cut me dead with a clear conscience."

"We might need to cut you, sir," the Earl said earnestly, "but I assure you we will regret doing so."

"I am pleased to hear you say that, my boy. I well remember your father and the scrapes we indulged in at your age." Sir Andrew's chuckle again rang out, and on this note their lordships took leave of their host.

The Earl and Lord Collingham went together to put in an appearance at Almack's. No one, seeing their nonchalance, could have supposed them on the eve of the most electrifying experience of their lives.

The Earl settled himself at the basset table, to play with his habitual, seemingly disinterested languor. Only those gentlemen not already far advanced in inebriety could observe the skill with which he disposed his cards, and had those other been in any condition to notice, they would have seen that, while he occasionally plunged deep, he seldom lost a hand. Nor did the brandy that brought grief to many of his fellows have much effect on the Earl.

Lord Collingham was not so fortunate. Opting for the pharaoh table, his lordship spread the skirts of his coat and sank onto a chair, called for wine, and proceeded to lose at reckless play with a hearty enjoyment his opponents found delightful. The Earl, watching from his own game and aware his friend was wallowing in the grip of boisterous excitement, at last rose from the basset table and sauntered to his side.

"No luck, Charles?" his lordship drawled.

A somewhat bleary pair of eyes tried to focus on his face, and failed.

"My dear Charles," the Earl continued, "I am weary. Yes, dear Charles. I am devilish weary. Come along." The Earl heaved Lord Collingham up from his chair. Firmly placing an arm about his shoulders, he guided their wandering steps toward the door. Pausing to clap his hat on Charles's unknowing head, he carefully set his own at an angle on his curling locks, and continued their erratic way down the steps of their club.

The cool air cleared Lord Charles's swimming head, at least a little, enabling the Earl to steer his friend to his address in Brook Street and to deposit him on his own doorstep. The butler had seen his master in like guise before. He accepted his lordship's nearly comatose person, remarked in a detached but most proper manner that my lord appeared a trifle unwell, and ended by saying he was sure his lordship was grateful for the Earl's assistance.

Going back down the steps, Drake very much doubted Charles would feel gratitude, or any other pleasant emotion, when he woke. He would very much more likely growl and curse, and hurl whatever came to hand at anyone foolhardy enough to venture within range.

Drake walked on down the street. It was by now four o'clock in the morning, no one was astir other than the watch and an occasional gentleman, the city was quiet, and Drake was acutely aware of the loneliness of his solitary stroll. Five days now apart from Annette! He felt the unluckiest man alive to have been wrested from her side. Why could he not have the common good fortune to pursue his intent, minus harrying distractions, the same as other men? And now this. Bodkin! Good God! What could he possibly tell Annette? She found the man repugnant and very well knew he was in complete agreement. He had, in fact, referred to him as a loathsome toad. How could he now suddenly profess a desire for his company? The whole thing was insane—Annette would not believe a word of it. The only course he could follow was to bluff it through, evading her questions and feeling like a traitor himself for thrusting Bodkin's company at her unwilling head.

"Drat and damn," he said aloud, to a startled gentleman encountered near Hyde Park corner. Drake did not notice his fellow stroller and remained unaware of the uncomplimentary epithet hurled at his retreating back. To do him justice, he would have offered his apologies had he realized his breach of good manners, but he did not. He proceeded on his way, lost to everything around him.

Somewhere in the inner recesses of his mind, another monster stirred. My Lady Ada Kinsley. God! What a coil. He was pledged to conduct her to a ball. But what would you? Her fiancé was posted abroad, his commanding officer hosting the affair; she had appealed to him for escort—food for the gossip, if ever there was. Society had believed them close, engaged in having an affair, in fact. It was never so. Friends only, neither had desired to alter their status. Another thought stirred in Drake's unwilling brain. It did not seem probable Annette would greet such tidings with any show of fortitude. Nor would she feel her pulses race to think that she had won from Lady Ada that best of all matrimonial prizes, himself. She would be more likely to remind him of the circumstances of their espousing and her own reluctant inclusion in the ceremony. He flected that it would undoubtedly be wise to say nothing of Lady Kinsley.

But fate is a flighty jade, at best. Lady Luck, so long his friend, now unaccountably cast him forth.

For Drake, having traveled through the night, unable to sleep, his thoughts soaring unbidden to delightful heights of fancy, crossed the threshold of Monkshaven—and entered into his private hell. Annette had gone.

She had boarded the early coach for London—and there the trail had ended. Drake returned immediately to the city to launch the search, but the hours stretched into days with no further word of Annette. He left Ardley House each morning, to return at evening, disconsolate, his face grim. He had exhausted every possibility of which he could think, had driven himself to the limit of his strength, and all without a glimmer of success.

How it would all end, no one dared to think.

CHAPTER EIGHT

Annette, dutifully seating herself opposite Mrs. Harrington with her back to the horses, tucked the fur blanket about her elderly employer's knees and handed her the long ebony cane without which the widow never ventured from her house. Mrs. Harrington, a comfortable female, and one of whom Annettè had grown quite fond, perched on the edge of her seat with a magnificent disregard for the comfort of the squabs provided as a part of her well-sprung carriage by a considerate and thoughtful son. That gentleman had, on the occasion of a somewhat spectacular success in business, established his aging parent in a house staffed by a larger number of servants than his mother could deem seemly and provided an allowance of a generosity to guarantee his mama's every comfort.

It was not many minutes before the widow embarked on a happy discourse of her favorite topic— her son and his affairs. With embarrassing candor, to Annette if not to the widow, she discoursed for the first time, and with great freedom, on her son's business acumen, even going so far as to reveal his number of pounds per year, while disregarding the coachman and groom sitting just beyond Annette's shoulder and easily able to hear the widow's every word. She then informed Annette in a very conspiratorial way that it was high time her son took to himself a wife. It seemed she felt that Annette could perform this office in a manner quite acceptable, though how her son would feel about abandoning his bachelor state, she had not troubled to ascertain.

Annette felt powerless. She bore the recitation with a tolerable equanimity, but when the widow became inquisitive in regard to her companion's feelings toward her son, Annette simply declined to comment. Mrs. Harrington then expressed her intention to refrain from further discussion along this line, beguiling the remainder of the drive with talk of the forthcoming church bazaar and her intended contribution to this yearly affair. Although this discussion put her in a great good humor, Annette felt certain her employer had not abandoned her matrimonial plans on behalf of her son. Attentive to Mrs. Harrington as the carriage rolled on through the sunshine, Annette missed seeing a gentleman staring at her from the doorway of a business building. She did not see him wave his arm or hear him call her name.

Sir Carlton, requesting and receiving from his associate the information he desired, returned to the inn where he was staying, instructed his man to pack with all possible dispatch, and in the space of a remarkably short length of time was en route to London and Ardley House. It was with a feeling of unreality that Drake heard him through upon his arrival. Afraid to believe, he stared at the slip of paper bearing Annette's address. "Manchester!" he said, stunned. "But what can she possibly be doing in Manchester?"

"She appeared to be filling the position of companion to a Mrs. Harrington."

Drake spoke over his shoulder as he hurried toward the door. "Be a good fellow, Bellamy, and order the coach brought around."

Four days later, Annette, not knowing Drake had discovered her whereabouts, made good her escape to the garden at the rear of Mrs. Harrington's house. Small and enclosed, it nevertheless contained narrow paths separating beds filled with vegetables and bordered by flowers. Strolling along the paths, she made her way to the bench beneath an apple tree. Mrs. Harrington was away with her son visiting a relative, providing Annette with a rare opportunity to be alone. Sighing, she leaned back and closed her eyes.

She was awakened from her dozing some half hour later by a voice saying her name. Still drowsy, she murmured, "Drake?" Her eyes flew open, and she blinked at him.

"May I sit beside you?" he asked with a humility she had not before heard from him.

Annette nodded, moving over to give him room. Emerging from the shock of his sudden appearance, she asked somewhat innocuously, "Sir, have you been well?"

"I'm fine. And you?" The niceties having been exchanged, an uncomfortable silence fell. "I've missed you," he said softly.

"You have?" she asked surprise.

"But of course. If you knew the sort of weeks I have endured, you wouldn't wonder."

"Drake, why have you come?"

He gazed at her in consternation. "You are my wife," he answered, unsure of himself.

"That is not sufficient reason to burden yourself with me."

"Burden myself!" he ejaculated, appalled. "Is that what you think? Good God, Annette!"

"You do think it," she answered hotly. "If you didn't, you wouldn't have—"

"Wouldn't have what?"

Annette took a deep breath. Thinking rapidly, she

decided to bring the truth out into the open. He had come seeking her to rid himself of the encumbrance she presented. A way must be found out of their imbroglio. "You have desired the company of other females. I do not censure you for this," she hastened to assure him when he would have interrupted. "You were certainly forced into marriage with me, and if your sentiments were previously engaged, I am sorry for it."

"Whatever gave you that idea?"

"You went to London for the express purpose of—Drake, do let us be honest with each other. I know of Lady Kinsley and do not hold it over your head."

Understanding dawning in his eyes, he gazed at her. "Annette, she used to be a friend, nothing more. She is betrothed to an army officer posted with his regiment abroad. She could not attend a ball unescorted, and since the affair was hosted by her fiancé's commanding officer, she applied to me."

"Well, but—"

"It was an opportunity for her to further his interests. I could not refuse."

"But people—s-said—"

"Yes, I know. She was never my mistress, Annette. I would not lie to you about this. I hope you will find it in your heart to believe me."

Staring into his eyes, she knew he spoke the truth. But she had not finished. "Why did you go, Drake? What business did you have to transact that was so important?"

"I am not at liberty to tell you, Annette. I would, but—trust me—I give you my solemn word you have no cause to mistrust me."

Glancing at his pallid countenance, she could not miss his discomfiture. She did not doubt he was laboring under a perfectly understandable tension; his smile seemed forced, but then it would, with the awkwardness of their situation.

"Annette, I have come to take you home."

She could not fail to realize his right to order her future, but what was to become of their marriage she could not imagine. With inherent honesty, she could not but feel guilty for having condemned him with an impulsiveness that had not allowed him to be heard. Drake did not in any way embarrass her with recriminations. They succeeded in arriving at a congenial understanding, leading Annette to think it probable they might someday hope for a return to their former easy relationship.

And so she finally yielded to his pleas, but said, "I could not leave with explaining to Mrs. Harrington. She has been kind to me."

"I will explain. You just pack your belongings."

It was, however, late in the afternoon before they entered their coach to depart. Mrs. Harrington had returned to find her servants considerably flustered by the presence of an earl in the house, but the widow, with her customary aplomb, remained unperturbed by the knowledge that a countess had served as her companion. She declared she had always known Mrs. Lloyd to be a superior sort of young woman. And whatever might have been her opinion of runaway wives, she did not express them, contenting herself with heartfelt best wishes for Annette's future happiness.

As their coach turned onto the main road, Drake said, "Mrs. Elizabeth Lloyd. May I inquire how you settled on that name?"

"Lloyd was Mama's maiden name."

"It is not to be wondered I could find no trace of

you." When he saw she intended saying nothing in reply, he changed the subject. "I do not know where we will pass the night. Are you familiar with the inns hereabouts?"

"No, I'm afraid not, Drake. Mrs. Harrington preferred the less traveled roads."

"Then we will select one at random."

"How did you find me?" she asked curiously.

"Bellamy had gone to Manchester on business and saw you passing in your employer's carriage. He obtained your address from his associate and brought it to me."

"Then he has been often at Ardley House?"

"You might say so," Drake grinned. "Wedding bells are in the offing, unless I am much mistaken."

A slight smile greeted this remark. "I told you they were suited."

Chuckling, he gently drew her against his side. "I, too, happen to own some wisdom," he murmured. "I have the sense to love you." He also had the wisdom to hold her lightly, smiling tenderly into her rather dazed eyes.

She was still rather shaken when the coach drew up before an inn. The door was opened, the steps let down, and Drake was helping her to alight. Drawing her cloak more closely about herself, for the evening had become chilly, she followed the bowing landlord through the door, passed through the tiny well-hall, and entered a private parlor comfortably furnished with a settee drawn up before the fire. Stripping off her gloves, she extended her hands to the warmth of the blaze while Drake bespoke their quarters and discussed the dinner menu with their host. Arrangements completed, Annette followed in the wake of the landlord's wife to a large chamber at the head of the stairs.

She bestowed a smile on the mistress, said she was pleased with the room, and was relieved to see a serving maid bringing in a can of hot water. Pouring some into the basin, she washed her hands and face and dried with a square of soft linen provided for this purpose. A tap sounded on the door, and Annette, crossing to open it, stared in surprise as the landlord and a young boy carried in their trunks and boxes. She had the impulse to point out that Drake's had been brought to the wrong chamber, but forewent it.

Opening her trunk, she ruefully inspected the gowns it contained. Only one was a lively color, a deep pink. She slipped it over her head and smoothed the skirts into graceful folds. Combing out her hair, she dressed it again and stood back to look doubtfully at her reflection in the long mirror. Thinking she looked as well as possible under the circumstances, she rummaged through a case in search of a fresh handkerchief, located one, and went down the stairs to the hall below.

The landlord was waiting to usher her to the private parlor. Covers were laid on a table set up in the center of the room, but of Drake there was no sign. Crossing to the settee, she sat down to await his coming. She owned to herself the chilliness she was feeling might owe its existence more to nerves than to the temperature of the room.

Drake entered and surveyed her somewhat enigmatically. She rose and walked to the table, to sit in the chair he held for her. She drank her soup and noted he finished quite half a bottle of wine by the time the fish was on the table. She felt decidedly uncomfortable when he ceased any pretense of eating and leaned back in his chair to watch her, but was more immediately concerned with his continued drinking. By the time the sweetmeats were on the table, she was finding his by now silent scrutiny more than a little trying. His face was expressionless, but his eyes glittered strangely and strayed often to her breasts pushing against the bodice of her gown. Inspecting the dish of sweetmeats with a care quite out of keeping with the selection, she chose the best of them and bit into it.

So taut were her nerves she jumped when he spoke. "Is it your intention to spend the rest of the night eating?"

"I will have another sweet," she temporized, and reached for a sugar plum.

Drake considered her silently while she ate it. When she finally laid down her napkin, he rose and moved to the door. "Well?" he said.

Annette stood uncertainly by her chair, staring at him. She was thinking fast. It was apparent that he was by now quite drunk; she did not care to risk annoying him to his present condition. But what to do? Retiring to her chamber seemed wise. By morning he should be restored to his customary conduct. Accordingly, she moved toward the door he was holding open for her and preceded him up the stairs.

Walking down the hall by his side, she had an impulse to run, but curbed it. She held out her hand when they arrived at the door. Her voice was pleasant. "I will bid you good night," she said in a carefully level tone.

"Will you?" he asked and threw back his head and laughed. Putting his hand at the small of her back, he pushed her into the room and followed her in.

Annette faced him bravely. "Your trunk was brought to my chamber by mistake."

He curled his lip. "A husband shares his wife's bed. You will grow accustomed."

"If you think—"

"You will become my espoused before this night is out."

"You wouldn't dare," she breathed in a suffocated voice.

There was no stopping him. He stalked to the bed and flung back the covers. He pulled off his coat and hurled it across the room. Annette gaped as his hand moved to unfasten the buttons of his waistcoat. She turned her head and debated what to do. Dashing from the room would gain her nothing—in his present condition he was entirely capable of pursuing her through the halls. She longed to box his ears.

"Well?" he demanded.

She slowly turned her head. The breath caught in her throat. The ruffled collar of his night robe brushing his chin only served to emphasize the air of recklessness about him.

He grinned (she thought he sneered) and walked to the bed. "Hurry up!" he ordered, and lay down with his back to her.

She waited, poised for flight, to see what would come next. When some minutes had passed without anything at all occurring, she whispered, "Drake?" He did not answer. Cautiously she approached the bed. Leaning over, she gazed at his averted face. He was asleep and breathing heavily.

She had a moment's quandary. They had no other chamber. It went against the grain to spend the night in a chair; the mere thought was intolerable, not, in fact, to be borne. Kicking off her shoes, she betook

herself, fully dressed, to the bed, scrambled somewhat haphazardly over his prostrate form, ensconced
herself comfortably, and waited for sleep.

Annette struggled slowly awake and blinked at the
sunlight pouring across the covers. Drake's face was
pressed against her shoulder, an arm encircled her
waist, a leg rode intimately on hers. Blushing furiously, she tried to ease her limb from under his but
abandoned the attempt when her slight movement
threatened to awaken him. Lying still, willing herself
not to move, she drifted back to sleep.

The morning was far advanced when Drake
groaned; he was staring at her in stupefaction, a
queer expression on his face. "Dear God!" he
breathed in disbelief. "What are you doing—Oh, my
God!"

She met his gaze bravely, a flush rising to the roots
of her hair. Then: "You are unwell!"

"Yes," he muttered, his voice hoarse.

Annette cast a furtive glance at his face and
crawled over him as lightly as she could. Crossing to
the washstand, she curled her toes away from the cold
of the floor and poured water into the basin, soaked
the linen square, and wrung it out. Returning to the
bedside, she placed the folded pad on his forehead.
He looked at her without speaking, his gaze falling to
the rosy, pink mounds completely exposed to his view
by her bodice gaping open as she bent over him. "For
God's sake, cover yourself!" he suddenly shouted,
wincing at the pain stabbing through his head.

Annette gazed down at herself, dismay written all
over her face. Desperately hauling the garment into
place, she backed away. Seeing Drake's brows drawn
down in a heavy scowl, she stood uncertainly, her eyes

skittering around the room, and wondered what to do. Her heart thumped heavily as his eyes raked over her. "Are you intending to stand there indefinitely?" he asked shortly.

She had enough knowledge to realize the passionate response of a man to a woman and sensed rather than knew the effort his restraint was costing him. Looking guilty, she scooped up her shoes and hastened from the room, taking care to close the door quietly behind her.

Late afternoon found her enjoying tea in the private parlor. She had spent the day walking over the hills surrounding the inn and had found she was hungry. The door opened and Drake walked in. As always he was immaculately dressed, his fawn-colored breeches and dark brown coat fitting to perfection. Annette was pleased to note his obvious recovery. "The tea looks inviting," he remarked in a pleasant voice.

"Do join me," she said ringing for the landlord as Drake drew up a chair to the table. "But I'm afraid the pot is cold. It will take a moment for fresh to be brought."

"We have the rest of the day," he said easily. "Or what is left of it. In any event, it is too late to set forth now. Did you find amusement in this place?"

"I explored the countryside. You will eat something, will you not?" she added as the landlord returned to place several dishes on the table.

"I'm hungry enough to swallow anything you put before me," he remarked, before exclaiming, "Strawberries!"

"The first of the season, my lord," the landlord beamed.

Drake chuckled and applied himself to the meal,

eating with gusto. Replete, he sighed, content. "An artist in the kitchen. Who would have thought it?"

"You are pleased?" Annette asked.

"I am pleased. Shall we linger here beyond tonight?" Brief though her expression of surprise, it did not escape his notice. "You need not be afraid, my dear. It was enough that I should have become drunk the once. I shan't repeat it." Looking at her carefully, he said softly, "I do not remember much of last evening."

"There is nothing to remember."

"Then I didn't—"

"No."

"I'm glad to know it." His eyelids drooped, veiling his expression. "When it happens, I don't want it to be like that." When she could not meet his eyes, he continued: "There is nothing to be ashamed of, Annette. You know yourself we have been treading on thin ice since the day we were married. Most husbands would have taken their wives to bed before now."

He wished he could read her expression.

"I am as other husbands, my dear. I want you, more than I have ever wanted anything before in my life." (Under his steady gaze she felt her pulses quicken.) "I have been patient, but I am much afraid—" He paused, his eyes studying her. "I want to make this clear. It is not my intention to force you against your will. I do not want that relationship. But I cannot much longer—" Having delivered himself of this somewhat incoherent speech, he rose and strode from the room, leaving her to blink after him.

Less than twenty minutes later, Annette, conscious of being very much exhausted by the emotional strain of the past twenty-four hours, left the parlor and went out into the hall. She was brought up short by the sight of Drake, booted and spurred and enveloped in a surcoat. He was giving his coachman instructions but turned at her approach. "I will be with you shortly," he said. "If you would be so good as to wait in the parlor?"

She went back into the room and walked to a window to look out on the courtyard. A stable boy was endeavoring to control a high-spirited animal and having rough going of it, to the amusement of his friends looking on and shouting encouragement. An outstanding piece of horseflesh, the large roan would require a hand of iron on the reins. A correlation between Drake's attire and the horse waiting out front suddenly struck her. He was leaving! Annette crossed to a chair and sat down.

Here he found her a few minutes later. He came in with an apologetic look on his face, saying that he regretted keeping her waiting.

Annette managed a smile. "It is not my intention to scold."

His eyes searched her face. "I have something to tell you."

"Yes, I know. You are leaving." At his look of surprise, she added, "Your mount is out front being walked."

There came a pause while he tossed the skirts of his coat out of the way and sat down. "I have made arrangements for you to continue on to Monkshaven."

"Are you for London?" she could not stop herself from asking.

"Why should you take such a notion into your head?" he asked, momentarily disconcerted. "Of course, I am for Monkshaven. Moore has been my coachman for years and can be relied on to transport you home in perfect safety."

"I do not anticipate the least difficulty."

"Are you vexed with me for leaving you?"

"I daresay you have your reasons."

"I do," he said firmly. "Not the least of them is the unavailability of a further chamber here. No harm has been done, but it will be best if I go on ahead."

"Oh!" she gasped. "No harm done, indeed! How abominable you are. I am removed from honorable employment in the most high-handed way imaginable, and you say no harm has been done!"

His control slipping, he said curtly, "The Countess of Ardley could hardly be said to be in need of employment."

"Oh!" she flared back at him, jumping to her feet. "You are the outside of enough! You have the—the," she sputtered, "nerve—" She stood glaring, her hands clenched at her sides.

His anger suddenly evaporated. "We are quarreling," he said.

She had the oddest desire to burst into tears, but sought refuge in rallying speech. "I hope I am not so poor spirited as to submit to villainy without defending myself."

"Villainy?" he repeated in a much calmer tone. "My good child, I have given you an uncomfortable time of it, haven't I? That was not my intention and I most humbly beg forgiveness."

"If I am to be martyred in this cause, let me first observe that you have a shocking opinion of my understanding the due consequences of my position."

"Between my horrid notions and yours, things appear to have arrived at a questionable pass. Shall we put them right? I will behave, if you will." Smiling, he put out his hand. "Is it a bargain, then?"

Placing her hand in his, she said, "It is a bargain. Are you ever put out of countenance?"

"Often," he replied with an inference she couldn't miss.

CHAPTER NINE

Altogether to Annette's surprise, the days at Monkshaven passed swiftly, so fully occupied she had little time for retrospection. She sat to have her portrait painted, to hang beside Drake's in the picture gallery; she rode with him most mornings; learning to play chess, she became adept enough to put him in check occasionally, if not checkmate. He did nothing to annoy her on the occasions when she was in his company; on the contrary he was so pleasant she was quite in charity with him. She thought it odd, those strange absences from the house that seemed to occur with disturbing frequency, and she had questioned him about them, but he brushed aside her inquiries, glib of tongue and secretive. While she did not know where he went or what he did, and did not seem in the way of finding out, she nevertheless trusted him—his very attitude toward herself made this mandatory. For Drake knew he had lost ground when she had fled from him, and, intending to regain it, embarked on a campaign to reestablish himself in her estimation, taking care to do nothing to antagonize her.

Annette found her thoughts becoming more and more interdependent with Monkshaven itself. She could not understand its fascination but vaguely recognized an intangible affinity for the older portion of the structure. Riding home with Drake in the mornings, her eyes would wander to the east wing with its ancient stones and narrow, high-set windows. Vast, gaunt, looming toward the sky, that part of the monastery left to become a part of Monkshaven exuded a feeling of loneliness quite at variance with the later additions to the house.

Annette wondered why Drake had never taken her to explore the east wing. He had accompanied her readily enough through the rest of the structure, but inquiries of that particular wing met with polite evasions and vague promises. She knew him well enough by now to recognize the signs of withdrawal that could descend on his face, leaving it expressionless, but had never before encountered the—could it be revulsion?—she had read in his eyes at her first mention of that part of the house. Being by nature more than a little inquisitive, Annette's curiosity was immediately aroused. The east wing was an anachronism, a specter from the past, exciting her mind and spurring her to action.

She had been back at Monkshaven for a month when they dismounted from their horses one morning. Drake having been particularly pleasing throughout their ride, she deemed the time ripe to mention the east wing again. She smiled prettily, and said, "I have yet to see the oldest part of Monkshaven."

"There is little to see," he answered evasively.

Placing her fingers lightly on his arm, she shook her head. "Do not let us quarrel about it, Drake. It is useless to try to dissuade me. Mind you, I am quite determined."

"Quite?" he echoed, looking amused.

"I hold it a bad thing for any female to retreat once she has made her desires known."

Drake threw back his head and laughed. "Being born a female carries with it certain prerogatives, abuse of the male among them. Well, come along, then. Though I am at a loss to know why you will poke around."

They had proceeded only a short distance before they arrived at a winding stair. Gazing upward, Annette resisted the temptation to turn and run back along the way they had come; the dimness of the lower hall seeped into a darkening void as the stairs rose upward. She took herself in hand. Drake led the way, their footsteps echoing hollowly through the gloom; narrow, twisting passageways arrived at blind corners, to continue on at different tangents; the very levels of the floors, with a few steps rising and others descending, delineated the additions to the building as the structure had been added to through the centuries. Annette peeped into numerous rooms as they passed by open doors. Empty and layered in dust, she could tell the entire wing had remained unoccupied for years.

At the end of a narrow hall, Drake lifted the latch of a door at the top of a twisting, stone stair. Cautioning her to place her feet with care, he held her hand and led her downward. They proceeded slowly, for the stair was steep and narrow and did not have a handrail, and was made treacherous by the treads having been worn uneven by the passage of feet through the centuries. By the time they arrived at another door at the bottom of the stairs, she was regretting her insistence on exploring the wing.

Following him through the door, she was surprised to find herself in a room of a luxury quite at variance with the portion of the ancient structure they had just traversed. High bookcases, the sunlight streaming across the vacant shelves, lined the walls. Wing chairs were drawn up before the hearth, while a large desk occupied the space in front of tall windows. Annette was astonished by the elegance of the room, staring in amazement at the opulence of an Oriental rug beneath her feet.

"This was originally the quarters of the head of the monastery," Drake explained, crossing to open the door of an adjoining room. Annette gazed around in silence at the huge, canopied bed and wardrobe as Drake added unnecessarily, "It has not been used in years."

"It was richly furnished for someone."

He crossed to a window and stood looking out. Annette was thinking he did not intend saying more when he muttered, "It was for my tutor. I was often in disgrace and ordered to these rooms."

"If it pains you—"

"I once spoke of his cruelty. He lived in these rooms, a petty tyrant lording it over the helpless boy left in his charge. At times he ignored me, at others he was only too attentive. His favorite form of punishment was banishing me to the part of the house we had just passed through." He paused, a shadow crossing his face. "I was locked in, without light, for days at a time. You can imagine the terror I endured, a small boy alone in the dark and victim to the imaginings of the young. If my father's death had not occurred while I was still a youth, I doubt not I would have been scarred for life."

"What happened then, Drake?"

"I went to live with my guardian. I have often wondered what would have become of me had he not entered my life. Nothing good, I suspect."

Annette rose and crossed to stand beside him, her hand in his. "We will banish your ghosts, Drake."

"How do you propose to do that?"

Looking around the room, she had an inspiration.

"Here! We will start here. Your memories of these rooms are unpleasant. We will replace them with pleasant ones. If we fill the shelves with books, and hang drapery, and—"

"Furnishings do not banish ghosts, my dear."

"But they make a room livable. We will take our tea here, and read together. Yes, and laugh together. You will come to love these rooms, Drake. I promise you that."

Warming to her subject, she talked at great length of pictures for the walls, and furnishings to be moved into the rooms.

"You will want to see the garden," he said when she appeared to have exhausted her discussion. Annette had not noticed a door leading from the apartment until he led her through it. She found herself in a garden enclosed by a high wall and shaded by trees trimmed in the shape of a cube. Boxwood lined the perimeter walls and flowers grew in beds between flagstone paths. The splash of water from a fountain mingling with the perfume of flowers and the hum of bees lent an air of content to the scene.

Annette gazed around. How lovely it was, this oasis made for love. There was no chattering of voices, only the soft trill of birdsong. The garden was very quiet, and yet the atmosphere was one of gaiety and a happiness that brought a lilt and gladness to the heart.

Drake put his arm about her waist and drew her against his side. "It was laid out by my mother when she came to Monkshaven as a bride," his deep voice mumured in her ear.

"It is beautiful. We will take our tea here."

Drake laughed. "Are we to spend all our time drinking tea?"

"What? Oh." Annette sounded angry. Actually, she was conscious of his body pressing against hers and felt slightly dizzy.

"Are you unhappy here?" His voice was sharp. "You sound irate."

It took her a moment to grasp his meaning. She looked at him quickly. "It wasn't that. I felt—strange."

"Are you ill?" he asked, immediately concerned.

"No." She dropped her eyes and tried to move away from him, but his arm instinctively tightened about her. Surprised, she felt his lips on her cheek and turned her head, her mouth close to his for a moment before his lips were on hers. "I won't beg your forgiveness," he said, his voice firm. "I have been wanting to do that for weeks."

It was several minutes before Annette could be restored to her usual composure, and several more before the effects of the kiss ceased to be felt. For a quiver had shot through her body, a feeling quite new and somehow thrilling.

It was, however, not until she sought the solitude of her bed that night that she was free to think of him without the distraction that his presence brought. She had had no notion early in their relationship that she would come to accept intimacies between them, but she now would admit she no longer took fright when he took her in his arms. More to the point, she found nothing to despise in his kisses. Blushing rosily, she felt a little throb of desire to feel his lips pressing hers once again. Almost she could wish him with her in her bed, she thought, and blushed more rosily still.

She could hear him moving about in his room and heard the murmur of his voice speaking to his valet.

He had never crossed the threshold between their bedrooms, but she could not help her nerves giving a little leap to hear his step pause before the door—

She squealed and jerked the covers to her chin. He stood gazing at her, a little strained perhaps, but otherwise amazingly handsome in his long robe.

"What are you—g-going to—d-do?" she whispered, feeling strange.

"Nothing you will object to," he calmly answered. "I am only going to sleep in your bed." Removing his robe, he slipped into bed and turned with his back to her. "Good night," he said quietly, steeling himself to lie without moving.

Annette drew in a quick breath, poised to flee should he touch her, yet excited. She waited, stiff, only gradually relaxing when he did seem to be going to sleep. Perversely, she felt disappointed to hear him breathing evenly and knew that, without a doubt, he had.

If Annette expected to find him beside her when she awakened on the morrow, she soon found him gone from her bed. His pillow still bore the imprint of his head and the sheet was rumpled, but a quick survey of the room failed to discover him lolling in the shadows. She found herself wishing he were, frowned, and climbed out of bed.

The day dragged by without any indication from Drake that the night just passed had been in any way different from any other night. The evening was harder to bear than the day had been. Expectation, alternating with foreboding, could only make matters worse. Annette, in fact, became quite jumpy.

This time when he slid into her bed, he did not turn his back to her, but lay talking quietly, his voice soothing. She scarcely noticed when he turned on his side to face her. Putting his arms around her, he felt her shiver, but gently persisted until she lay clasped against his side. Could he hold her close and still manage to control himself? he wondered. God! he thought. He must. And somehow did.

He was still beside her when she woke. Her eyes flew wide as she stirred in his arms. "I trust you slept well," he murmured in her ear, and kissed it.

Annette pinked. To her surprise she found herself enjoying the novelty of lying in his arms. She felt warm and content and didn't want to move.

"What are you thinking?" he asked softly.

"That I like being here with you," she said, incurably truthful, and, with a queer little sob, buried her face in his throat.

He wondered later why he hadn't taken her then.

CHAPTER TEN

Later that morning Annette appeared on the front steps feeling rather shy, her cheeks delicately tinged with color, and found Drake waiting for her. He mounted her on the mare, his hand lingering on her ankle a moment before he turned away to his stallion. The devil was in his gray eyes and there was a jauntiness to his step that warned Annette a change was coming to their marriage. He turned in the saddle to smile at her—no one was quite sure how it happened—Annette sneezed and the next instant he lay sprawled on the steps. His eyes were open and he was looking at her, but Annette saw his dazed stare and knew he did not see her.

She did not permit herself to give in to the dread that threatened to overwhelm her. She conferred with Watkins, saw Drake carried to his room (fortunately he fainted), and sent for the surgeon. She thought the doctor was taking an unconscionable time in arriving, felt chilled by the pallor of his face, but brightened when his eyes fastened on her in recognition.

"He threw me," he said weakly. "I've never been thrown before."

"Do not try to talk, Drake," she said anxiously, and drew up a chair beside his bed. "We have sent for the doctor. Until he arrives, you really must remain quiet."

"I don't need a doctor," he grunted, and made a

move to rise. Wincing, his face gone dead white, he sank back on the pillows.

"I trust you are now prepared to do as you are told," Annette commented in a businesslike way.

"Are you intending to become one of those bossy females who must have her way in everything?"

"I have little doubt you are intending to be a querulous patient."

"The devil you say."

"You need not be alarmed, Drake. I am sure the doctor will not make you any more uncomfortable than necessary."

He regarded her speechlessly, closed his eyes, and seemed to ignore her. She merely folded her hands in her lap and waited. But when the doctor finally came bustling into the room, he insisted she leave (the slight smile on Drake's lips caused hers to tighten), and desired someone to inform him why his lordship lay propped up on pillows. There was nothing Annette could do but pass through the door Watkins was holding open for her.

The doctor's ministrations left Drake too sore to refuse the laudanum poured somewhat dictatorially down his throat. Two ribs were cracked and tightly bound, but otherwise he had escaped serious injury. The surgeon delivered himself of a few pungent remarks on the foolishness of bestriding an uncontrollable beast, ordered his lordship not to stir from his bed without his, the doctor's, permission, said he would call again, and departed.

Drake slept throughout the day and most of the night. He awoke twice, swallowed the medicine held to his lips, and lapsed back into slumber without knowing it was Annette who held the glass. It was close upon dawn before he was resting easy and she could seek her own repose.

Returning to his room at noon, she found him half-sitting up in bed, propped against his pillows, a truculent expression on his face. "Tell this fool to bring my clothing," he immediately demanded.

"Certainly not," she returned composedly. "I instructed Fisher not to do so. You may direct your recriminations at my head."

"Annette," he began awfully.

"I have little doubt you wish to consign us all to the devil," she said without any visible signs of trepidation, "but you will remain where you are."

His lordship glared, bereft of speech.

She continued in a reasoning tone: "Pray do be sensible, Drake. We will make you as easy as possible. I have ordered a nice broth for your lunch. I am sure—"

"Broth!" he exploded. "So I am to starve!"

"I am sure," she continued imperturbably, "you will enjoy the roast fowl that will follow, and Cook has prepared your favorite custard."

"Well, be that as it may," he said in a more mollified tone. "In future, I will have my orders obeyed. Is that clear, Fisher?" he added to his valet with a restraint that left Fisher feeling he had just been doused with a basin of cold water. "As for you," he went on, his gaze swinging back to Annette, "I do not wish to offend you, but you will refrain from issuing orders to my servants."

She was not noticeably chastised. "Very well," she said obediently. "I will only suggest to them what I think best for your welfare." She walked slowly to the door, and said quite sadly, "I only hope you do not bully them into assisting you in damaging your health."

"Come back here!" he demanded rudely.

Annette looked at him, seemed to hesitate, and then said with a sigh his lordship thought exaggerated, "I have no desire to plague you."

"Yes, you have," he grimly contradicted her. "I would like to box your ears."

Annette laughed. "I don't doubt it, sir. You have taken an aversion to a female in your sickroom. Well, the obvious course to follow to rid yourself of my invasion is to stay in bed like a good boy."

"Annette, my dear, quell your tongue. It's unbecoming. And sit down!"

"Yes, indeed, my lord," she said, and sat.

"Stay with me," he begged, reaching for her hand. His fingers closed on hers, and, grasping hers tightly, he closed his eyes and went to sleep.

As it turned out, it was a fortnight before the doctor would permit him to leave his bed. He had a number of trenchant remarks to make, but otherwise submitted with less objection than Annette would have thought likely. But she found herself powerless to prevent callers from being admitted to his chamber. On two separate occasions, the oddest-appearing visitors remained closeted with him; nondescript of appearance, and obsequious in demeanor, they crept through the house and into his room, only to leave some hours later, their departures silent and secretive.

Annette found she had not the courage to question Drake. She was burning with curiosity and was several times on the verge of mentioning the strange visitations with a hope of discovering what business they could possibly have with him, but the opportunity to introduce the subject did not arise.

She entered his room one morning to find him sitting at a table partaking of a platter of rare roast beef and a tankard of beer. Politely refusing his offer to share his breakfast, she accepted a cup of coffee from Fisher, waited until the valet had left the room, then said she wasn't aware the doctor approved of his patient imbibing spirits.

"As a matter of fact," Drake grinned, "he forbade it. But don't let that disturb you, my dear. It doesn't disturb me."

She knew it would do no good to argue and changed the subject. "I have been thinking, Drake. You will need something to relieve the tedium of your recovery."

"I agree. What do you have in mind?" he asked with the devil in his eyes.

"We could plan the east wing," she plunged on, avoiding those eyes and the glint in them.

"We could, but I have a better idea. Would you like to hear what it is?"

"I think not," she managed to reply, chagrined at her failure to keep her cup from rattling against its saucer. She knew very well the meaning behind his teasing words.

Drake laughed and picked up his tankard. He took a sip, watching her over its rim, and turned in his chair to face her. She was disturbingly aware of his scrutiny, and of the fact that his eyes had dropped to her breasts.

For something to say, she remarked, "You are making an excellent recovery, Drake."

His amused gaze moved upward to her face. Then his brilliant smile flashed, disarming her completely. "We will follow your ideas during the next few days, my dear, for mine must wait upon my recovery. It is folly for a grown man to want to cry, but that is just what I wish to do. Of all the damnable luck—"

She did not speak, but only sat there, wondering what he would say next.

"You are no longer afraid, Annette. I know that."

She subjected the dish of roast beef to a minute inspection before finally braving his gaze. "No, Drake, I'm not," she admitted. "I have been slow to banish my fears, but they were real to me. You have been very understanding."

"You're mighty generous, ma'am, but I had no choice. That will soon be remedied," he added, chuckling.

CHAPTER ELEVEN

Not altogether to Annette's surprise, the refurbishing of the apartment in the east wing had become prolonged. She had been promised the drapery at an early date, only to be informed the shipment had been delayed and further time would be required before delivery could be made. She had experienced further frustrations of a minor, though annoying, nature in assembling volumes for the bookshelves and in locating artworks she deemed perfect for their setting. She had, however, enjoyed the undertaking, her days having been thus full and busily occupied. And when at last she declared the project complete, and Drake stood in the rooms, now fully recovered from his injuries and in the best of spirits, she raised anxious eyes to his face and waited breathlessly for his comment.

"It does you honor," he finally said. "We will take a deal of pleasure in such surroundings."

"You said that very prettily, m'lord. If you will be seated, tea is about to be rolled in."

Laughing, he offered his arm and led her across to the table overlooking the garden. "I knew you would be surprised at tea the first time you stopped by," she remarked smugly as she settled into her chair.

"You are behindhand, my dear. I have already ordered flowers for the table. Did you not know me to be uncannily omniscient?" he added with a twinkle at her startled look. "I felt you would bespeak tea. No, I will correct myself. I knew you would bespeak it."

"I can't decide whether you are acute, or merely conceited."

"A little of both, perhaps. Though my thoughts of you have never been attended by any secrecy."

Annette threw up her hands in mock surrender as the tea cart was rolled in. Watkins placed a floral arrangement of pink roses in the center of the table, and, with a flourish, set a cake before Annette. It was her turn to chuckle. For the confection was in the shape of a horseshoe, frosted white and sprinkled with coconut.

She leaned forward, her face serene. "The symbol of good fortune, I believe."

"You are a resourceful female," Drake said. "I am impressed. I am also hungry."

She cut a piece and arranged his plate. Passing it to him, her eyes were full of laughter. "What you are, my lord, is worsted."

He looked so pleased with himself she could not but wonder at his next sally. She was not to wonder for long. "Drink your tea," he said in a self-satisfied drawl. "You've not much time."

She took a sip and contrived not to question his meaning, only succeeding in amusing him the more. "No questions," he coolly persisted.

She shrugged with a careless gesture. "Oh, I don't suppose it is of any import."

As if to deny her allegation, Watkins approached the table. "The phaeton is at the door, m'lord."

"We're coming," Drake nodded and looked at Annette, his eyebrows raised and with a wide smile on his lips.

She rose and moved toward the door, only restraining her curiosity with an effort. She did not think she could keep from asking their destination, but determined to try. She was perfectly sure he had planned some surprise, and, like a little boy, was wanting to tease her into asking questions which he would pretend to misunderstand.

He led her out to the phaeton and assisted her up, all obsequious attention and loving glances. Annette paid not the slightest notice, settling herself comfortably and smiling unconcernedly.

They soon turned off from the main highway and followed a narrow road winding through picturesque hamlets and green undulating hills to the village of Shibbingstone. As they passed the last cottage, Drake sent the horses down a rutted lane toward an open field crowded with people and conveyances of an astonishing and motley variety. As they neared the area, Annette could see over the heads of the gathering from the height of the phaeton and turned to look at Drake in amazement. "It's a horse fair!"

A rough ring had been contrived around which horses were being led; more animals were off to one side being groomed by their owners waiting their turn in the ring. Drake drove his grays around the crowd to where the cattle came into the ring, winding his way in and out among the gaitered farmers and shifty-eyed agents moving back to make room for the phaeton. Taking up a position at the entrance, he laid a restraining hand on Annette's arm as the young groom jumped down and hurried to the horses' heads. "We will remain where we are, my dear. You will be able to see perfectly well, and I do not want you mixing with the types you see around you."

"It would be a pity to miss an animal that is really good, wouldn't it?" she suggested hopefully, then pinked at his ready grin.

But he only asked, "Do you see anything that catches your fancy?"

"That one might come up to scratch," she answered, pointing to a young stallion in the center of the ring.

"Georgie," he ordered, flipping a coin deftly caught by the tiger, who in turn pressed it into the palm of a young boy, who in his turn ran to the horses' heads while Georgie hurried forward to inspect the stallion.

Returning, the tiger shook his head. "Too nervous by far, gov'nor. E'll go off sad in a year."

"You may rely on Georgie, Annette," Drake said. "He is never wrong about a horse."

"I may rely?" she asked, startled. "Are you saying—"

"Exactly my dear. We are here to purchase a mount of your choosing. To tell the truth, I know of a mare that will be put up for sale and thought you might care to make the decision."

Feeling dazed, she turned her eyes back to the ring, carefully inspecting each animal brought forth and conscious of the weight of her decision. And then she saw the mare. It was frightened by the noise and rearing a little, but Annette knew at a glance she was a lovely creature. Drake, noting her reaction and pleased she had singled out the horse he had brought her to see, motioned to Georgie, flipping a coin to go the way of the first, to the grinning delight of the young lad falling heir to such unexpected largess. The tiger strutted importantly up to the mare, but there was no sign of cockiness about him when he finally looked across at the Earl and nodded.

"Wait here, Annette," Drake said, climbing down from the phaeton. "I will have a look at her."

When they returned, the groom was leading the

mare by her bridle. "Georgie will take her home for you," Drake said as he swung up to his seat.

Annette smiled at him as Drake set the grays in motion, and craned her head as they moved off for a last glimpse of the mare. Sighing happily, she cuddled close against his side and looped her arm through his. "Thank you, Drake," she said earnestly. "She is such a dear."

He put up a heroic struggle, and lost. "There is nothing for it," he murmured against her hair, "I am going to kiss you."

"Drake!" she protested, striving to sit erect. "Someone will see."

"Let them," he replied and made good his word with the utmost disregard for a yokel gaping at them from a field beside the road. Annette, seeing the vacant grin on the face of this witness, tried to control her features, failed, and went off on a peal of entrancing laughter that caused Drake to grin delightedly and repeat his assault on her lips.

She said, when she had opportunity for speech, "The very idea, sir, behaving in such a way. And in broad daylight, too."

He gave a low laugh and released her, commenting, "You liked it. Now confess that you did."

Finding no answer, she said thoughtfully, "I wonder what I should call the mare. It should be a name worthy of her beauty. A flower, perhaps? No, that won't do." She was silent a moment, pondering. Then: "Heather!" Drake looked at her in surprise as she continued: "Yes, that shall be her name. I remember thinking it the prettiest sight the first time I saw it."

What he thought of such a name for a black filly with a white fetlock, he kept to himself.

On their return to the house, Drake took himself off on business with his secretary, and Annette, finding herself at loose ends, returned to the apartment, curling up in a chair with a book. It wasn't long before the warmth of the fire, in combination with the silence around her, made her drowsy. Only gradually did a faint sound penetrate her consciousness. She was more curious than disturbed. The east wing had been unused for years and she wondered who could be moving about in that labyrinth of gloom. A servant, no doubt, she thought, though what one could be doing there, she was not interested enough to find out.

She thought later she should have guessed that something was wrong.

Shortly after dinner, Drake sat at his desk in the library absently rolling a quill back and forth in his long fingers, his eyes on Annette. She was seated by the fire, an open book on her lap, her head lowered in pensive thought.

"What is it, my dear?" he asked quietly.

Annette looked at his handsome face and said in a rather dreamy voice, "Must you ferret out my secrets?"

His eyebrows rose. "If you would rather not say—"

"Always so polite," she murmured, still languid.

"You have a scheme in mind."

She crossed her legs and swung one foot. "Very true."

"Perhaps you will tell me in your own good time."

A mischievous giggle bubbled from her throat. "What will you give me if I do?"

"It is what I'll give you if you don't."

"You will have me whipped?"

"No," he said, and waited. (She wrinkled her nose

at him, much pleased with herself.) "I would permit no man to touch you. I would administer it myself."

"Would it be best to have a care?" she wondered.

"It would be best not to tease. I am recovered, and you have much to learn. I will be your tutor."

She colored but met his look. Rather bravely, she thought.

He relented. "We were speaking of a scheme you have in mind."

"You won't think—it was only a party."

"I think it an excellent idea, my dear. A dinner, perhaps, to be followed by cards. Shall we compose the guest list?"

Annette crossed to his desk and drew forward a chair. "There is Lady Ellen, Paul, and Harriette. And Sir Carlton. Then—"

"Not so fast," he interrupted, pulling forward a sheet of paper and dipping a quill in the inkpot. "Let me get these first ones down." The quill scratched busily. "Now, who is next?"

"Agatha, of course. Do you think she will come?"

"I will see that she does. Who else?"

Annette opened her mouth—and closed it. Who, indeed?

Drake raised his eyes to her face. "May I make some suggestions?" he asked quietly. "There is my good friend and neighbor, Lord Charles Collingham. You have yet to meet him, but I'm certain you will like him." He wrote the name down. "Lord and Lady Ington and daughter Melissa. Their estate is west of here, some five miles, I believe. Lady Ington was a friend of my mother. Now, let me see. Sir Markham and Lady Scott. Our lands march with theirs on the south. We have thirteen on the list, my dear, including ourselves. Seven women, and six men. It will not serve. We will add another gentleman." He paused and glanced at her. "Lord Bodkin," he said, his eyes now carefully on the paper.

Annette gave a shriek. "What!" She stared in disbelief. "You could not have said Lord Bodkin!"

"He will partner Aunt Agatha. The table will be balanced. I think, my dear, this will comprise our list. The state of our mourning—"

"Drake, you needn't think you can quick-talk me into submission. I would like an explanation."

"I told you, my dear. We need a gentleman to even the number."

"I am sure you have some acquaintance who would do nicely."

"One should be friendly with one's neighbors. Lord Bodkin—"

"But we despise him. You know we do."

"Perhaps when we know him better—"

"Fiddle!" she said rudely. "He would be no less detestable had we known him for years. If you are nourishing thoughts that I will welcome him, permit me to correct the illusion."

"Ah, but you will, my dear. I wish it, you see." Beneath his gentle tone, she sensed the steel.

Suddenly Annette's eyes were swimming in tears. She rose. "I should have known," she said bitterly, and turned for the door.

"One moment, my dear. You must forgive me, but I have something further to say." He picked up the quill from the desk and examined it with unusual care. "At times one is not at liberty to explain one's reasons. One must be accepted on trust."

"If one wishes trust, one should give it."

"I am aware of that, certainly. But there are times—" He placed the quill back on the desk. "I would not request you accept Lord Bodkin's company if I thought you would be harmed by doing so."

"That I do not wish to do so does not interest you?"

He turned his head. "You mistake my motives."

"I am to understand, then, that I have no say in the matter?"

"I am very much afraid I am unable to correct your thinking at present."

"That being so," Annette said through her teeth, "have the goodness to excuse me, sir. I have nothing further to say."

He stood and crossed to the door, and held it open. She walked past him into the hall, her eyes smoldering dangerously, and swept up the stairs, to indulge her agitating reflections in the privacy of her chamber.

Feeling justly incensed, she sat herself down in her elegant little French chair to consider the perfidiousness of all men in general, and of one man in particular. It was small wonder she should not wish to talk to him; she did not care, and should he beg for further audience, she would not scruple to refuse. She would, instead, remain where she was and work on her embroidery.

She remained ruthless in her determination—for quite two hours she continued to ply her needle. The commonest civility should have brought his lordship to her door. His neglect was intolerable. The unwelcome suspicion crossed her mind that she was destined to forego the satisfaction of denying him admittance. By the time she had spent the evening without word from him, she was sure of it. Sighing, she gave up the struggle and went to bed.

During the days remaining before the party, she

held herself aloof. The preparations might very well not have gone forward at all for all the attention she paid them. She busied herself with her own affairs (all of which she had to invent) and assumed an air of indifference quite at variance with her heavy heart. Drake, failing twice to soften outraged indignation, silently cursed and gave over the day—it must be left for time to remedy the harm forced secrecy had done.

Annette continued to brood in fruitless solitude. It was not to be wondered she would take exception to his conduct. His behavior was unpardonable, his refusal to relent utterly despicable. He was dictatorial and overbearing, and she herself little better than a shrew.

Such artless musings produced confusing results. She found that she was trembling, her composure set aside. What passed through her mind during the remainder of that day, she did not divulge. She emerged from her rooms for dinner, pale but determinedly pleasant, and had the small comfort of not having the impropriety of her behavior commented on.

The approaching party naturally made inroads into her newly acquired and quite blameless demeanor. No gown would do. This one displayed too much décolleté, that one not enough. One should think a wardrobe of numerous selection would be sufficient to demands placed upon it—it was not so. A knotty problem, surely.

Annette was so taken up with the vagaries of her toilet, she had no time to spare for thoughts of Lord Bodkin. It was just as well. Otherwise the night of the party might have found her in a dangerous mood. It found her, instead, smiling and expectant as she descended the stairs to the brilliantly lit hall below. In a gown of emerald crepe, and with diamonds at her throat and on her arms and fingers, she was a vision to dazzle the most exacting critic.

It still lacked ten minutes to the hour, and although Paul and Sir Carlton were present to witness her descent, of Drake there was no sign. It was left to Sir Carlton to come forward, as indeed he did, but Annette had never felt more disappointed in her life. The first guests were announced and she moved in some confusion to welcome them, assisted by Sir Carlton who generally filled Drake's absent shoes. Annette had no idea where he could be and hoped every moment to see him walk in.

Free for the moment, she threw Watkins an expressive look which brought him to her side. Replying to her query that he believed his lordship to be conversing with the new gardener, the butler carefully kept his eyes from her thunderstruck face, inquired if he could be of further service, and returned to his post by the door.

Annette was recalled to a sense of her surroundings by the arrival of Lord Bodkin. He stood before her, a quizzing glass on a long stick held in negligent fashion some eight inches from his eye. He came mincing forward on ridiculously high-heeled shoes to make a flourishing bow. "My dear Countess," he said expansively. "My very dear Countess."

Annette sketched the briefest of curtsies. "My lord."

Lord Bodkin gave a high-pitched titter. "You look ravishing, m'dear. 'Pon my soul you do."

"Thank you," she murmured in tones of dulcet sweetness. "Shall we join the others in the salon?"

My lord gave another titter. "Why, certainly. Certainly. As you wish, dear lady."

Annette's eyes lingered for a moment on his face, then she turned to lead the way. The glow of the candles in the huge chandeliers shimmered on the gown flowing about her slim form and struck myriad points of darting light from the diamonds about her throat and arms. Lord Bodkin's eyes glittered queerly and swept over her as she went before him, but he did not speak.

The drawing room was a charming apartment. Exquisite gilt furniture brought from France by Drake's father stood about on the large Savonnerie carpet; masterpieces of the Italian school looked down from walls especially upholstered for them in the palest of straw-colored silk; great bowls of roses placed artfully about sent their perfume into the air. The room set off the ladies to advantage and had been the object of some envy, and indeed a few attempts, abortive though they may have proven, to copy it in several aspiring ladies' homes.

Annette and Lord Bodkin entered to find the company standing about in little groups, chatting and sipping superlative wines from Monkshaven's excellently stocked cellars. Annette looked around for Sir Carlton and moved resolutely forward.

"Luck always favors me," he bowed to her, an appreciative twinkle in his eye. "Ah, Lord Bodkin. I trust you are well?"

"Tolerably, my lord. Tolerably. Where's Ardley?"

"I am just behind you, sir." The Earl's quiet voice spoke at Annette's elbow, causing her to make a little jump. "You are acquainted with our other guests, I trust?"

Annette ground her teeth at hearing Lord Bodkin's annoying little titter for the third time. "But, Ardley, most assuredly I am," he simpered.

Drake transferred his attention to a gentleman standing by his side. "Annette," he said, placing his hands on her shoulders and turning her about, "this is my friend, Lord Charles Collingham. Be kind to him, my dear. He's a lonely soul."

"I'm dashed if you're to think it." Lord Collingham grinned, bowing over her hand. "You didn't do her justice, Drake, my boy. If she were my wife, bless me if I wouldn't lock her away."

Drake looked amused. "My dear Charles," he lazily drawled, "you cannot have considered the mettle of your adversary. But think a moment, dear boy, before you fly in the face of danger."

"I do not understand," Lord Bodkin interjected. "Why would his lordship wish to lock Madame away?"

There came a short silence. Drake's eyes flicked to Bodkin's face. "It was intended as a joke," he said dryly. "If you will bear with us, sir."

"Are you French, Lord Bodkin?" Annette suddenly asked.

He made a hasty movement, and was still again.

Annette added contritely, "I don't know why I said that, sir. Of course you are not French. How could you be? It was the way you said 'Madame' that took me by surprise."

Bodkin shrugged. "Doubtless many Englishmen use the term."

"But you sounded so French," she persisted. "Have you known many Frenchmen, Lord Bodkin?"

"I passed some time in France," he answered shortly.

"I declare, that must have been a trial, what with that terrible Bonaparte, and all," Lady Ellen said vaguely, losing interest and looking around the room.

"Great heavens. Where did Lettie find jaconet in just that shade of blue? I have been all over—I positively must ask her—" And Lady Ellen fluttered away in a swish of silk.

Lord Bodkin turned from watching her departure and smiled ingratiatingly at Annette. "A charming lady," he murmured in honeyed tones.

But she felt his smile forced and tried to put a name to the strange expression that had flickered for a moment in his eyes when she made her thoughtless remark. Perplexed, she watched but saw no further outward aspect of a like nature before they went in to dinner. She was seated some distance from his place at table but managed to observe him closely. She read a potpourri of emotions on his face, but concluded that none of them seemed in any way out of the ordinary.

Throughout the remainder of the evening, as Annette moved graciously among the guests, her thoughts returned again and again to Drake's insistence on Lord Bodkin's presence here tonight. She could understand tolerating his company, albeit unenthusiastically, if such a meeting took place in some other locale. But in their home? At Monkshaven? Drake would not in the general way socialize with such—she was shrewd enough to see that Lord Bodkin did not belong with the elite, his title notwithstanding. There was a mystery here—she would seek its solution. It would be poetic justice, she thought, and smiled.

It was regrettable that Drake could not read her thoughts.

CHAPTER TWELVE

Late the next afternoon, Annette sat in the apartment of the east wing listening to the stillness. Its vibrant quality lifted her spirits, made her feel gloriously alive. Idly crossing to a window, she looked out upon the garden; evening was fast approaching, casting long shadows and obscuring the view. She came away from the window and wandered around the room, finally settling herself comfortably with a book. Reading on and on in the darkening room, drowsiness slowly overtook her; her eyelids drooped, were forced open, drooped again.

Gasping, she struggled up from sleep. Her mind fuzzy, only partially conscious, she blinked her eyes—and stared. "W-who—" She tried to rise, willed her limbs to move—and sank back. She gazed in stupefaction. "W-what—w-who—" She couldn't take it in. A man sitting in a chair, looking at her?

"Drake!" she whispered. "Drake!" her mind sighed—

She woke with a start, for a moment feeling suffocated, and remembered seeing the man. A vague uneasiness, the strangest feeling she couldn't define, insinuated itself over her. She held her breath, her pulses racing in sudden terror.

Fear spurred her to action. She slipped through the door and crept along the hall, feeling her way in the thickening dark. Skirting the console, she paused to listen. Above the sighing of the house she detected a sound, a soft swishing as of footsteps moving. A dark form loomed in the dark, a glimmering of light—

Annette screamed, the sound tearing through the silence, reverberating off the walls, bouncing back to mingle with the whimpering coming from her throat. From out of the pool of light the startled face of a footman emerged, coming closer as he stared, stupefied by her frightened face.

Drake burst from the library and tore along the halls. Shoving William aside, he rushed to take her trembling body in his arms. "My God! What is it?" he asked in a shaking voice.

"I s-saw—" she gasped, clutching frantically at his arms. "The g-ghost. I saw the ghost!"

Without another word, he lifted her in his arms and carried her back to the apartment, through the sitting room and into the bedroom. Annette tried not to cry—failing this, she buried her face in the folds of his neckcloth and dampened it beyond repair.

He lowered her gently to the bed and removed her clutching hands from the lapels of his coat. "You are quite safe, Annette," he said, seating himself beside her. "Try to control yourself."

She made an effort to choke off her tears. "I'm s-sorry to be so poor spirited," she managed to utter. "But I was so frightened. A man—no, a ghost—"

"Annette, there is no such thing as a ghost."

"Then who was he?" she demanded truculently.

"I haven't the slightest notion," he calmly replied. "Tell me about it."

"Well, I was reading and dozed off. Then I woke up and s-saw—"

"Yes? What did you see?"

"The ghost!" she insisted defiantly. "He was sitting in a chair watching— Oh, Drake!"

"I would much prefer to discuss this sensibly, but for the moment we will assume you saw a ghost."

"Are you suggesting I imagined him?" she asked disgustedly.

"I am not suggesting that, no. But I do think you may have been dreaming. My dear, you should now forget this."

"Forget what?" Paul demanded, coming hastily into the room. "What the devil is this about? Watkins couldn't, or wouldn't, say, but I heard the disturbance. What's amiss?"

"We will discuss your execrable manners, but not in my wife's bedchamber," Drake said unpleasantly.

"Damme if I care," Paul said, staring at Annette's pallid countenance. "She looks ill to me."

"It is most improper—"

"Please do not make a scene, Drake," Annette intervened. "Paul will need to know."

"Know what?" Paul demanded.

His lordship sighed and motioned Paul to a chair. It did not take long to repeat the tale. Paul exclaimed once during the telling, but generally heard it through without indulging in distracting questions. He was then able to state that it was his opinion Annette had the right of it, that there was no question about it, she had had an encounter with Monkshaven's ghost. Drake cut short further remarks along this line with a few stringent remarks of his own. He thought he had put a period to the whole affair, but he had not, for Paul departed to seek the council of his long time friend and cohort, Dickie Beauchamp.

Silence reigned supreme in the room following his departure. Drake stood looking down into Annette's face, a hungry gleam creeping into his eyes. Suddenly he bent and, before she could protest, swept her up into his arms. Her struggle was brief and soon over— she was returning his kisses with an ardor to match his own. He raised his head to stare into her eyes before his mouth again closed on hers, his arms crushing her against his chest. She felt him molding her soft body to his, grinding her thighs to his, and pressed closer still. He undressed her slowly and lay her gently on the bed, the breath catching in his throat as he gazed down at her.

She watched him strip away his clothing, his body quickly emerging to view, and stared. But he was soon beside her, his lips on hers, and she forgot her fear in the thrill of his seeking hands and searching lips. He was slow and gentle, touching her intimately, caressing her softly, and finally when at last he claimed her, she clung to him, and knew his passion, and sighed softly when it ended.

She held him tenderly, her limbs entwined with his, feeling a dreamy content as his lips brushed lightly across her cheeks, touched her eyes, softly pressed against her mouth. Half-smiling, he idly traced a finger around her face and down her throat to a breast, cupped the breast with loving hand. Lying back against the pillows, loving the newness of his loving, the sweet teasing of his fingers, she felt she did not wish to move again, to leave the splendor of his loving.

CHAPTER THIRTEEN

Lady Ellen rapped briskly on the library door and hurried in. "Do I find you busy, Ardley?" she asked somewhat breathlessly. "Well, never mind if you are, for I need your support. As head of the family, you may feel obliged to put an obstacle in our path, but I apprehend you won't. I only hope you won't ask provoking questions."

The Earl had risen to his feet at her entry and now came around his desk to pull a chair forward for her. "What will I not obstruct?" he asked in his leisurely way.

"My coming nuptials," she thrilled, perching on the edge of the seat. "Dearest Carlton says he does not in the least intend being put off any longer. So really, Ardley, you must give your consent."

"But, of course. Did you expect I wouldn't?"

"Well, no. But Carlton wished you informed."

He regarded her with a devilish grin. "Should I ask his prospects before I grant permission?"

"Good gracious," she said, laughing in return. "Carlton is the stickler. I could care less for that, now you and the children approve."

"May I inquire if your plans have progressed beyond this stage?"

"We did hope the ceremony will take place at Monkshaven. And I needs must go to London for my trousseau, I dare swear."

"Annette and I will be pleased to place

Monkshaven at your disposal. And you will have all bills sent to me."

"My dearest Ardley—"

"Do not embarrass me with a surfeit of praise, I beg you."

"Very well," she replied, moving toward the door, "but you will permit me to say you are the most complete hand?" she tossed over her shoulder, and vanished through the door.

Smiling to himself, he started back around his desk. Glancing through the window, he saw Hodges in the gardens, and went, instead, from the house and down a path.

"Sir Andrew told me to put this in your hands, m'lord," Hodges said softly, surreptitiously pressing a folded paper on the Earl.

Drake thrust the missive in a pocket and bent over a shrub with every appearance of studying it. "Do you know what the note contains?"

"No, m'lord. Sir Andrew didn't say and sealed it with wax." Hodges suddenly grinned. " 'Tis his way of telling us not to meddle."

"I have a message for Sir Andrew. You will go to London, ostensibly to purchase a replacement for this bush. Tell Sir Andrew that her ladyship asked Lord Bodkin if he were French. She told him the thought occurred to her when he pronounced the word 'Madame' as a native-born Frenchman would. I have no idea why, but from the expression on Bodkin's face, I would say her chance remark touched a nerve. —Yes, Hodges, it definitely must be replaced," the Earl suddenly said in a louder voice. "It is not a healthy plant. Ah, my dear," he continued to Annette approaching down a path, "have you come to see the gardens?"

"I saw you from the house and wondered what you were doing."

"Conferring with our new gardener. You have not met Hodges, I believe. He was a real find, my dear."

"I am sure he was," she replied, looking at him strangely. She remembered Watkins having said Drake was conferring with the new gardener when he should have been on hand to greet their guests on the evening of the party. "We are glad to have you on the staff, Hodges. The gardens are in need of a knowing hand."

"I'll do me best, m'lady," he answered, clutching his cap in both hands.

"That will be fine," she said pleasantly, and turned to Drake. "Will you walk with me? There is something I wish to tell you."

They wandered down a path and came to the lake. Drake helped her to a seat in the skiff and put the oars in place. "Are you sure you know how to work this thing?" she asked with mock severity.

His lordship seemed incredulous. "You ask me that!" he demanded. "Me, an oarsman of the first stare!"

Annette giggled. "Sir," she said. "You have all my sympathy. I know nothing of your past."

"My present, Madam, is the thing that should concern you."

"The mystery grows."

"It will soon be solved, my love. Land approacheth."

Her eyes widened. "It's the island!"

"True."

"But there is nothing on the island!"

"On the contrary," he replied, stepping ashore and holding out his hand. "Shall we proceed?"

Wonderingly, she placed her hand in his and looked around in bewilderment. A path led inward from the water, rising gently through the gorse, to round a curve and disappear. "One would never know it here," she commented, and followed along behind him. "Where does it go?"

"Patience, my dear. You will like it very well."

A half-mile farther and a clearing was reached, a peaceful spot overhung with widely spreading limbs of oak. Sitting serenely in the dappled shade—Annette could only stare—was a Chinese pagoda, and looking much at home in its English setting.

Drake slipped an arm about her waist and led her forward. "You find it to your taste?" he asked softly.

"It is so unexpected, Drake. Who built it?"

"My grandfather, some fifty years ago. Pavilions were much in the mode at the time, but few were hidden away like this. It leads one to wonder at my esteemed forebear, wouldn't you say?"

"No, I wouldn't. I shouldn't care to give you an opening to say something outrageous."

"That will not do, my dear. All these weeks I have remained a man of considerable resourcefulness. I have not needed an opening."

"You have only to add that only the most determined considerations of honor compelled you to break your silence."

"You are quite out, you know," he replied, and she knew she had given him his cue. "It was not until I recognized your determination to avoid my company that I dared to entertain the notion you viewed me in a loverlike way. It put a delightfully different complexion on the whole affair." His lordship, having reduced her to the condition of total speechlessness, chuckled, ignored her belated remark on the lost art of chivalry, scooped her off her feet, and carried her inside.

One room comprised the entire ground floor. Seen from the circular center of the room, and set at the four main points of the compass, were alcoves hung with silk and furnished with settees. A patterned marble floor and tile on the walls depicting scenes of mythological origin—Annette caught but a glimpse as Drake strode across the floor and mounted the circular stair.

Reaching the floor above, he stepped forward—and stood still, gazing around in disbelief. The room, which should have reflected the serenity and order of its cultural form, displayed, instead, a state of disorder he had to admit lamentable. The bed, a delightful concoction of bamboo carving, and (until now) the target of this visit, could only be described as rumpled, a prospect his lordship found not pleasing. Nor could the remains of a meal left moldering on a table imbue its viewer with any strong desire to linger long amid the litter.

Drake, who had no idea of the identity of his lackapenny guest, made not the least attempt to search about the room to discover it, not, indeed, from any lack of curiosity, for he had that, but because he held close to his heart an unrepentant bit of fluff whose feet had seldom trod the righteous path of rectitude. That Annette was displaying no tangible sign of unholy glee brought him little comfort. He knew his love. For her to hold her tongue in the face of so much temptation was too much to expect. Nor did he. He turned on his heel and stalked back down the stairs and did not stop until he reached the lake.

Annette stole a look at him from under her lashes. She found her view limited to a glimpse of ear and square-cut jaw, and withheld comment until he had lowered her into the skiff. She then said innocently, "One must admire someone's resourcefulness."

He undoubtedly would have met with further remarks of a like nature had he dallied along the way. He did not. He rowed them back across the lake at a goodly clip, walked beside her up through the gardens to the house, saw her inside, and retraced his steps to relate his discovery to Hodges. "I am sure I don't know who it can be," he finished, looking off toward the island, "but I am inclined to think we should find out."

"If I may so say, m'lord, Mr. Peale could go to London while I keep m'eyes open here. Unless ye think it could be young Sir."

"Lord Wrexly? He could never be guilty of slovenly habits. No, someone is using the pavilion for a purpose. Ask Peale to bring instructions from Sir Andrew. The course we follow upon discovering the identity of our trespasser could be vital. And do have a care, Hodges. I would hate to lose you." The Earl's smile gleamed. "I have become accustomed to having you around."

His lordship went immediately to the library on his return to the house. Arrived there, he sent for his secretary and spent the next hour answering correspondence. This task completed, he leaned back in his chair, remembered the letter Hodges had brought him earlier in the day, fished it from a pocket, and spread it open. The message was brief, without salutation or signature:

Lady Ada Kinsley will be included in the list of guests staying at Monkshaven for the wedding of Lady Ellen and Sir Carlton.

Drake drew in his breath—and read the missive a second time. He couldn't credit it. Nothing he could have imagined would have prepared him for this. Rising, he crossed to stand staring out of the window at the sunlight shimmering in the haze. "Damn!" he ejaculated aloud, and ran his fingers through his hair. "I should refuse," he muttered to himself. "God, if only I could!"

Cardwell watched without speaking. He had been his lordship's secretary for enough years to know when to hold his tongue. Ardley was as reasonable an employer as he could hope to serve, but he had seen the Earl in his many moods and recognized the symptoms. He would have given much to know the contents of the letter but thought it as much as his position was worth to ask.

Drake stood glaring at the missive as the minutes ticked away on the tall case-clock in the corner. How could Sir Andrew have known of the coming nuptials when he himself had known only since this morning? He had not, in fact, as yet informed Annette! Annette! His face softened as his thoughts veered to her. Cardwell, seeing his changing expression, sighed mentally in relief.

Drake sighed audibly. "Mark, will you tell Watkins I wish to speak with her ladyship?"

"May I inquire if your lordship desires my further service?"

"No, not today, Mark. I am in no mood for work."

Cardwell gathered his papers together and went in search of Watkins. Whatever the news that had disturbed the Earl, it was apparently not of a nature to disrupt the evenness of their days.

In this he was mistaken.

Annette informed Drake she had known of the

coming nuptials, had indeed intended to speak of it but (with a gleam in her eye) events on the island had put it out of her mind.

"I plan to give Cousin Ellen a free hand," he commented dryly. "With Monkshaven and its staff at her disposal, we should escape the preparations she will no doubt deem necessary."

"I daresay they will take her to London."

"Within the week. A trousseau looms large as the first order of business."

"And Paul?"

"He finds himself able to withstand the temptation in favor of the many diversions Monkshaven has to offer."

"Is it possible to feel sorry for a ghost?" she asked pertly.

"Annette," he said seriously, "he has sought permission to hunt for it, but I wish you won't mention it. It can do no good, and Paul might be thought foolish."

"Very well. I shan't speak of it."

Something in her manner caught his attention. "I trust you expect to remain aloof from his plans?"

"You wish me to?"

"Unless I'm permitted to join the quest."

"You shall lead the way." Moving to the door, she could not resist the temptation. "I see you are not above making yourself look foolish," she flipped at him as she crossed the threshold.

Drake stared broodingly at the door through which she had vanished. He did not cavil in the performance of his duty as laid on him by Sir Andrew. It was, rather, in the way of its performance that vexed him. There was, first, the necessity for secrecy, and its attendant trauma in keeping the truth from Annette.

Then secondly, dammit, came Bodkin's unavoidable
company, a bitter pill to swallow. Other than her ini-
tial reaction, Annette had been a trump about it. But
could she be prevailed upon to accept cheerfully the
addition of Lady Ada to their charming little group?
He could not bring himself to see that there was any
particular likelihood of this. His instinct for danger
seldom failed him, nor did it now.

As he had predicted, they were not unduly involved as the date for the wedding approached. The
magnitude of their escape became apparent when the
bills began arriving at Monkshaven with an appalling
regularity. If the Earl was surprised by the amount of
his money passing into the eager palms of an army of
tradesmen, he kept it to himself, only remarking that
if all that was expected of him was providing the
blunt, he was well enough content.

It was some time before the storm clouds gathered.
Drake (taking care not to provoke Annette) readily
gave his consent to any suggestion she put forth. He
did not mention Lady Kinsley, cowardly (he admitted to himself) delaying the disclosure until the last
possible moment. Annette, accustomed to meet in the
past with denials of at least a part of her schemes,
was left bewildered. The problem possessed her
thoughts for many days before an explanation
presented itself.

Having accompanied her on a stroll through the
gardens, and leading her through the maze to a
bench at its center, Drake seated her (she thought
with unusual solicitude) and spoke in an offhand
way. He said, "No rose in the garden is prettier than
you, my dear."

Annette, no fool, smiled, said, "You are gallant, my
lord," and waited.

"I have a favor to ask. We are invited to a dinner and I am hoping you will wear your rose gown."

"I have not before known you to make such a request. Who is giving the dinner?"

His tone was remote. "Lord Bodkin," he said.

"Certainly not," replied her ladyship, promptly and with finality.

He sighed. "I imagined you would say that, though I had hoped you would not."

"Are you intending to insist?"

"I'm afraid so, my dear."

"You will do better to save your breath."

"I see no need for you to speak in an unladylike way."

"I thought my words extremely apt."

"They were excessively vulgar," he answered crushingly. "In any event, I have accepted the invitation."

"You have accepted—" Annette sputtered. "Are you telling me that—"

"You will need to decide which jewels to wear so Cardwell may take them from the safe. I am sure you know that either the rubies or the pearls would be equally suitable." He looked at her a moment, then glanced away. "I would recommend the pearls. They are quite fine and would not only complement the color of your dress, but would glow against your skin."

"I much prefer the rubies," she said instantly. "They are also quite fine and will be infinitely better with the rose gown."

"I really wish you would wear the pearls," he gently persisted.

That determined it for Annette. "I am sorry to be disobliging," she said with a smile that belied her words, "but you will be good enough to instruct Cardwell I will require the rubies."

The Earl stood. "As you wish," he said without expression, leaving Annette much pleased with her victory.

Her pleasure was of short duration.

Crossing the hall later in the day, she met the secretary just emerged from the library. "I imagine his lordship has instructed you to take the rubies from the safe, Cardwell," she said serenely. "I will wear them tomorrow evening," she added, bestowing on him a somewhat self-satisfied little smile.

The secretary looked startled. "I have already done so, my lady," he said in some surprise. "His lordship instructed me to have them cleaned."

Annette regarded him steadily. "And when was that?" she asked quietly.

"A week ago, my lady."

CHAPTER FOURTEEN

Annette entered their coach and said breathlessly, "I made it."

"I shan't be unpleasant and scold," Drake said sardonically.

"Oh, dear," she said, and shot a mischievous look at him from under her lashes, "I hope that doesn't mean you are going to be tiresomely agreeable?"

"My dear, I refuse to be drawn into a discussion I cannot possibly win."

Annette smiled and said, "I see."

"You will forgive me— What is it, my dear? Are you chilly?"

"A little."

"Move over here and let me warm you," he said, wrapping his arms around her. "Would you like the throw over your knees?"

"Yes, please, Drake. I seem to be c-cold."

He picked up the fur rug from the other seat and wrapped it around her legs. "I don't understand it," he said, puzzled. "The evening is really quite warm."

"I—I forgot to put on my—my chemise," she admitted, and flushed at his incredulous look. "I was r-rushed—"

"You are naked under your gown?" he demanded in disbelief.

"If we return home, I could put on—"

"There isn't time," he said grimly. "How you could have forgotten—" His lips set, he withdrew to his corner of the seat and sat without speaking, unmoved by

Annette's infuriated flounce and corresponding silence as they rolled on through the evening.

The coach drove slowly forward in the press of traffic, the coachman obliged at times to pull his horses almost to a standstill before moving on again at little better than a crawl. "It appears Bodkin is entertaining on a large scale," Drake remarked from his corner of the seat.

Annette turned her head and tried to see his face in the darkness of the interior. "One can only hope the company respectable," she said somewhat waspishly.

"Oh, it will be, my dear. Depend on it. But brilliant, no."

She made no reply; beyond smiling slightly, which she could not see in the dark, neither did he say more.

The coach pulled in under the canopy before the house and stopped at the bottom of a red-carpeted flight of stairs. A groom scrambled down from his seat, the steps were let down, and the Earl stepped forth, turning to hold out a hand to Annette. Only imperceptibly did she hesitate before placing her hand in his.

Her eyes raked the facade of Lord Bodkin's ancestral seat. "He does himself proud," she remarked with a contemptuous smile.

"He has not needed to, my dear. His forebears did it for him."

"The only thing that surprises me is that they did not drown him at birth."

"I have no doubt there is a good deal in what you say, but I hope you will not repeat it."

Annette raised her eyes to his. "Do you expect me to disgrace you?" she asked quietly.

"I think you place too much emphasis on what I say."

"Think what you will, this evening is a mistake. I would like to return home."

"We cannot in honor turn back from an engagement," he said only, and stepped back for her to precede him up the stairs.

They found a crush of people inside. Annette's impression was of spacious rooms, lively chatter, glittering jewels, and a great deal of lace. The rooms were very much too warm.

"Our host approaches," Drake's voice murmured in her ear. "Do try to bear up."

She turned with a start to see Lord Bodkin mincing forward. When he stood before her, and had furled a lace handkerchief through the air, he bowed with a flourish. Annette took an involuntary step backward, trod on Drake's foot, turned to beg pardon, and hopelessly entangled the strings of her reticule around a button on his sleeve. She stood mortified, and had the impression he was laughing at her. She did not know his enjoyment was directed at Lord Bodkin. For fashion had not seen fit to smile on mine host. His shoulders were too narrow, his girth too wide. He resembled nothing so much as an overripe pear posturing about on spindly legs.

His bow completed, Bodkin raised his eyeglass and surveyed Annette through it. She feared he would kiss her hand, couldn't abide the thought, and kept it resolutely at her side. "So," he said, "the Ardley rubies. I have heard much of them."

She had no idea what to reply. She could not think the remark other than ill-bred and momentarily regretted a certain fastidiousness that would not allow her to say so.

His lordship's unbounded conceit prevented him from seeing her distaste. "You grace them well," he continued with the subject in what was taking on all the earmarks of a monologue. "It is a great piece of nonsense for Lady Emily to think the Arlington rubies can compare, for anyone can see they can't. I assure you I have been at great pains to point out the error in her thinking, but she will not allow it to be so. Such imperiousness I find shocking, and I do not care who hears me say so."

"I dare say you don't," Annette ventured when he paused.

"If I live to own a finer set, I can die content," he declared with all the drama of a thespian upon the boards. (The thought crossed Annette's mind that he was indeed acting a part.) "Heaven forbid that I should not."

Drake, who had heard a surfeit of the rubies, felt forced to intervene. "Perhaps you will show my lady your picture gallery?" he inquired, having no idea the impact his chance remark would have on their future.

"Well, yes, if it comes to that, I will be pleased to do so. I apprehend that my art, at least, ranks with the best. I trust I have no patience with anything inferior, no matter what it is. Are you not in agreement, my lord?"

"In that respect, yes, we can be thought to be in agreement."

"But, of course. It will be my pleasure, Lady Annette, to conduct you about following dinner."

"May I hasten to include myself?" Drake said carefully.

"Certainly, my lord. If you wish," Lord Bodkin replied.

A silence no one seemed inclined to break was

saved from prolongment by Drake calmly marching Annette off to inspect a cabinet of porcelain.

Upon their gathering in the salon following dinner, the only annoyance Annette had to endure was the sight of a somewhat overblown beauty casting out lures in Drake's direction. She thought her making a public spectacle of herself and enjoyed the sight of Drake paying her not the least heed as he hurried to her own side. "You are positively purring," he leaned toward her to remark.

"The beauty is the cat. Her claws are showing." She threw him a saucy look, and stared. "You didn't notice," she gurgled in delight. "You really didn't notice."

"May I share the joke?" Lord Bodkin inquired, coming up to them.

"It wasn't very amusing," Annette said quickly. "May I be presumptuous and prevail on you to show us your pictures?"

Lord Bodkin seemed to hesitate, but they could not be sure. He lifted his quizzing glass and surveyed her through it. "Pray allow me the honor," was all he said.

She could not think the gallery either more or less than that to be seen in other great houses. Long lines of Bodkin ancestors marched down the walls, each portrait of the then lord of the manor being accompanied by a companion piece of his lady. Annette had seldom seen a family resemblance so strong as to repeat itself through each succeeding generation. The Bodkins were a handsome lot with their blond hair and blue eyes, and from the expressions on the painted faces, Annette gained the distinct impression they were of a restrained, even retiring, inclination.

Lord Bodkin was talking all the while. It was seen

he desired nothing better than to extol the merits of each painting, and he soon sought Annette's opinion, obviously expecting corroboration.

"I hardly could say about the entire collection," she said earnestly. "You must not expect such knowledge from me. I am able to tell you of my preference for the fourth Lady Bodkin. Her expression is so gentle, I know I would have valued her as a friend."

Lord Bodkin pursed his lips and simpered. "My ancestress is honored, my lady."

Annette took a few steps back along the row of pictures and stopped before the portrait of the third Lord Bodkin. "I do believe this gentleman is the handsomest of them all. Do you not agree?" she asked Drake.

"It would be difficult to single out any one of them," he answered in some amusement.

"They are all so blond—" she said, and turned to look at Lord Bodkin. Blinking, she glanced from his face to the portraits, and back. "And you so dark," she murmured thoughtfully. "Tell me, sir, how could that be?"

Lord Bodkin glanced sideways at the Earl. "I don't take your ladyship's meaning," he said shortly.

"You do not in the least resemble your ancestors. I merely wondered at it."

"I should not think that remarkable."

"But other families seldom present such consistent similarities through successive generations."

"I am at a loss to discover why you should be concerned."

"Well, but—" Annette had a puzzled frown between her eyes. "Are you quite sure, sir, that you are a Bodkin?" she asked impulsively, and gasped. "I had no intention of saying that," she confessed in great confusion.

"Your inference was plain," Lord Bodkin said with a sneer. "I resent it, I might add."

Drake had been covertly watching Bodkin's face, taking particular note of the expression in his eyes. There is something here of moment for Sir Andrew, he thought. Aloud, he said, "Her ladyship made no intimation that should disturb you. Hers was but a natural reaction to the obvious."

"On the contrary," retorted Bodkin, "you will admit that various traits have a way of popping up from time to time."

"I am aware they do," the Earl said soothingly. "It was from my grandmother that I inherited gray eyes, or to be more accurate, from her family, for hers were blue. I am told the color was to be found among her relations, with none following since, until my own."

"You are right," Annette agreed. "Papa used to tease about my hair. He laid it at the door of some black-hearted pirate who had wandered onto the family tree. I was used to shiver with it until I learned I came by it in a most proper way."

Lord Bodkin had regained his self-assurance. "I am sure you found more pleasure in the thought of pirates than in gentlefolk," he said with a smirk. "Or am I at fault?"

"Indeed you are not, sir. You have a sure understanding of the female brain."

Bodkin was naturally pleased with this remark. To move in the company of the Earl and Countess of Ardley was a privilege to be prized.

At the conclusion of the evening, Annette was still worrying their conversation around in her mind. She settled down in her corner of the coach and leveled her gaze at Drake as he came in beside her. "Well," she began immediately, "what did you think?"

"I think you have every intention of talking at the wrong time."

"Well! I should have thought—"

Drake wasted no further time. He took her in his arms and buried her face in the folds of his cravat. "Don't be difficult," he whispered in her ear. "Bodkin's groom rides with ours."

She turned her face up to gape at him. "But I don't see—"

"You are talking again," he reproved softly. "Shall I silence you?"

"You are impertinent—" she began, and found herself being ruthlessly kissed.

She said, when she had opportunity for speech, "You are displaying a shocking conduct, sir."

"Yes, I know."

"To own the truth, I have not the least objection to having you repeat it."

His eyes gone dark, he pulled her onto his lap and ardently sought her lips, his large, warm hand sliding under her skirts. She rested against him, quivering with pleasure at his teasing fingers, until the coach arrived at Monkshaven and he reluctantly put her from him.

He was surprised to find his coachman waiting to speak to him when he turned from assisting Annette to alight. "My lord," said Moore, "could I have a word with your lordship?"

Moore had not before climbed down from his seat before driving the coach on to the carriage yard. The Earl looked puzzled, but nodded. "But, of course."

"My lord, if you would, how much run of the stables should we give Lord Bodkin's groom?"

"But all of it, Moore. Why do you ask?"

"He says he's here for training, my lord."

"He is, Moore. Train him." The Earl went on up the steps, and checked. "One thing further, Moore. The groom will freely come and go between Bodkin Hall and here."

"I am not to question his movements, my lord?"

"Precisely," said his lordship, and passed on into the house and up the stairs, to enter Annette's bedroom unceremoniously.

She was standing before the dressing table, her hands lifted to the clasp of the ruby necklace. Her eyes widened at his gesture to her maid, and she stood looking at him rather strangely as Marie hurriedly departed. A few quick strides and he was before her, his hands brushing lightly over her shoulders. He was smiling in a way he had and she knew his intent. "Drake, my gown. You will rumple it."

"It doesn't signify," he said, and picked her up and carried her to the bed. She stared up at him as he lifted her skirts and quickly moved over her. "All I've thought about all evening was you—naked—"

"Forgive me," he whispered when he had finished. "I wanted you so, I couldn't wait."

The thought of him contrite made her smile. "Come, sir," she said in a rallying tone, "I am quite content. It may not be quite the thing to be pleased with one's own husband, but for my part, I do not find the prospect boring."

"When I think of the trouble I have been put to, I should think you wouldn't," he replied with a grin, his hand moving from her waist to cup her chin. "To own the truth, my dear, until this moment it had not occurred to me you might have been put to some bother yourself."

"No," she agreed pleasantly. "I expect it hadn't."

"Annette," he said in a persuasive voice, "tell me the truth. Did you leave off your chemise on purpose?"

"Now how should I answer that?" she pertly inquired. "If I say I didn't, you will think me careless. If I say I did, you will know me wanton."

"I would say you did," he said, his amused glance sweeping over her. "You look the veriest trollop with your gown up to your waist."

"You are hardly one to comment," she answered pointedly. But she made a move to lower her skirts.

"Oh, no," he protested. "You look particularly splendid just the way you are."

"Is this the way you were accustomed to have your mistresses?" she shot at him.

His lips twitched. "Not at all, my dear," he drawled, eyes gleaming. "They would have had on nothing at all."

"Are you laughing at me?"

"Dearest girl, I have not had all that many mistresses. No, do not interrupt. I am baring my soul for your inspection." He grinned wickedly at her. "I am sure that my ideas of propriety are at least as nice as yours."

But she only said, "Fiddle!"—which caused him to kiss the tip of her nose. Unfastening the buttons of her gown, he removed it and tossed it on the floor. "I am inclined to think jewelry sufficient cover for any female," he murmured in a reverential tone.

"If you are expecting me to sleep in nothing but these rubies, I cannot imagine where you got such a bird-witted idea."

"Don't quibble," he replied, rising to strip off his own clothing. "It is more than I will wear."

Annette drew up the sheet to her chin and gazed approvingly on his muscular figure emerging to her view. "I shall do nothing of the sort," she purred. "Quibble, I mean," she added, and gave her enchanting gurgle of laughter.

Neatly turning the tables on her, he told her to take either the front of the bed or the back, he wasn't particular which, and said he hoped she had no objection since she could not expect to occupy the middle. She looked at him a moment in a speculative way, seemed about to say something but changed her mind, and moved over to the back. Looking amused, he slid in the front and pulled up the covers.

"Actually," she said sweetly, "if you feel crowded, I have no objection to your seeking your own bed."

"I like it this way," he returned, his amused expression widening to a grin. "You keep me warm."

Acknowledging his hit without obliging him by putting it into words, she snuggled into his waiting arms. "Oh, well," she said. "I had intended asking your opinion of Lord Bodkin. Now is as good a time as any."

"You have a strange notion of the purpose of a bed."

She chose to ignore this remark. "There is something very wrong, Drake," she insisted.

"You cannot go about suspecting people of—whatever it is you are thinking. You really must be more careful, Annette."

"People who won't tell other people what they know about other people are more odious than people who won't volunteer what they know about other people."

Drake pondered this statement. Composing his countenance, he said he was at a loss to know how it fitted him. But if he sought to evade a further query with such weak-spirited denial, he soon found it would not serve.

"He has all the outward trappings of the quality," she said in a ruminating tone. "And it is not as if he did anything perfectly dreadful. But there is something—one must see he is not of the ton. I daresay you know all about him. Tell me, Drake, just who is he?"

"I don't know all that much," he admitted reluctantly. "He was living abroad when he came into the title."

"He said Paris, to be precise. If you did not know him, I doubt very much that others did. And I just cannot conceive how the heir of an old and respected family could be unknown."

"I believe the relationship was distant," Drake answered, feeling goaded. "The Bodkin line has never been prolific."

"Well, that's as may be, but it still does not answer my question. And there is another thing. How does he come by such dark hair and eyes when all the Bodkins were so fair?" she asked expectantly. "And don't speak of distant relationships."

"What are you driving at, my dear?"

"It's as plain as the nose on your face, Drake," she said dramatically. "He is illegitimate!"

He first looked startled, and then grim. "You cannot go about making such statements, Annette. Bodkin's claim to the title was upheld. It won't do at all to question its legality."

"A mistake could have been made," she insisted doggedly.

"Good God! You cannot know what you are saying. Why don't you just ask Bodkin if he is an impostor?"

"I thought about it, but he would be bound to be put on his guard."

"Annette," he said, raising up to bend over her. "I have not the slightest intention of continuing this conversation. Kiss me!"

"Insufferable," she said, and moved her body voluptuously against his.

CHAPTER FIFTEEN

A few days now would bring the wedding upon them. Lady Ellen set forward on the journey from London, departing Ardley House not more than two hours later than she had originally intended. As it was, fate smiled on the radiant bride, and with no mishap to mar her passage, she arrived at Monkshaven by five o'clock in the afternoon.

It seemed the next day the front door continually opened and closed, admitting houseguests being set down from the stream of coaches arriving before the house. By midafternoon Drake went in search of Annette, declaring the place a shambles of trunks and boxes and milling people. The staff could sort it out, he said, and escaped with her to their apartment in the east wing.

He was dozing on the sofa, his long legs stretched out before him when Annette heard a sound. She frowned and listened intently. Had she imagined it? She finally concluded that she had. Rising quietly so as not to disturb Drake, she tiptoed across the room to look out of the window. The roses were beginning to fade, a sign of summer's passing. Birth, flowering, death. The cycle of life. Annette turned to gaze upon Drake's slumbering form. The flowering of her life, stretched out and snoring softly. She nearly giggled, but choked it off.

She was returning to her chair when she heard it again—a soft, bumping sound. Her body trembling, she crept across to shake Drake's shoulder lightly. His eyes flew open as she placed her fingers to his lips, shook her head, and rolled her eyes upward. A frown creased his brow as his glance went to the ceiling and returned to her face. Annette leaned close, her lips to his ear. "I heard the ghost," she breathed quietly.

He gazed at her, his expression incredulous. "What—"

"Shh!" she whispered. "Listen!"

He gathered her in his arms, but it was some time before he convinced her that her fears were groundless. It was hard to rid herself of the impression that something sinister lurked in the east wing, something evil that would reach out to blemish their lives in some blasphemous way. As they left the apartment together, Annette looked back at the lovely room and asked herself if it would ever seem the same.

By dinnertime the majority of the guests had arrived. Lord and Lady Enright were particular friends of Agatha, and while taciturn, Lord Enright nevertheless occupied an enviable position in society. The Marquis of Auxley was of another turn entirely, amiable and with a gentlemanly address the ladies found irresistible. It could be seen that Lady Pease lost no time in shepherding her daughter before him in an effort to thrust this lamentably unattractive hopeful in the path of the Marquis, a mother's fond hope doomed to failure from the outset. Lord Sutterfield, in spite of a tendency to converse in a loud way, was, with his store of anecdotes to amuse his fellow guests, always an acceptable addition to any gathering. And Paul, clapping eyes on Miss Judith Annis for the first time, stared at her in a dazed way and spent his every effort in trying to attach her notice. The other some fifty persons present must always be considered ac-

ceptable guests, chatting in an amenable mood and
perfectly willing to enjoy themselves.

Lady Pease bore down on Annette and begged
leave to present her daughter. Rising from her curtsy,
Miss Lilly Ann stammered a greeting ignored by her
mama, who said to Annette, "I have frequently
desired that dearest Lilly Ann see the splendors of
Monkshaven. Surely nothing can equal its elegance."

"If this is her first visit, perhaps I can find someone
to show her around," Annette said politely.

"You are most kind. Perhaps Lord Wrexly—?"

Annette hardly knew where to look. She dare not
meet Lady Pease's glance, lest that lady see the understanding in her eyes. Having failed to attach Auxley's
interest on behalf of her daughter, Lady Pease was
casting about for an acceptable substitute.

Paul could not fancy the assignment. Many matters
required his attention: he had engaged to show Lord
Tolson the cabinets of Oriental art; Lady Wor-
thington was waiting his company in the cardroom;
and in all events, there was no denying his presence
was needed in the salon. Annette introduced the
thought of the addition of Miss Annis to the tour;
Paul immediately deemed the idea to be an excellent
one, even going so far as to agree to Miss Lilly Ann
being a member of the party.

Free for the moment, Annette moved quietly
toward the door. She would seek the solace of her
rooms, for the need for rest loomed large if she were
to brush through the coming days in form.

It was just upon dusk when a coach pulled up before the door to deposit yet another guest upon the
step. From the flurry surrounding her arrival emerged
Aunt Agatha. She looked about to see who was
present, and had the satisfaction of finding numerous

close friends in attendance. Rustling around the room, she engaged the entire attention of the party in a manner wholly her own.

Her wanderings eventually brought her to Annette's side. Standing on tiptoe to kiss her cheek, Lady Agatha said, "Well, I'm here. Are you pleased to see me?"

"I'm happy your sense of duty brought you, but I will admit to some surprise. We felt you might remain in London."

"I must confess this house gave me pause, but I could not fail dearest Ellen. So here I am." Tucking her arm in Annette's, she led her to a sofa. "Now, sit right here and tell me what has been transpiring within these dreadful walls."

"They aren't dreadul, Aunt Agatha. We have been happy here."

"Well, I daresay you have, dear. You have the knack for it, but I haven't. I clearly recall the horrid time I had of it on my last visit. It was two years ago now, but it seems like yesterday since I heard the specter."

Annette well remembered hearing noises in the east wing and her own fears that they emanated from some unearthly source. Drake's assurances to the contrary, she was not entirely convinced. She could not rid herself of the feeling that something was very wrong, but she kept this reflection from Agatha, turning the conversation to a discussion of entertainments projected for these last days before the wedding.

The next morning Drake shook her awake a full hour before their customary time of rising. She peered at him blearily through half-opened eyes, then rolled over to snuggle back down. Leaping out of bed, he tossed back the covers and turned to pluck his robe from a chair. Annette sat up and clutched the blanket to her chin, pulling it over herself as she sank back comfortably on the pillows. "No, you don't," he told her, and snatched the cover away. Grabbing her ankles, he hauled her to the edge of the bed. Giggling and threshing her legs, she tried to hold onto the side of the mattress, but he pulled her off and stood her on her feet. "Sleepyhead," he grinned, and whacked her on her bottom.

"Brute," she pouted, vigorously rubbing her posterior. "May I ask why we are up at this hour?"

"You forget you have an engagement with your husband today. Don't get back in that bed," he admonished. "You have thirty minutes—no longer."

Annette rushed to dress and present herself in the dining room on time. She found him partaking of a substantial breakfast. Rare roast beef, kidneys in cream, and lamb chops formed the nucleus, but other dishes were contributing their fair share to his repast. She slipped into her chair on his right and requested tea and toast. At his insistence, she allowed Watkins to place a lamb chop on her plate. Drake leaned toward her and murmured low, "I find my nighttime activities necessitate an adequate diet to keep up my strength."

If Paul noticed her blush when he came rushing in, he chose not to mention it. Stammering that he wished to speak in confidence, he waited until Watkins had followed the footman from the room, and launched into an obviously prepared speech: "You may have noticed Miss Annis? She is of a delicacy of principle that cannot fail to please. She is a gently nurtured female, and—"

Drake was in the act of raising his cup to his lips.

He lowered it. "Are you speaking of an attachment?" he asked in some surprise.

Paul leaned forward eagerly. "I want to marry her. You do grant permission, do you not?"

Drake studied him. "I fail to see what this has to do with me, Paul. I am not your guardian. Bellamy will shortly be your stepfather. I would suggest you speak with him."

"I had much rather have your approval."

"That I cannot give you. As things now stand, I much doubt the lady's parents could be expected to turn their daughter over to you. However, that may soon change. I am turning the Middlesex property over to you. I have discussed it with Bellamy, and he will give you whatever advice you need."

"You are the most complete hand. That is a lucrative estate. Are you sure?"

Drake was looking at Annette and smiling at the approval he read in her eyes. Turning back to Paul, he said, "I'm sure. And now I will be obliged if you will address yourself to your breakfast."

"I was sure I could depend on you," Paul declared radiantly. "Well, I'll be off now," he finished happily, and took himself off.

Annette looked at Drake, a smile in her eyes. "I don't know whether to felicitate you or Paul."

"Pray don't give me more credit that I deserve. The property came to me through my maternal grandmother. I have always intended Paul should have it. His declaration only precipitated my telling him. Perhaps it will serve to gain sympathy with his chosen's papa."

"I am astonished at your forbearance," she said, smiling. "No offer to wager a monkey?"

"Love," he murmured, raising her fingers to his lips.

"Well!" Agatha spoke from the doorway. "I never expected this at table."

Annette pinked, but Drake calmly rose to hold her chair, seating her on his left. "Where are the servants?" she asked as she unfolded her napkin. "I must say I didn't expect such laxity from Watkins. Will we ever unravel the tangle this wedding has precipitated!"

"I sent the servants away," Drake replied. "Paul required privacy. He has determined to marry."

"Good God!" Agatha said, overcome. "I hope you quashed it."

"The thing is," Drake answered calmly, "Paul will shortly be within the scope of Bellamy's supervision."

Watkins reentered the room at that moment, drawing Agatha's attention to himself. "You have worn well through these past weeks, Watkins," was her comment to him as he came forward to serve her.

"I trust so, my lady," he bowed, pleased. "May I suggest the lamb chops? I believe your ladyship was ever partial to them."

"Trust you to remember, Watkins. Well, and what is this you are putting on my plate. Coddled eggs? I believe not, thank you. Serve them to the guests. And that reminds me. Where are they?"

"They will breakfast in their rooms," Annette answered.

"Good. Keep them out from underfoot. Your wife is talented, Ardley. Never forget it."

"I won't," he promised, the gleam in his eye causing Annette to look away in some confusion. She could only hope he would not say anything indelicate.

He didn't. He said, "If you will excuse us, Aunt, Annette is driving out with me. We won't be back until late this afternoon." As they left the room, he looked back at her with the hint of a smile. "We leave you in charge. Feel free to boss everyone to your heart's content."

CHAPTER SIXTEEN

It was as well that Annette was not present later in the day to witness the arrival of Lady Kinsley. Agatha, however, did witness it. Turning a stern eye on her relative, she said severely, "I think, Ellen, you have taken leave of your senses. How you could have been so misguided as to inflict that woman's presence on us, I'm sure I don't know."

"Now, Agatha," Lady Ellen protested with a sigh. "Do not fire up, I beg you. Nothing would have induced me to do so. The very notion was repugnant. It was Ardley."

Agatha stared in disbelief. "Well!" she said. "I will speak to him!"

"I declare, Agatha, I don't know how you find the courage. Ardley is all that is amiable, but I shouldn't care to cross him."

The prospect of incurring his displeasure was one Agatha would not consciously pursue, but now it came down to it, could she fail to express her sentiments? The dear boy needed guidance.

The Earl, it seemed, had returned to the house. Agatha hesitated before the door to the library. She reflected, not for the first time, that the room was too austere, and contained too many scholarly tomes. Resolutely, before her courage deserted her, she tapped on one of the panels of the door and promptly entered.

He was seated at his desk in his shirt-sleeves, and looking particularly harassed. "Now, don't bother,

Ardley," she said as he rose and reached for his coat. "I shan't keep you."

"Had we an appointment? My dreadful memory, you know."

"You know we hadn't, and there is nothing wrong with your memory. Don't be patronizing, please."

He surveyed her briefly. "How may I serve you?"

Agatha, attempting to get comfortable in her chair, gave it up and looked at him with a steady gaze. "I will admit," she said, "that you will not fancy what I am about to say."

"Then perhaps you will leave it unsaid."

"I have never been a coward and do not intend becoming one now. Someone must speak, and as there is no one else, I must be the one."

"Instinct tells me this interview may become disagreeable. Are you sure you wish to continue it?"

"Quite sure. You will believe me, Ardley, when I tell you that seeing Lady Kinsley enter Monkshaven has given me a shock."

"If I seem rude, Aunt, forgive it. But I do not intend explaining my action."

Agatha took a deep breath. "We seem at cross-purposes, and we really should not be, you know. I do not know how much you build on Lady Kinsley's presence here—"

"You may rest easy on that score."

"Pray don't mistake me, dear boy. I do not suppose she means anything to you, but others may not be so charitable. Her presence may, in fact, occasion gossip. What have you told Annette?"

There came a brief silence. Agatha stared at him, a glint coming into her sharp eyes. "She does not know. I never would have believed you could be such a fool."

"You don't understand the situation at all."

"That I can believe. And neither will Annette, the minute she claps eyes on the fair Ada. Or does she not know of her?"

"Unfortunately, she does."

"What in God's name possessed you?"

"If I found myself at liberty to tell you, you would probably refuse to believe me."

"You will be wise to confide in me."

"You see," his lordship said apologetically, "I do not intend giving more notice to Lady Kinsley's presence than to the presence of any other guest. Annette will find nothing to remark."

Agatha looked faintly surprised. "For an experienced man-about-town, my dear nephew, you can be remarkably naive. Your relationship with Lady Kinsley, whether rightly or wrongly, was generally assumed to be of a most intimate nature. You know this very well, and you are mistaken if you think Annette will accept her without demur. It is folly, Ardley. Admit it."

"I should be excessively sorry to upset Annette. Perhaps you will be so good as to tell her?"

Agatha sniffed. "Since you are determined, manlike, to avoid unpleasantness of any sort, I suppose I must."

"Thank you. I will be grateful. And now, Aunt, you must have much to occupy you. I won't keep you."

Agatha gave it up. He could be obstinately tight-mouthed when he chose and would not be teased into disclosures he did not wish to make.

Annette could be very nearly as uncommunicative. She was in a negligee when Agatha waited on her in her sitting room, and by the time Agatha took her departure, she was in a frame of mind to appear down-stairs dazzlingly gowned to cast Lady Kinsley in the shade. She was too clever to cut her before the others, but one looking carefully would have surprised an expression that was not a smile in her eyes.

As for the Earl, he betrayed nothing. Well aware of the speculation in the minds of some of the guests, he trod the thin line between a courteous interest in Lady Kinsley's conversation and a dividing of his attention among the other guests. Not even the most inveterate scandalmonger was able to fabricate a tidbit to propound. The end of dinner found the company inclined to believe the previous gossip mere fabrication.

When the Earl led the gentlemen to rejoin the ladies following the ritual of the port, Lady Kinsley made her way to his side. "I need to have a word with you," she said too quietly to be overheard.

He glanced in Annette's direction. She was laughing at some sally just imparted by Lord Collingham as if she had no other thought in the world. Drake raised an eyebrow, and, admitting to himself the demon jealousy astride his back, turned his attention back to Lady Kinsley. "We will stroll in the gardens where we will not be disturbed."

But Annette was not so unaware as she appeared. Seeing him take Lady Kinsley's arm to lead her through the doors opening onto the terrace stunned her. She felt suffocated, and bit back the sob rising in her throat. Her hand fluttering unconsciously to her breast, she stood like one caught in a trance.

"Dash it, Annette," Lord Collingham murmured in her ear. "Buck up. You feel affronted, and it shows."

"How odious you are, to notice."

"The others will," he said dryly. "Smile. That's a

good girl. Pretend we are having a merry coze. You will get the hang of it."

"I do not wish to 'get the hang of it,' as you say."

"He is deeply in love with you, you know," he said, thinking ruefully that Drake was in for it.

She looked frigidly at him. "I am certain this conversation is most improper and I refuse to continue it. Good evening, sir."

He took the snub in good part, and did not budge. "Don't talk fustian, Annette. I can't tell you what Drake is doing, but it doesn't touch on you."

"Do you think me a fool to be fobbed off with half-truths?"

"Do be sensible, Annette. And for God's sake, trust Drake."

Agatha was extremely fond of Annette and had been watching with a growing sense of alarm. First Ardley disappearing with that hussy, and now Annette engaged in a tête-à-tête with his friend, and all before a most interested audience. Coming up to them, she said abruptly, "Your other guests would no doubt enjoy at least a part of your attention, Annette."

Annette flushed and looked guilty. Agatha relented and reached out to pat her hand. "Run along, then, my dear. I will entertain—Lord Collingham, is it not?"

His lordship bowed, his eyes following Annette as she moved away. He was not, however, to be let off so lightly. Fixing him with a stern eye, Agatha relieved herself of a few brief but caustic remarks, quickly reducing him to the stature of a recalcitrant and somewhat backward boy.

The reason for the controversy, meantime, sank onto a garden bench beside Lady Kinsley and looked down at her provocative face. When he had first known her, he had been drawn by her exotic beauty, but early into their acquaintance the attraction faded. Behind her celestial good looks dwelt an intellect almost childlike in its simplicity.

Lady Kinsley, for her part, had displayed a surprising understanding in her dealings with him. Unable to attach his sentiments, she settled for what he was willing to give—friendship—and found, when Thomas McClerity entered her life, that friendship was enough. She now said, her voice low, "I am truly sorry that Sir Andrew thrust my presence on you, Drake."

"You have something of import to tell me?"

"Sir Andrew has planted additional false information in an effort to bring matters to a head. The thing is, Drake, the hunt has been expanded. Soldiers under temporary attachment have been stationed up and down the coast, along with navy patrols and law enforcement officers. They are watching at every creek and cove."

"What is your role in this?"

"Lord Bodkin has long had a tendre for me." She glanced at him and looked away. "I am the bait to induce him to spend a great deal of time at Monkshaven."

"Good God!"

"Please do not raise objections, Drake. Bodkin is a loose screw, I know, but I do not anticipate any difficulty with him."

"Have a care, Ada. He can be damned indiscreet. I hate for you to be subjected to his addresses."

"Well, as to that, I daresay it won't be for long. Sir Andrew only wishes him under surveillance in case a contact is made that will lead to others involved in the treason. And he has added another to the team. The groom Lord Bodkin recently hired is his heir and should prove most useful."

"Do you mean to tell me Bodkin would be unaware of that? For it won't fadge, you know."

"The relationship is distant, Drake. They had never met."

He stared at her, a speculative gleam coming into his eyes. "Bodkin was out of the country for some years. It could just be. But to get back to the matter at hand, I will not see you placed in danger. I will cooperate in inviting Bodkin to Monkshaven, but if you are going to flirt with him and appear to accept his attentions, I will afford you my protection."

She tilted her head to look up at him. "Tell me," she said quietly. "What has your wife heard of us? I see," she added ruefully. "Still the adventuress."

"When this is over, everyone shall learn the truth."

"But in the meantime, dearest of all dear friends, you will do nothing in a misguided effort to spare my reputation."

"No," he replied, and stood. "We should return to the house now, Ada. Your interest in Bodkin must appear sincere."

Annette had sustained the shock of Lady Kinsley's presence at Monkshaven, she had dressed with unusual care, she had been witness to the seeming ease with which Drake had been charmed, and still she had thought their departure for the gardens a kind of horrid wonder. Holding her head proudly erect, she looked toward them when they reentered the room and managed a smile.

Drake, not privy to Annette's thoughts, strode over to her quickly. "You are looking particularly lovely this evening," he said caressingly.

"Thank you, kind sir."

He looked at her searchingly, the thought that she might be thinking him unfaithful occurring to him for the first time.

He found it difficult to curb his impatience during the remainder of the evening, and followed her to her rooms immediately she retired for the night. She tried to hold him off, but he had no notion of permitting her to doubt his love.

His lips were so warm and his hands so gentle, she was swept along on the tide of his passion until she cried out in her response and held him to her with all her strength. And when she finally went to sleep clasped against his hard body, no doubt at all remained in her mind.

CHAPTER SEVENTEEN

Watkins opened the door the following morning to find the Honorable Dickie Beauchamp upon the step. Looking tired and somewhat morose, Dickie inquired the whereabouts of Lord Wrexly, and upon receiving the intelligence that his lordship was to be found partaking of breakfast, resolutely crossed the threshold. It was a devilish early hour to come calling, he knew full well.

"Where have you been?" Paul demanded of his reluctant guest the instant that gentleman was shown into the breakfast room. "I should think you could have arrived before this."

Dickie gazed at him with feeling. "M'father doesn't approve, old boy. Says only barbarians are about at this hour."

"Well, let me tell you, ghosts ain't barbarians."

Annette looked up from her plate and fixed her eye on Paul. "Am I to understand you plan to search for our ghost?"

"Well, yes," Paul admitted. "But don't fancy Ardley will disapprove. He gave me the office—well, he did say I wasn't to involve anyone but Dickie, so I won't."

She cocked her head and looked at him in a speculative way. "I have no plans for the morning," she remarked pleasantly.

"Now, see here," Paul gasped. "It ain't that we don't want you, Annette. Lord, no. But Ardley—"

"I'm sure he won't mind."

"Well, I ain't," Paul shot back. "And I don't intend to find out. Frankly, m'dear, I daren't."

"He will know nothing about it," she insisted. "I will just change into something suitable."

"Oh, very well," Paul recklessly agreed. "But do hurry," he called after her receding back.

Dickie's worried eyes fastened on Paul's face. "I can't think we should go against the Earl's wishes," he said faintly.

"Dickie, you ever try to stop Annette when her mind's made up? Well, I have. Forget it, my boy. It can't be done. What concerns us now is, how are we going to intercept the ghost?"

Dickie ran his hand through his hair, and pondered deeply. "I thought ghosts only came out at night."

"We can't wait for him to show. Damme, we must make the fellow come out."

"Out of where?" Dickie asked, much intrigued.

"Out of wherever it is he comes out of, of course. What in thunder is keeping Annette?"

"Ladies can't dress without a great deal of fuss. Wouldn't be reasonable to expect it. Take m'sister, for instance—"

"Dashed if I could ever see why they take so long. Well, come along. We've wasted enough time."

They arrived in the hall just as Annette was descending the stairs. Paul led the way. An hour later their enthusiasm had cooled. The unused east wing was dusty, cold, and drafty. Dickie felt wretched, but hesitated to express dissatisfaction. Paul, had his companions but known, felt much the same, for his plans had been rewarded with a notable absence of success. The hunt had about reached its conclusion when, at the end of a particularly gloomy corridor, a closed door came into view. Drawing to a halt before it, Paul greeted the discovery jovially. "Damme if we ain't getting somewhere," he exclaimed happily. But the aspect before them was unsavory. A narrow flight of stairs rose immediately the door was opened. What lay beyond the uppermost step could not be ascertained from their vantage point at the foot of the stairs.

Dickie plucked at Paul's sleeve. "You know," he whispered, "poking about—not at all the thing. I shouldn't think the Earl will be best pleased."

"Of course he will be pleased. No one wants a ghost lurking about, let me tell you. Now stop talking and come along."

They trooped up the narrow flight to the floor above, to find the way blocked by a further door. Paul squared his shoulders and slowly pushed it open. "The attics!" he whooped, much relieved not to be confronted by a sinister and unearthly being.

The eaves came down at steep angles, enclosing an enormous space, dimly lit by dormer windows and interrupted by the mighty columns of Monkshaven's many chimneys. The spot on which they stood afforded them an enchanting sight. Trunks and boxes of every description jostled for space among the furniture and bric-a-brac cast off and forgotten by past generations. It was not many minutes before they were about the business of exploring the trunks, nor many more before the floor became strewn with their contents.

Annette suddenly gave a shriek. "It's he," she cried, dragging forward a painting in a heavy gold frame.

The portrait depicted a man well into his middle years. Hard hazel eyes gazed upon the viewer with unmistakable malice, echoing thinly formed, sneering lips. One satin-clad arm rested on the table beside his chair, the hand clasping a book between long fingers. Softly glowing emeralds in the lace at his throat introduced the only pleasant note to be found in the painting.

Paul whistled. "Well, what d'you know?" he said. "It is Ardley's tutor."

"His tutor!" Annette exclaimed in tones of profound disbelief.

"None other. I wonder what a portrait of him is doing here."

Annette felt as if the breath had been knocked out of her. Her hands shook. "Oh," she said faintly, "it is the man who was in the apartment when I woke."

Paul stared at her and bit off the oath rising on his tongue. "Are you saying," he demanded with more violence than Dickie could think seemly, "that we have been moving heaven and earth to find a ghost, when he ain't a ghost at all?"

His attitude restored Annette's sense of equilibrium. The world ceased its reeling. "I could not have known," she said firmly.

But Paul remained indignant. "Could you not!" he gritted.

"It doesn't matter," Dickie faltered. "Mustn't make a big thing of it, Paul. Won't do at all, you know. Won't do at all."

"Pray do not attempt to reason with him," Annette besought Dickie. "He is not in the mood for it. I do not wish to seem uncivil, but I will leave you now."

The silence following her departure wore on. Dickie broke it. "Paul, dear boy, what will you do?" he asked, aghast.

"Do?" snorted Paul. "The devil take it, tell Ardley, of course. What else can I do?"

Annette was ready to go down to dinner when Drake entered, dressed for the evening in green satin, with an embroidered waistcoat, and white satin small-clothes. "I trust," he said, his eyebrows raised questioningly, "that you were entertained this morning?"

"Yes. Though I would never have thought the attics—" She came to an abrupt halt, appalled by her slip.

"Paul has made a most praiseworthy confession," he said, his eyes twinkling. "Forgive me, my dear. The temptation to tease was one I found myself unable to resist. Your nose twitches so adorably when you contemplate a lie."

"It does?" she murmured, stealing a glance at him from under her lashes. "Did he tell you of the portrait?"

"He did. Because of its discovery, I find myself able to endorse the escapade."

She turned the full force of her gaze on him. "Why would there be a portrait of your tutor here?"

He came forward to stand before her, and gathered her hands in his. "I have a favor to ask, my dear. I very much wish you will not leave the house unaccompanied."

She blinked her eyes at him. "But why?"

"Don't press me, Annette. Just do as I ask, this once."

She stared up at him, the thought of Lady Kinsley entering her mind. "You do not wish me to interfere with you. Very well. But you shan't interfere with me!"

A frown was gathering on his brow. He deliberated a moment before saying, "You force me to command you to obey. Do not compel me to take steps to ensure your compliance."

"You wouldn't!"

"Ah, but I would. Make no mistake about that."

Her face hardened. "As you say, my lord," she muttered, and, whirling, left the room.

It was not an auspicious beginning for the evening. The very sight of Lady Kinsley was enough to fan Annette's wrath to a flame. She could not take her eyes from her, a look of undisguised hatred on her face. It was not many minutes before Lord Collingham was at her side. Talking in his inconsequential way, he interspersed his conversation with outrageous flattery that soon had her in more happy spirits.

Drake, who had been watching, strolled over to them. "May I spirit Charles away, my dear?" he calmly asked. "I have something in particular to discuss with him." There was something in the sternness of his expression that forestalled interrogation.

He led Lord Collingham to the library and carefully closed the door. "Our problems may be unsought, Charles, but they are damnably recurrent. Bear with me while I fill you in. You have heard of Monkshaven's ghost. While searching for it with Paul, Annette came across a portrait of my former tutor. I need only add that she had before seen him in the east wing. The question is, dear boy, what was he doing here? I see I have your undivided attention."

"You have. He could be involved with—"

"Bodkin."

"He lives close by. They could have met."

"Precisely, Charles. I am inclined to believe they are in this together. Wadding—the tutor—knows the countryside like the back of his hand. It would be the greatest piece of folly to look to apprehending them through surveillance alone. I am convinced the best chance for success depends on surprising them in the act of treason."

"Have you any idea of places Wadding favored to visit? Any haunt, or the like?"

Drake pondered. "It has been so many years. I seem to remember—he did spend his holidays—by all that's holy! Eastbourne! He visited Eastbourne!"

Lord Collingham shook his head. "Eastbourne is a resort town. The thing is, it's too public."

Drake's eyes narrowed as he meditated. "I seem to remember a relative," he murmured. "A brother, or—an uncle? Wadding once mentioned a farm. Unfortunately, however—"

Lord Collingham threw up his hand. "You've hit on it, Drake. Farms away from the towns are isolated and surrounded by hills. Boats coming in from the sea on a dark night would never be seen."

"With Sir Andrew watching at coves and creeks! You may be sure it is Wadding's plan. Bodkin hasn't the wit."

"Well, for m'self, I'll be off first thing in the morning to see Sir Andrew, but tonight I mean to entertain your wife."

Drake's lips twitched. "In that case, my dear Charles, I think I will remain by Annette's side."

CHAPTER EIGHTEEN

Two mornings later Lord Saxton sat facing the Earl before the fire in the library. "I am not an unreasonable man, Ardley. My wife may deck herself out for the wedding in any way she might choose. But I do not see posting off to London to bring back sapphires when I have already made the trip to bring back diamonds. Tell me. Would diamonds really be out of place at the wedding?"

"What color gown will your wife be wearing?"

"Pale gray, I believe."

"Then the sapphires it must be, Saxton," Drake said with the glimmer of a smile. "She would do you credit, you know. Look at it from her viewpoint. She would not disgrace you before your friends."

"Do you mean to say that sapphires— Oh, I see. You are pulling my leg."

"Not at all, dear boy. I am keeping you in favor with your wife." Drake grinned, regarding his friend with an amused expression. "I will remind you that when it comes to the distaff side, I am considered something of an authority."

At this moment a tap sounded on the door, and Annette came hurrying in. "I have the most delightful news, Drake," she began, then paused, her eyes discovering Lord Saxton. "Oh," she said, "I did not mean to interrupt."

Lord Saxton stepped forward. "In any event, Lady Annette, I was just on the point of departure. It seems I must journey to London. If I am to return in time for the wedding, I'd best be off."

Annette waited until he had left before coming swiftly forward to stand in front of Drake, her face radiant. "I've a notion you will be pleased with what I have to tell you," she said happily.

"If you are pleased, I am sure I will be."

She gazed at him tenderly, savoring the moment. "Oh, my dearest. We are to have a child."

He was staring at her, his eyes widening. "Are you sure?" he asked, reaching out to draw her into his arms.

"I have just come from the doctor," she said, and found herself crushed in an embrace that immediately slackened. "You needn't be so careful, Drake. I will be fine," she told him between kisses. "Are you happy about the baby?"

She heard the catch in his voice. "Happy?" he repeated. "I have never been so happy." His fingers closed over hers, to press hers to his lips. "I wondered why you were looking so splendid."

Annette gave her irrepressible chuckle. "You'd be wise to postpone your glee until you know the result. It could be a girl."

"A daughter will suit me fine."

"No, it won't," she said with a smile. "You will want a son. You may not say so, but you will."

"All I really want is for you and the baby to come through safely. When do you expect it?"

"Around the middle of May."

He was struck by a sudden thought. "What did the doctor say? Are you quite the thing? Do not scruple to tell me if—"

"I am in the best of health, Drake. Women have

been having babies for simply ages. There is nothing to alarm you."

"Knowing you, my dear, there is. You will take especial care not to do anything rash, will you not? I want you to promise to be careful."

Her hands moved in his, returning the clasp of his fingers. "I promise I will. Though you must know I cannot spend the next months languishing on a sofa. Now, do stop fussing, Drake. You will never brush through this in form unless you do."

Laughing, he crossed to the table bearing the decanter and poured out two glasses of wine. Returning, he handed one to her. "You may not feel the need," he said, eyes glowing, "but I do."

"May I propose a toast?"

"I would deny you little at this moment."

"To Redding, our son," she said, smiling into his eyes over the rim of her glass.

He did not guess that her meek acquiescence to his orders sprang from a desire to allay any concern for her health that he might harbor. The doctor had instructed her to continue in her customary activities, and this she thoroughly intended to do. In happy unconcern, she went about her affairs.

Coming upon Paul beside the lake late in the afternoon, she stood watching him disconsolately skipping rocks across the water. "What is bothering you?" she quietly asked.

He hurled a stone into the water. "We're not to become engaged for one year! One whole year, mind you."

Understanding dawned in her eyes. "You have spoken with Miss Judith's father."

"I told him about the Middlesex estate. You know

what he said? He said when I found myself in a position to support a wife, he would consider my suit."

"I daresay he will agree in the end, Paul."

"You think so?" he asked, brightening perceptibly.

"Indeed I do. Fathers usually cavil at letting their daughters go." She searched her mind, and said, "Paul, when I was with Drake one day, we found someone had broken into the pavilion on the island. Do you think we should row over to see if he has been there again?"

Her ploy met with success. Paul was immediately interested. "We'd best be about it," he said, hurrying toward the skiff.

"Don't be offended, Paul, but—do you know how to row?"

"I ain't offended. Watch what you're about now. I don't fancy being dunked in the water."

Annette carefully crawled around him and settled herself on the seat. To her intense relief, he fetched them up on the shore of the island without mishap.

Again she was struck with the manner in which the path had been concealed from view. Following along behind Paul, her vision was limited. It was thus that she bumped against him when he suddenly halted.

"Good God!" he gasped. "What are you about, coming up on us like this?"

Annette peered around his shoulder to see Hodges facing them on the path. He stood nervously casting his eyes about as if seeking an avenue of escape. "Beg pardon, m'lord," he said weakly.

"Don't try to flummox me," Paul advised him. "What are you doing over here? I should think you'd have enough to do at home."

"If ye'll just let me pass, m'lord, I'll get back to me

roses." Hodges eased around them, bobbed his head at Annette, and hurried off.

Paul stood watching his receding back. "Damme if I can make head or tail of him," he muttered with the deepest misgivings.

Annette turned her gaze from Hodges and looked onward up the path. "He is only the gardener. Come along, Paul, do."

When they came to the clearing, she became conscious of a strangeness to the quiet. "I have the queerest feeling we are being watched," she said, looking around behind them.

"Probably some small animal. If you want to see inside, we'd best be about it. It will be dark soon."

As she followed Paul within, she was aware of a prickling sensation running down her spine. He cast an appraising look around. "Someone has been here, I'd say. From the look of it, the place has been cleaned."

Annette felt a great sense of relief. "So that was what Hodges was doing here."

"I daresay he'd as soon we didn't know he's been about female work. The only thing—" Paul broke off speech in midsentence. They turned their heads to see the gardener close the door and lock them in.

"Well!" Annette exclaimed, breaking the silence. "I must say, I have never been so surprised in anyone."

"Devil a bit," Paul replied, flinging himself into a chair. "I suppose you will next say you didn't know Ardley keeps a gardener who, from what I can make of it, ain't a gardener at all."

"Do you think he will leave us here for very long?"

He sat looking at her, his brows contracted in a frown. "I expect he will release us soon. More likely he's drunk. I daresay he will sober soon enough once Ardley hears of this."

Annette sighed and looked toward the door. "You don't think you could break it down?" she asked, then gave a shriek as it swung open.

"Dickie," Paul gasped, gaping at his friend blinking at them in a bemused fashion. "I've never been so glad to see anyone in my life."

"M'pleasure," Dickie returned, crossing the threshold. "Why did that fellow lock you in?"

"We don't know. How'd you open the door, by the way?"

"The key was in the lock."

"Blister me if that don't beat the Dutch!" Paul exclaimed disgustedly. "Just wait until I get my hands on him!"

"I say, Paul, just who is he? I mean—"

"He says he's a gardener. But that ain't the point. What we need to do is get after the fellow." His glance happened on Annette. "You're sure it was the tutor staring at you when you woke?" he asked, and looked satisfied at her nod.

Dickie asked, much interested, "Why'd you think the tutor had been here?"

"Someone had," Paul explained. "Stands to reason. No one else about, except the gardener." A thought struck him. "Find the gardener, you'll find the tutor. Which way did he go?"

Dickie pondered. "South," he said positively.

"Then let's be off. Annette, you go back to the house."

"I will do nothing of the kind," she said with considerable spirit. "I suggest you waste no further time discussing it. Hodges will surely lose us if you do."

Paul looked severely at her. "You'll get us in a scrape," he declared flatly.

Annette made a most unladylike sound in her throat and went toward the door. "I will be dreadfully late if I wait for you," she said loftily.

"Confound it!" Paul ejaculated fiercely. "I just hope this night's work don't come to Ardley's ears. He'd have my hide."

They rowed across the lake without mishap and proceeded to the stables. Paul wondered aloud at a faradiddle they could spin for ordering mounts so close upon the dark, but they bluffed it through and rode off out of the stableyard.

They had not gone far before Paul asked, "Where the deuce are we headed, Dickie?"

"I expected you would know."

Annette appeared to have her attention fixed on smoothing the pleats of her skirt. "In which direction is Bodkin Hall?" she asked in an offhand fashion.

Their attention immediately became fixed on her. "Why?" they demanded simultaneously.

"Bodkin is just the sort to make a friend of Drake's tutor."

"What if he's at home?" Paul asked.

"He won't be. He is forever at Monkshaven."

And so the matter was decided. The remainder of the ride was accomplished without incident, except that the distance to Bodkin Hall was farther than Annette remembered and dark had descended before they reached their destination.

"The house is just beyond this hedge," Annette said, whispering. "I have been thinking it will make things far easier if you go around to the front, Paul. Dickie can check the stables, and I will slip around to the back. We will return here to report our findings."

Paul, unconvinced, said that he thought not. "For what if you come across him while alone?" he asked in a reasoning tone.

Annette regarded him briefly. "I will face him down. After all, he is only a gardener. I shan't have any trouble, but if I do, I can always scream." Slipping from her horse's back, she said, "I will see you back here in one hour," and, before they could move to stop her, hurried off.

The night had by now become quite dark, with an overcast obscuring the moon. Annette felt a trifle nervous, but, upon discovering she could move about easily among the darker shadows cast by shrubbery, and reasoning that no one else could see one whit better than she, stepped forward bravely to take up position in a larger shadow, her eyes on the rear of Bodkin Hall. Time, however, began to drag. A breeze sprang up, chilling her. In growing vexation she blinked her eyes (they were developing a tendency to droop) and flailed her arms to ward off the increasing chill.

It may have been that inactivity dulled her senses and lulled her thoughts. For whatever reason, she was taken unawares. A darker shadow disturbed the corner of her vision—a fraction late. She was seized from behind and held immobile, a hand clamped over her mouth smothering the scream rising in her throat. Though her muscles bunched to struggle, she could not move.

A softly indrawn breath whispered above her head as her eyes caught a movement in the gloom; a darker figure separated itself from a shadow, to move furtively to the house and disappear around a corner. "If I release you, will you be quiet?" a voice murmured in her ear. "I won't harm you, my lady. You have seen me at Monkshaven. I am Lord Bodkin's groom."

"But what—why in the world—"

"It is not safe for you to be about tonight, my lady."

"Lord Wrexly and his friend are with me. I will be perfectly safe, I assure you."

"I sent them home," the groom answered mildly and seemed to be debating with himself. He said he thought it best she remain for now at Bodkin Hall. He would secret her safely in the servants' quarters until she could return to her home without danger.

Annette eyed him with considerable disfavor. "I do not intend your telling me what to do," she said quellingly. Recalling her earlier impression that he did not in the least resemble any groom she had had occasion to know, she edged a further nervous step away from him.

"I regret I am not at liberty to confide in you, my lady, but you will not be ill-advised to put your trust in me. The Earl does, you know."

Annette had to concede this. Her head by now was in a whirl. What Drake had to do with the man before her was not at all clear, and she did not think she was in the way of finding out. Appearing to fall in with his plan seemed the best course for her to follow. She would return to Monkshaven immediately the Bodkin servants went to sleep.

To her surprise, the staff accepted her precipitate addition to their number without comment. The butler and housekeeper, two very superior persons, condescended to be pleased. No further recommendation was required.

Annette, pitchforked belowstairs with not the least notion of how to go on, rather wished Malveney had refused her refuge the moment her strange benefactor voiced his odd request. The butler's failure to act in an expected manner suggested two possibilities: either the groom was of sufficient standing to enjoy a considerable amount of Malveney's deferential respect, or the butler remembered her from the evening she had dined at Bodkin Hall with Drake. To her great relief Malveney offered the groom a glass of port with so much condescension that Annette reasoned she ought not to go too far in dwelling on alarming thoughts.

To one unacquainted with life in the servants' hall, the opportunity to observe its workings at firsthand undoubtedly had its surprises. One such instance came at dinner, and with a thoroughness impressive in its condemnation. In total disregard of the niceties of loyalty, the assembled company trampled on their master's character with a candor that was at once as amazing as it was unjust. No one could be that black-hearted. Annette, taken unawares, thought the gossip of the ton quite tame when compared with the tongues of servants. She retired to the chamber assigned to her at the conclusion of the meal considerably vexed. She herself harbored no kindly regards for Lord Bodkin, quite the reverse, but to be held up to such ridicule by one's employees, however much deserved, and all without the slightest notice of a stranger in their midst, left her feeling daunted. She sat down in her room to wait for the household to quiet, anxious to leave her unhappy surroundings.

Annette had never before wandered over a strange house in the dead of night. The thought of the impropriety of doing so now did not deter her. She stole out into the passage just as the kitchen clock was striking twelve. Moving swiftly to the narrow staircase and up its cold, stone treads, she pushed open the door at the top of the flight and cautiously stepped forward into a large hall. At the same moment, across the shadowed chamber, a gleam of candlelight suddenly fell upon an opened portal. Lord Bodkin and the tutor came in view. Annette did not hesitate. In an instant she had whisked herself back down the stairs. She would remain in her room at Bodkin Hall until the morning.

The appearance of the groom at breakfast made her doubt her very senses. Looking exceedingly smart in a beautifully cut coat and gleaming top boots, he cast a driving cape and tan gloves on a chair and sat down opposite her at table. "Well?" he chuckled as she stared in a fascinated trance.

"But—but, is it you?" she inanely asked, feeling at a loss for words.

"I have been laboring under that impression," he grinned, and turned to nod at Malveney, who, with every indication of respect, was waiting to serve him.

Annette's mind suddenly woke from its bemused state. This groom, in truth, was no groom at all. He was a Bodkin. But a servant? An explanation obtruded: he had no legal claim to the name.

The coach pulled up in the stableyard bore no crest upon its door, but was for all that a comfortable conveyance. Annette's brows went up. "Doing it rather brown, aren't you?"

"Yes, I know," the groom murmured gravely, controlling an errant tendency of his lips to smile. "But I will contrive to deposit you at your door without incident. This is the least conspicuous means of doing so, you will agree."

Making the best of the situation, she allowed him to assist her to a seat inside the coach. Questions were burning on her tongue, but she found it impossible to ask them. She could not, after all, introduce a subject that could well be a painful one for him. It was, in fact, the groom who, surprisingly, brought up the matter by telling her, while grinning at her in a way she could only interpret as indicating he knew what she was thinking, that he was indeed a Bodkin and a legitimate one at that. But beyond cutting his eyes at her in a most amused manner, he seemed content to settle into his corner and lapse into silence. Annette stared at his averted face, disappointed, and had to be satisfied. There was no finding out more from him; she would question Drake.

A shot split the quiet, jerking them upright in their seats. Annette, striving to keep her balance in the rocking of the vehicle caused by the coachman dragging his horses to a standstill, turned frightened eyes to the door hauled open by a mounted ruffian. "Stand and deliver," he growled, leveling a pistol in the face of the erstwhile groom. His eyes widened. "Well, well," he said, perceiving Annette. "What have we here. The Countess of Ardley. Your servant, ma'am."

"Now, see here—" began the groom, only to have the firearm motion him to descend to the road.

"If you will be so good, my lady," the highwayman said to Annette, leaving her little choice but to follow the groom from the coach.

"You are welcome to my purse," said the groom. "You will find little in it, I'm afraid."

Cruel eyes surveyed him from behind a mask. "I haven't the honor of your acquaintance," spoke a cold voice. "But if you will bear with me, sir, I will be with you in a moment."

The groom seemed on the verge of further speech, but, his worried gaze going from the pistol held by the ruffian to Annette's face, he remained prudently silent.

The highwayman's eyes swung to Annette. "The Earl is careless, I see," came his hateful voice. "Or does he not know his countess is larking about the countryside in the company of another?"

Annette gasped. "How dare you!" she stormed, momentarily forgetting her fear.

"Well, well, a termagant."

"You mustn't speak to her ladyship disrespectfully," the groom protested in her defense.

The words had scarcely left his lips when the ruffian's pistol fired, the shot spinning the groom around before he crashed in a lifeless heap upon the ground.

Annette stared, horrified, numbed by the sight that met her eyes. The groom lay so still, the blood rapidly spreading across his chest, his now sightless eyes turned toward the sky. A scream tearing from her throat, Annette set off down the road, running wildly, her skirts whipping about her ankles. Mindless, in the grip of a terror such as she had not known before, she did not hear the highwayman thundering down on her. An arm snaked out, and she was snatched from her feet, to be flung across the back of a wildly galloping horse.

CHAPTER NINETEEN

The Earl stumbled to a chair. The draperies were drawn against the night; there was a bright red glow from the fire, and the flickering of candlelight. He seemed not to notice. The cold hand of fear clutched at his heart.

"Drake, old boy," Lord Collingham's voice spoke shakily. "Drink this."

But a shattering anxiety gripped the Earl. He sat as though carved from stone.

Lady Agatha, watching him, abruptly rustled across the room. "Do be sensible, Ardley," she said, taking the glass from Lord Collingham and holding it out to him. "The port will do you good. My dear, you must pull yourself together. You cannot continue on like this. I cannot imagine how they made such a mistake, for that is all it is, I'm sure. You will find that Annette is perfectly safe."

"You cannot know the circumstances," he replied with difficulty. "It does not signify talking."

There was a moment's silence. "What nonsense is this?" Agatha asked. Receiving no reply from the Earl, her gaze swung to Lord Collingham. "Sir?" she demanded.

"Nothing—upon my honor—you must wonder, I daresay—" Acutely uncomfortable, Lord Collingham ground to a halt.

Agatha stared, speechless, from one of them to the other. Clamping her lips together, she walked to a chair and sat down. "I will not move from this spot until I am told what is going forth in this house," she declared with strong feeling. "I am well aware I lack the strength to force your confidence, but I assure you I have the fortitude to wait you out."

Drake was stung into replying, as she meant him to be. "Do you imagine I would not give my life to have Annette safe?"

Agatha shook her head in a gesture of denial. "It occurs to me that you have a strong reason for feeling so positive that she is not. The news that reached our ears did not strike me in just that way. What are you keeping from me?"

Drake looked steadily at her before replying. "For some time now, we have been engaged in tracking down traitors selling information to the French. Lord Bodkin was known to be involved. I will tell you now that Lady Kinsley was the lure that drew him here. We were sworn to secrecy, with these results. Annette and Paul went hunting for our ghost—and found him, or more accurately, his portrait. Wadding had been making free with the east wing."

"The tutor!" Agatha gasped, her mind reeling.

"There is more. For some reason, Annette and Paul went to the pavilion on the island. Hodges, who is actually an intelligence agent, saw them there, and, fearing Wadding might turn up, locked them in and went in search of me. But Dickie must have released them, for they all turned up at Bodkin Hall. Bodkin's groom, Benji, came across them there. Had it been Bodkin—"

"You said the groom came across Annette," Agatha prompted.

"He thought it wise to secret her in the servants' hall until morning. He was returning her home when their coach—"

"I can only say it is your own affair if you wish to abandon hope. I am very sorry about Benji, but we should not assume that Annette met with—an accident. She more probably will return when she is able."

"You have forgotten Wadding? I find myself unable to do so."

The flat way in which he spoke had its effect on Agatha. "We should discuss what is best to be done."

"Hodges is at present scouring the countryside for Annette."

"And you are expecting him to return empty-handed?"

"I have sufficient reason to expect it. Ask yourself how Wadding has made his living during all these years. I don't cavil to say he is capable of robbery." The Earl took a restless turn about the room, fetching up at the window. "If you are wondering if he is capable of murder, he is. He is capable of anything."

Agatha had gone white. She voiced the only hope left to her: "He has never seen Annette."

The horror of it stared from Drake's eyes. "But he has," was all he said.

They spent a wretched hour waiting for news. The least sound in the house brought their eyes to the door; a footfall in the hall brought them to their feet. Agatha did her best to reassure Drake, but her own alarm was evident.

"We should hear something soon," Lord Collingham said, trying to speak calmly. "Do not fear the worst, dear boy."

"You know I have reason to fear the worst. I have been recalling Wadding's hatred of the family and the vicious things he said when discharged."

"But even Wadding could not hold Annette responsible."

"That is the thought I cling to."

Lord Collingham gazed upon his friend with compassion. "I'm sure you will find her—otherwhere."

Drake's voice was scarcely audible. "Otherwhere is forever."

At this moment a tap sounded on the door and Hodges entered. "I came as fast as I could, m'lord. I wish I had better news."

"Nothing?"

"Not a whisper, m'lord. We'd best be on our way to Eastbourne. Sir Andrew expects the landing for tomorrow night at Grantley's farm. It'll be real dark, what with the moon behind the clouds, and all. Ye'll find yer lady there, m'lord. Where else could she be?"

Thirty minutes later they were riding at a gallop on the road to Bodkin Hall, bestride the swiftest cattle in his lordship's stables. At about the moment they were thundering through the village of Heathfield, Annette was being shoved into an attic room at Grantley's farm, to stagger forward against a table, bruising her hip. She was so shaken she had to hold onto it to steady herself. To her intense relief, the door slammed shut behind her, and she dropped exhausted into a rickety chair beside the narrow window. She scarcely saw the narrow pallet standing against a smoke-blackened wall or the tattered curtains hanging limply at the window.

The breeze stirring the curtain brought with it an odor. Annette wrinkled her nose and turned to look out of the window. Scrawny chickens scratched amid the litter strewing the ground between house and outbuildings. A malodorous aroma emanating from the barnyard mingled with the scent from the sea. It was becoming quite dark, with black clouds boiling in, obscuring the moon and carrying with them a surfeit of rain. Annette drew her cloak more closely about herself and struggled to throw off the megrim threatening to overcome her.

The part of her that was aware of her predicament heard the voices. They sounded harsh—a strangled sob caught in her throat. She could envision their faces, boorish and coarse, yet infinitely preferable to those others. She closed her eyes, reliving her terror at finding herself in the tutor's power, and her greater terror of Lord Bodkin's intentions. His face, flushed, the beginning of lechery staring from his eyes, rose up to haunt her. Whatever the tutor's plans for her, an assault on her person was not among them. Had it not been for Wadding—

Annette hardly dared to breathe. She tried not to make a sound, crouched there in her chair. Perhaps, the footsteps would go away. Perhaps she could plead, could reason with her captor. The thoughts raged feverishly in her brain. Before her frightened eyes, the door swung open; the moment she dreaded had come.

He came in then, grinning, like a wolf in the night. His eyes, what she could see of them under a curling lock of hair, were cold, dispassionate, traveling slowly, insultingly, over her. He spoke slowly, his voice implacable: "If you are entertaining thoughts of escape, *mignonne*, forget them. One does not waste one's francs, *n'est-ce pas?* I bought you," he added conversationally.

The room was very still. Annette, staring at him, was appalled. She gasped, "You're French!"

"But, *oui.* What else would I be, mademoiselle?"

"Madame!" she shot at him.

His eyebrows rose. "Fifty thousand francs. Wadding

is a ruthless devil. Tell me, *mignonne*, is your body *magnifique?*"

She reached out to clutch the arms of her chair. She looked up into his face, hoping to read compassion in his expression. But all she saw was a very evident content with his bargain.

"And now, *mignonne*, it is time to leave. We must sail with the tide, *n'est-ce pas?*"

His voice seemed to Annette to come from a long way away. Was she in the clutches of a smuggler? In normal circumstances, such a one would be illiterate. Unless she was very much mistaken, the man before her had received more than a modicum of learning. She was thinking fast. Could she reason with him? One thing was certain. She would not meekly board a French vessel. Looking at him as appealingly as she was able, she said, "I haven't any money with me at the moment, monsieur, but I can pay any sum you care to name. You say you w-were out fifty thousand francs. I will gladly restore this amount to your pocket."

To her chagrin, he threw back his head and laughed. "You are an original, *mignonne*. Our association should prove most pleasant."

"It is not quite accurate to say that I am able to replenish your funds," she hastened to say. "Rather, it is my husband who will do so."

His eyes were brimful with amusement. "May I inquire the identity of this so wealthy gentleman?"

"Why, the Earl of Ardley, of course."

He achieved a beautiful leg. "My lady," he grinned.

"You must believe me," Annette said desperately. "I am the Countess of Ardley. Ask Wadding."

This gave him pause. "Wadding?" he asked, surprised.

"He was my husband's tutor. And a more vicious, a more despicable—" She drew a deep breath.

He was staring at her, thunderstruck. "You have an excellent understanding of his character." A thoughtful expression came on his face. "You could, however, have gleaned the impression during the past two days."

"Will you just listen! Wadding was discharged for the unspeakable cruelties he inflicted on Drake. He is only using me to make him suffer. He is using you, too, you know."

Her bald statements had their effect. He sat down on the edge of the pallet and absentmindedly ran his hand through his hair. Annette waited while he pondered. She was weary, exhausted with emotion, her endurance about depleted.

"Madame," he said, rising. "We sail with the tide."

"Oh, please—"

"Quiet!" he roared, much annoyed. "You are perhaps that which you claim. I do not know. You make easy with Monsieur's given name, madame. But still I do not know. Time will tell, n'est-ce pas? A ransom paid means much, n'est-ce pas?"

"But if you take me to France, how can Drake pay? You could not collect, and—"

"Madame, you try my patience. It would be a pity to feed you to the fishes. You now see fit to obey, n'est-ce pas?" He turned away and stood waiting for her to precede him down the stairs.

It seemed a long way from the house to the beach. She noticed they kept to the shadows of low hills running nearly down to the water until they came to a pebbly beach. Stepping into a boat drawn up to the shore, he held out a hand to steady her aboard, and shoved off for the open sea. Annette craned her head for a last backward look before her abductor, with a few deft strokes, fetched them up in the lee of a ship.

No lights showed to pierce the dark. A rope ladder dangling over the side was thrust into her hands. Pushed from below, and pulled from above, she negotiated the swaying contrivance to the blessed stability of the ship's deck. She then sank down to the planking on the portside, bereft of all emotion. Shadowy figures swarmed up the rigging, silently and efficiently setting the sails to catch the breeze. The ship, standing out to sea, ran before the wind, the hum of the shrouds and the slapping of water against the hull heralding her eager assault of the rolling swells.

No sound of her passing reached the ears of Sir Andrew's forces converging on Grantley's farm. Situated a few miles out from Eastbourne in the low-lying land between the hills, the farm was reached by a narrow, rutted road snaking its way between ancient hedgerows enclosing it in a wall of impenetrable growth. The hills, rolling and barren of vegetation other than gorse, covered the area, ending abruptly in ragged cliffs a few feet from shore. Strange odors hung in the air, noisome with the scent of sea wrack from the beach mingling with the stench of moldy growth from the hills.

Men of His Majesty's navy approached from the east, the law enforcement officers from the west. Few words were spoken, and those at a whisper. They crept up one hill, to slither down, and creep up another. There was, surprisingly, no sentry to hear their coming. They swarmed around, now in position and hidden behind the nearest hills, and waited.

A line of wagons approached the farm, swaying and creaking along the rutted road. Burly men filled the lurching vehicles, with others trudging along in their wake. Each was violent-looking and armed. They passed without challenge to the yard of the farm. Sir Andrew's men had their orders; the assault would come in the farmyard, and after the carts were loaded. The smuggler's guilt would be undeniably established.

Shadowy figures swarmed between barn and wagon, bent nearly double under heavy bundles, the weight balanced precariously on shoulder and hip. The work went on at fever pitch, silent and furtive. Sir Andrew lay stretched full-length upon the scraggly turf, his head raised cautiously over the brow of the nearest hill. His position afforded him an excellent view, being not more than thirty yards away. The sound of hoofbeats moving fast came to his ears, growing louder and louder as a solitary rider approached from down the road. Sir Andrew's lips spread in a humorless smile: the leader of the band of cutthroats drew near.

The horseman swept into sight, astride a lathered beast. His voice rang out clearly over hill and farm. "What did I tell you, lads? Quite a haul, eh?"

One of the smugglers stepped forward. "We been talkin', ye see," he said. "We been takin' all the risks, and we wants more'n ye're givin' us. Ye been lyin' up safe and tight in Eastbourne whilst us does all the work."

"I have not been idle while in Eastbourne," the rider said with dangerous quiet. "You have not the wit for intercourse with the ship's captain. Not a solitary one of you has the wit."

"Us still wants our fair share," the spokesman held stubbornly to their demands. "Ye may plan the smugglin', Wadding, but us carries it out."

"Damnation!" stormed the tutor. "You're a scurvy bunch, the lot of you." Beside himself with rage, he dragged a pistol from his belt and leveled it at the spokesman. "You'll find I'm a match for you, you murderous dogs. I'll put a ball through the first man of you who stands in my way. There's more to this than your paltry smuggling. You'll ruin us all, you fools."

"Now, ye just wait," the spokesman said, backing off toward his fellows. "Ye can't talk like that. Us just—"

He got no further—Wadding fired, blowing away his face where he stood. An angry growl rose from the throats of the others, and, before the spokesman's body went crashing to the ground, another shot split the air. Wadding staggered back, clutching the hole blown in his chest, a look of profound disbelief spreading across his face.

Sir Andrew blew a piercing blast on his whistle. "Throw down your arms," he called. "You are surrounded."

All pandemonium broke loose. Death or penal servitude awaited the smugglers were they captured alive. Surrounded as they were, the battle raged furiously, but swiftly concluded. Sir Andrew had no trouble at all in drawing intelligence from the now subdued and cooperative captives, but they were ignorant of Wadding's traitorous activities. He was forced to stake his slender hopes on the skill of the navy surgeon striving to keep Wadding alive.

CHAPTER TWENTY

The Earl, as it happened, had no idea the tutor lay close to death. Coming into the parlor of the inn at Eastbourne, he stood looking at Lord Bodkin. To do him justice, he had not contemplated taking Bodkin's life, though his companions would have understood had he done so. It had been a fruitless day. The Earl and Lord Collingham, along with Hodges and Peale, had come upon Bodkin Hall just at dawn. Rousting Lord Bodkin from his bed, they had questioned and threatened, to no avail. For Bodkin, not dreaming that anyone, least of all the Earl, had any idea of his traitorous dealings, saw no need to make disclosures detrimental to himself. He would not be made to talk.

The Earl now walked up to him, looking at him in a way that caused Bodkin to cower in his chair. "You may now know," said his lordship, "that presently you will tell me what you have done with my wife."

Lord Bodkin gave his nervous little titter. "I cannot understand what makes you so sure I have done anything with her."

A chilling smile touched Ardley's lips. "Your recollections are no doubt—shall we say—a trifle imperfect?"

Lord Bodkin struggled to appear at ease. "Forcing me to come with you is of grave moment, my lord."

"But, of course. If you say so."

Lord Bodkin flushed, but spoke with a great deal of bravado. "Were it not for the fact that I hold you in the greatest esteem, my lord, I would be inclined to lodge charges against you."

"Your motives are no doubt very fine, but I must remind you that unless you tell me what I wish to know, you will be in no condition to lodge charges."

A plan was taking form in Bodkin's mind. If denials would not win the day, perhaps a scapegoat would. "I had hoped to spare you, my lord, but I now see it my humane duty to apprise you of the most unpleasant tidings." He paused, and said with drama, "How devoutly do I wish it otherwise."

His audience did not seem much moved. Ardley continued looking at him levelly, as still as a statue. Those others sat without moving, their collective stares on his face. Bodkin, however, was not daunted. The journey here (forced upon him as it had been) had brought him excellent counsel.

When these gentlemen had first swooped on him (there was no better word for it), he had felt very much puzzled by the accusations hurled at his head. He had always considered Ardley's wife a jade; for his part, he had not been at all surprised to learn she had been apprehended on the return home from spending the night with a lover. He had no doubt at all that she would have lain as willingly in his own arms, had it not been for Wadding's untimely interference. The man was altogether too intent on vengeance. For his own part, he could not see it made the least difference whether the soiled dove was first had by himself or by a Frenchman. He, Bodkin, had been very much more concerned that Ardley had gone seeking his errant bride at Bodkin Hall. That seemed very odd to him, for there was no obvious explanation to account for it. Ardley could not know of his and Wadding's activities. It seemed stranger still that Ardley had brought him to this place. The man could have no idea what was going forward a few miles to the east. Bodkin was inclined to think disaster could not befall—he need only keep his wits about him. "Two days ago—I beg pardon—two mornings ago, at nine of the clock to be precise, I had occasion to be upon the road to Hawkhurst."

"A strange hour to venture forth, surely?"

Bodkin drew himself up. "There is nothing strange, I should think, in setting forth on an errand of mercy, regardless of the hour. I was on my way to lend succor to a tenant, little dreaming chance would intervene. I came upon a coach stopped right across the road. Picture my surprise, if you will, my lord, for what did I perceive but a robbery in progress!" He paused, shaking his head in a gesture of lament. "You may be sure I did not flee—I immediately proceeded forward to the scene."

"Such resolution does you credit," Ardley remarked dryly.

Lord Bodkin gave his little titter. "I do not claim to have done more than any gentleman would," he said virtuously. "The rogues perpetuating the abomination were vastly put out to perceive me bearing down on them, I will tell you. I stepped right up to demand they desist, but you will understand they were in no mood to follow my instruction."

"I should think not," Ardley murmured wearily. "And then?"

"The leader of the thieves—I had no trouble in singling him out—spoke in a most deplorable manner, considering there was a lady present."

Ardley's eyes were on Bodkin's face, a chilling expression in their depths. "And?" he said softly.

"I expostulated, you may be sure, but he paid me

no heed. My attention became distracted by another cutthroat turning his pistol on me, and so I saw not what next occurred. I can only tell you of my shock, my lord, at hearing a shot. A body lay on the road, my lord. A dead body."

Ardley's brows rose. "The lady?" he leisurely inquired.

"No, no. A gentleman. An occupant of the coach." Bodkin turned innocent eyes upon the Earl. "The lady's companion, sir."

"And could you identify this gentleman?"

"I had never had the pleasure."

Ardley's smile was bland. "Pray continue."

"Again I expostulated with the malefactor. You may be sure, my lord, I did all I could, but to no avail. The lady was pulled from the coach and placed before the cutthroat upon his horse. Had it not been for the fact that my pistol was at home, I would have persevered. As it was, I could only stand idly by and watch them ride off."

"You have concluded?"

"It may appear that I have, my lord. However—I did not wish to speak, you will recall."

"You had better," came the grim reply.

"The lady was your wife, my lord. I tried to save her. I—"

He got no further. His arm was seized in an iron grip. "You lying cur," the Earl spat, jerking him to his feet. "Where is Annette? Tell me, or I'll kill you."

Bodkin read death in his lordship's eyes. "I don't know. I p-protest—" he sputtered, his body shaking uncontrollably.

For answer, Ardley yanked him toward the door. "Say your prayers," he growled menacingly.

"No. Wait. I tried to stop him. He wouldn't listen,"

Lord Bodkin babbled, out of his wits with terror. "He sold her. I couldn't stop him. He—"

"Oh, dear God!"

"The Frenchman bought her. I tried to stop them. I—"

The Earl had gone dead white. In one swift movement Lord Collingham was out of his chair. Lord Bodkin goggled and babbled on. "France. She's gone to France. They sailed from Grantley's farm. I beg you—"

A moment only the thunderous silence held: Lord Bodkin went reeling back, flung from the Earl, to fall crashing to the floor. A moment more: Hodges and Peale stood over the cowering traitor, pistols drawn, listening to the sound of Lord Collingham and the Earl galloping wildly off into the night.

CHAPTER TWENTY-ONE

The Earl sat down in the room next to the one in which Wadding lay and contemplated the fare set out for his inspection. A slice of mutton, charred on the outside from being cooked too near the fire, a dish of porridge, grayish in color, two hard-cooked eggs, and a pitcher of ale comprised the offering. Not surprisingly, he picked up the tankard and waved the covers to be removed. Lord Collingham, standing silent by the window, shot him a quick, shrewd glance. To sit about kicking their heels, with only the vaguest hope that Wadding would regain consciousness, was not his notion of folly. The idea that Drake could lose his head and act the fool never occurred to him.

"He won't last long," said the doctor, coming into the room. "If you wish to question him?"

The Earl moved forward. "A few answers will suffice."

Wadding was lying very still, his face drained of color. Though his eyes were closed, his face seemed less cruel than the Earl remembered ever having seen it. "Do you hear me, Wadding?" he asked, taking the chair beside the bed just vacated by the doctor.

The tutor opened his eyes; they were dark with pain, but focused on the Earl's face. His lips worked; the breath wheezed in his throat at the effort to speak. The Earl leaned forward to catch his words: "Forgive—wronged you," the dying man managed to whisper.

"To whom did you sell my wife?" the Earl asked, his eyes steadily on the tutor's face.

"Frenchman." Wadding's voice was growing weaker. A gray shade had crept into his face.

The Earl bent over him, his ear close to Wadding's lips. "His name, for God's sake!" he begged, agonized that time could run out before he learned what he must know.

"Arnaud—" The tutor's voice sighed away to silence.

"His last name! Wadding—for the love of God—his last name."

The tutor's eyes were going opaque. Putting forth the last, weary remnant of his strength, he gasped, "Ducienne. Le C—Comte," and lay still.

An hour later, the Earl and Lord Collingham were ushered into the private parlor of the inn at Eastbourne by a beaming landlord. Never had so many distinguished personages seen fit to patronize his establishment. He withdrew and hurried to the kitchens. No fault could be found with the beef and kidney pie eventually served the guests, nor need the landlord apologize for the wine left on the table at the conclusion of the meal.

Sir Andrew set his glass down and sighed. "I am inclined to hazard the opinion that a ransom will be demanded. You will not be so foolish as to personally attempt a rescue, Ardley. I will send my best operative to France. If Arnaud Ducienne is, as Bodkin claims, an aristocrat currying favor with Bonaparte, it is reasonable to assume he will make all haste to Paris to lay the memorandum before him."

"And you think we should accept Bodkin's word?"

"He was obliging enough, once captured. No doubt he hopes for leniency by disclosing what he knows. Whatever his real name, he had known the real Lord

Bodkin in Paris for years before his death. Our false Bodkin had acquired sufficient precise and complete information about the Bodkin family to pass himself off as their heir. He had intended returning to France immediately upon concluding his spying activities. Bonaparte had promised possibly a title, should the information prove useful."

The Earl had the sensation of having received a blow in the pit of his stomach. "The memorandum this Arnaud Ducienne is taking to Bonaparte—if it is discovered to be false—"

"Your wife will be restored to you before that can occur."

Annette would have been much comforted had she been able to console herself with that thought.

She had remained huddled on the deck, very close to tears, but choking them back, as the ship sailed on. Instinct told her bravery could be a credential in future dealing with the smuggler. She was unutterably weary. The figures of sailors going about their work swam before her eyes, but she scarcely noticed, so sunk was she in misery. Her captor appeared in front of her, and, before she realized his intent, grasped her arm and hauled her to her feet. She was aware of the curious stares of several of the rough-looking men busy with coils of rope, and tried to hold back, but the smuggler marched her to a steep companionway, and down it.

The cabin was a fair size for so small a ship. There was a table and chair set beneath the porthole, a seaman's chest, and a bunk against the bulkhead. Annette sank down on the chair, feeling extremely weak, and carefully kept her eyes from the bunk. Not so, the smuggler. He strolled across to it and sat down, a most alarming gleam in his half-closed eyes. A flush rose in her cheeks, and she turned away from the insulting smile on his lips, and the way his eyes ran leisurely over her body. Laughing and lounging back at ease, he drew one leg up and hooked his heel over the edge of the bunk. "You will find it more comfortable over here, *mignonne*," came his hateful voice.

Her hands were not quite steady. She clasped them tightly in her lap and sat very upright. "We need to discuss my ransom," she said with a control he must admire. "I do not as yet know our destination, but—"

"You go to Paris with me, *mignonne*."

"Don't call me that," she said chokingly.

"But Madame sounds so—how does one say?—stiff? *Non*. Formal is a better word, *oui*?"

Annette strove to marshal her wits. It dawned on her that he was leading her on. "Your use of the English language fails on command," she said tartly.

He gave a low laugh, and produced a snuffbox from a pocket. "You have not inquired after my name, *mignonne*."

She shrugged carelessly. "As you say, monsieur."

He only chuckled. "You will come to accept more than my name. I am not so ill-looking, eh?"

She glanced at him fleetingly, but quickly turned her eyes away. "You need not insult me, monsieur. You will remember I am here against my will." There was a tremor in her voice, but she continued doggedly: "You said we would speak of ransom—"

"I did not say that, *mignonne*. You did."

She continued in a failing voice: "I've no idea of just how you will contrive to contact my husband, but I am sure it will be better accomplished if we remain near the Channel."

"You may think what you wish, *mignonne*, but we

go to Paris. You will enjoy Paris, *n'est-ce pas?* It is so charming, so gay. You will do well there," he added, his eyes roaming over her. "Your face, your body—you will see."

"Monsieur," she said desperately. "I will be in no condition to enjoy Paris. I am to have a child."

He sat up and stared at her, startled. "Whose is it?"

Her cheeks flamed crimson but she answered steadily enough. "My husband's."

He looked so grim she could not but believe his thoughts of her had taken another direction. She sat very still, therefore, and waited. She felt quite unequal to a further battle of wits and could only hope he would not resume a verbal fencing.

He spoke softly: "You may be at ease, *mignonne*. I was born a gentleman and will not take a woman carrying another man's seed." His eyes studied her keenly. "Wadding lied," he said candidly. "You were not en route home following a night in a lover's arms?"

She looked stricken. "No!" she managed, feeling suffocated.

"You have never had any man, other than your husband?"

"No," she replied simply.

He was silent for a moment, watching her. "What were you doing out early in the morning with another man? I want the truth, *mignonne*."

"We—a cousin and his friend—followed Wadding to Bodkin Hall. It was—" (her eyes skittered away from his face) "—not very wise. But he had been sneaking into Monkshaven and we thought to discover what he was about. We thought that whatever it was, Wadding and Bodkin were in it together. Lord Bodkin's groom came across me and insisted I spend the night in the servants' quarters. He was escorting me home when Wadding stopped our coach. He murdered the groom and seized me. You know the rest, monsieur."

"Not quite, *mignonne*. Your husband approved the escapade?"

Annette flushed. "He had, as a matter of fact, requested I not leave the house unescorted. But I was, you see. Paul accompanied me."

"You dissemble, *n'est-ce pas?* No, *mignonne*. You acted foolishly in disobeying your husband."

"If you will arrange passage home for me, I am sure he will reward you most generously."

"You forget you will shortly arrive in a country at war with your own. A French ship could not so carelessly sail into a British port, eh?"

"Could not this one turn about—"

"Your throat would slit as easily as mine, should we attempt to turn this crew about." He rose from the bunk. "Come," he said, "you will find the mattress comfortable."

The cabin suddenly seemed stifling. She closed her eyes to shut out the sight of him. "Please," she whispered.

When he spoke, his voice was furious. "I have no notion of molesting you, *mignonne*. But you will admit you are at least partially to blame for being thought a trollop?"

Her eyes flew open. "Yes, I know. But I had no idea anything really serious was going forward." She looked at him questioningly. "Something is, isn't it?"

"I have no intention of laying my affairs before you for your inspection. You might act the fool, madame, but I do not. And while we are on the subject, I will inform you that your conduct from start to finish has been rash and ill-judged. If you were right now lying sprawled in some man's bed, it would be no more than you deserve."

"My conduct is at least as good as yours," she shot back. "I do not take helpless females to foreign countries against their will."

"You are about as helpless as a pregnant jungle cat," he answered coldly. "Your husband would have been better advised to cage you."

Her swift smile flashed. "You are trying to make me believe you virtuous?"

"You would be advised, madame, to tread with care. If you do not wish to find yourself in circumstances you might find unpleasant, you will know not to tease. We go ashore at eight," he finished, and went out, slamming the door behind him.

CHAPTER TWENTY-TWO

The light was very dim, but she was able to distinguish the outline of a table and chair drawn up under a porthole. With a start, Annette sat up in the bunk, her memory flooding back. She peered distrustfully around the cabin, and, to her relief, found she was alone. This did not particularly surprise her. She had last evening reached the conclusion that her abductor was a most peculiar person. She had no doubt that in some way or other he would contrive to justify his conduct while at the same time dragging her off to Paris. Had she anything to fear from him? His hated lips might say terrible things, but she could not think he would actually harm her. Considerably buoyed by these encouraging thoughts, she rose from the bunk, smoothed her skirts and hair as well as she was able with her hands, and crossed to the chair to sit down.

It seemed she waited an interminable time. The light in the cabin only gradually became brighter. She had not anticipated being left alone for so long and wondered uneasily how she would be able to return to England, had the smuggler abandoned her. She had no money and knew full well the reception she would receive should she appear before a fisherman begging transport across the Channel.

In the middle of these dismal reflections, the door opened to admit the smuggler. "You're ready, I see," he drawled. "The mate is bringing coffee and rolls."

Annette eyed him, annoyed. "Have you not heard it is polite to knock?"

He was watching her in some amusement. "I daresay I have," he said carelessly, and laughed. "You will forgive me, eh?"

"You could offer me some courtesy," she snapped, stung. His very attitude stripped away her defenses, pitiable as they were. He lounged at ease, hands in pockets, his very posture an insult. Her color rose.

"You have given me no reason for doing so, *mignonne*," came his hateful voice in reply. "A wench must earn her keep, *n'est-ce pas?* I slept cold last night, *mignonne*."

She dared not look at him. "You said you would not molest me," she said in a voice that shook slightly.

"Put your mind at ease, *mignonne*. Fruit easily plucked always tastes sweeter."

"Stop calling me *mignonne!*"

"When I cease calling you that," he said, "you should take fright." His eyes studied her averted face. "You need taming," he remarked, rising to his feet.

She forgot her role of bravery. "Don't c-come near m-me!"

"Our breakfast has arrived. Would you not prefer eating it at table?"

She looked wildly around, to see the mate standing in the open door, a tray in his hands. She had a very fair idea of the thoughts running through his mind—she saw his sly grin—and kept her eyes averted. One further insult was in store: neither man made any move to assist her. She seated herself, and, with hands unsteady, poured a cup of coffee. Having second thoughts, she served her captor.

A smile lit his eyes. "Your conduct improves, *mi-*

gnonne. I make you my compliments. I'm no more an object of infamy, eh?"

She took another sip of the hot brew, and found it helped. "You have not served me ill, sir," she said. "I am sure you will wish to arrange my passage home. It is unfortunate that—"

"No, *mignonne.* You go to Paris with me." He came to his feet. "You don't think it now, but you will like the city very well. Come. We go ashore."

Annette climbed up the companionway with dragging feet. She felt that in leaving the ship, she left all hope of returning home behind. The smuggler led her up the gangway and to a chaise drawn up by the quayside. There was nothing for it but to allow him to hand her in. Sitting as far in the corner as she could contrive, she had, perforce, to share the warmth of the lap robe with her companion, for he entered behind her and settled himself beside her on the luxuriously upholstered seat. The steps were put up, the postilions mounted to their saddles, and the chaise moved off down the cobbled street.

She leaned back, staring through the window with unseeing eyes. The man beside her remained silent, only occasionally glancing absently at her averted face, until the chaise drew out of town and set forth on the road to Paris. He then said softly, "Are you weary, *mignonne*?"

She remained silent, too drained of strength to find a reply. Had she the courage, she would hurl herself from the rapidly moving vehicle. Such a thought had not before entered her brain—she shrank from it. She had the child to think of now. She was roused from her abstractions by his voice inviting her to rest against his shoulder. "What!" she ejaculated, horrified.

"It would be more comfortable, *n'est-ce pas?*"

She sat bolt upright. "Not for the world, sir!" She perceived that she had offended him, but turned her head and looked away for all the earth as if unaware of his presence by her side.

It was a mistake. She found herself hauled onto his lap, too surprised to protest. Fury blazed from his eyes; his grip crushing her against his chest made her wince. "You will learn to obey," he gritted in her ear. "I'll tame you!"

She cringed back, but there was no escape. His hand moved over her arm and down to a breast, cupping it and kneading. His eyes stared into hers, daring her. She heard his low chuckle and came alive, clawing at his face in her desperate struggle to be free. "So that's the way it is," he growled, his fingers working at the buttons of her bodice.

"Please," she whispered, "I've learned my lesson." But he paid her no heed. She heard the material of her chemise part and felt the cool air on her bared flesh.

He was not rough. He caressed her slowly, his hands lightly brushing over her breasts, gently cupping the soft mounds. Through half-opened eyes he studied her closed face, saw her nostrils flare, and bent his lips to suckle at her breast. The ecstasy rising in her frightened her and she struggled to free her hands. "Don't fight me, *mignonne*," his voice murmured against her throat. He put her from him then, and leaned back against the seat, his face inscrutable.

Annette collapsed in a sobbing heap, desperately hauling her garments into place. "You promised I should be safe," she choked when she was able.

"I have only fondled your breasts, *mignonne*. I could have enjoyed you more."

A heavy silence fell. She averted her tear-streaked face from his view. "You will not again?" she asked, conscious of his scrutiny.

"I regret you put me to the trouble, *ma petite*. If you obey in future, I will endeavor not to lay hands on you."

The journey continued for four days and neither Annette nor her captor very much enjoyed it. The one thing commending itself to her was her blessed relief each night to enter her bedchamber alone and turn the key in the lock. Her fluency in the French tongue enabled her to glean an understanding of Napoleon's France and she was appalled. The nation had set itself gleefully on a collision course with disaster, with herself caught up in it, willy-nilly. The only betrayal of uneasiness she permitted herself, however, was the maddening calm with which she greeted each new inconvenience.

They came upon the outskirts of Paris in late afternoon. Proceeding through the narrow streets, they arrived at last before a tall, stone house situated near a marketplace. Annette gazed around curiously as they passed through an iron gate and mounted the steps. They were admitted by the rosy-cheeked housekeeper, a lady of ample size whose face became wreathed in smiles.

"*Bonjour, M. le Comte,*" she beamed, dropping a curtsy.

Annette seemed to sigh. What next? She opened her mouth to speak, saw Madame's eye upon her, and had the wisdom to shut it again.

Ducienne bowed. "Madame Tourell will show you to your room, *mignonne*. I trust it will meet with your approval."

With a start, Annette realized he had addressed her

in French. Questions were burning on her lips, but she had a notion he would fob her off, and didn't ask them. She saw nothing for it but to follow the housekeeper up the stairs.

The bedchamber was a goodly size and situated at the front of the house. Annette crossed to the window and gazed in astonishment at the scene that met her eyes. Stalls set up for the sale of vegetables were enjoying a brisk trade. An altercation between a farmer and his prospective buyer over newly skinned rabbits, their furry paws still in place, drew an immediate and interested audience. It appeared to Annette that each sale was accomplished only after extensive haggling.

"Pardon, mademoiselle," the housekeeper interrupted her reverie. *"Déjeuner est servi."*

"Did Monsieur le Comte request my presence?"

"Mais, oui, mademoiselle."

He was waiting to seat her upon her entrance into the dining room. "Did Madame supply your needs, *mignonne?"*

"Oui, Monsieur le Comte."

His eyebrows rose. "No doubt you will address me as Arnaud in your own good time."

"Why did you not tell me?"

"Being addressed by the title is of course gratifying, though inaccurate at present."

"May I inquire why?"

"You will perhaps call to mind, *mignonne,* that I dislike being interrogated."

She shot him a quick look. Their entire conversation since entering his home had been conducted in French. She did not wonder at this in public, but in the privacy of his own abode? The Comte was leaning back in his chair, toying with his wineglass, his eyes on her in such a way that she looked full into them. His earlier demonstration of his power over her came to mind, and she paled. She felt advised to have a care, and folded her hands in her lap.

He turned in his chair to survey the pullet being offered for his inspection. "I believe not, Monsieur Tourell," he said lazily. "Serve Madame. This, *mignonne,* is one Monsieur Tourell, Madame Tourell's husband, I will inform you."

M. Tourell was unlike any servant Annette had before come across. He turned a stern eye on his master, and said, "Why have you done this thing, Monsieur le Comte? What do you need, now of all times, with a woman in your house?"

"As you doubtless know, Monsieur Tourell, I have been without such a one for no little time." He smiled, his gaze roaming over Annette's face. "She could prove a pleasant diversion, *n'est-ce pas?*"

"Surely you do not intend keeping her, monsieur?" M. Tourell persisted.

"As you so sapiently remark, Monsieur Tourell, I intend keeping her." A hateful smile curled his lips. "I will continue to do so for so long as it pleases me, eh? The question is—I am sure you will agree—do you intend feeding her?"

M. Tourell shrugged his shoulders, the gesture eloquent in its brevity, and moved around the table to place a slice of chicken on Annette's plate. Picking up the decanter, he poured out a glass for her, set the wine down close by the Comte's hand, frowned, and stalked from the room.

The Comte sipped his wine and looked across at Annette's crimson face. "A most instructive interchange, you will agree. Monsieur Tourell may expostulate, yes. But—he does obey. Strive to bear that in mind, *mignonne.*"

Temper and mortification warred within her breast. Temper won. She snapped, "Pray spare me a homily, Monsieur le Comte!"

"I have no intention of lecturing you, *ma petite*. I am past the age of drama." He took a further sip of wine. "Now, what were we discussing? Ah, yes. Obeying. I will instruct you, *mon ange*, to remain within the house."

Annette looked startled. "But where would I go?"

"I have not the least notion, *mignonne*. But you will refrain from journeying there."

"I have meant to ask you, sir. What am I to do all day?"

"I am sorry to disappoint you, but formulating an agenda for virtuous ladies is a thing quite beyond me."

She smiled at that. "How am I to act up to your expectations if I do not know your requirements?"

"My requirements?" His lip seemed to sneer a little. "If you were to contrive to please me, *mignonne*, you would find me generous. The rewards of virtue, eh?"

"I wonder how you reconcile your actions with your God!"

"I haven't one, *ma fille*. I thought you understood that." He rose and crossed to the door. "Perhaps," he said as he passed from the room, "you will restore my faith in yours."

CHAPTER TWENTY-THREE

The days sped past, and still Annette saw very little of the Comte. He seemed to absent himself from about midafternoon until a time of the clock long after she had retired for the night. She spent many hours below stairs in the kitchens with Mme. Tourell, becoming accustomed to being there long before M. Tourell became accustomed to finding her there. It was not many weeks before Annette became disconsolate. The exhilaration of preparing new dishes in anticipation of surprising Drake began to fade as her hopes of being restored to him began to wane. Meeting le Comte in the hall early one afternoon, she found him in excellent spirits, and, thinking the time ripe to once again broach the subject of her ransom, found the courage to speak. He was more than usually urbane, saying that he would shortly set the wheels in motion, but she could not but think his thoughts elsewhere on some private concern of his own.

If the situation was sad, it was soon to become sorrier.

Annette sat at breakfast (she had fallen into the habit of partaking of it at the large table in the kitchen) listening with rapt attention to M. Tourell's rather more than usually graphic description of the doings of the aristocracy. They seemed to Annette to litter Paris with their overwhelming numbers and to keep those of lesser station entertained with antics quite unknown to those whose titles had not sprung from Napoleon's pen.

M. Tourell was saying: "The Chevalier d'Anjou is reputed to have given the Duchesse de la Buchard a white coach with pink cushions. Bah! Has *la petite* before heard such folly?"

"*Non,* monsieur. Pink cushions must assuredly be thought strange. But tell us, monsieur. We are wondering at Monsieur le Duc."

"And well you might, mademoiselle. Monsieur le Duc is reputed to have only remarked on the quality of the fittings. They are of silver, *ma petite.* Monsieur le Duc feels only gold worthy of la Duchesse. A freak, is it not?"

"What will they be at next, I wonder?"

"A duel, *mon ange.* Over a parrot. This is very silly, *n'est-ce pas?* But I say it is so, mademoiselle, *je vous assure.* It seems le Comte de Sereau carried a parrot to Madame Vallier's soiree, to the disgust of le Comte de Poussard. He does not favor the bird, mademoiselle. They carry disease, he claims, but that I leave others to judge."

"It's inconceivable. You shock me, Monsieur Tourell."

"Almost inconceivable, *ma petite.* Possibly they suffer from ennui."

Into this contented domestic scene walked le Comte, the wooden sabots on his stockingless feet clacking on the tiles of the floor. The coat he had donned looked none too clean, and a rend could be seen in the trousers he wore. His audience gaped.

M. Tourell was first to find his tongue. "What new start is this, monsieur?" he asked sardonically.

"We will pass over that," the Comte replied briefly,

and held out a pair of sabots for Annette. "Have the goodness to put these on, *mignonne*."

Annette accepted them gingerly. "Put them on?" she repeated stupidly.

Mme. Tourell's bosom swelled. "*La petite* has tender feet, Monsieur le Comte. What do you intend?"

"Nothing alarming, madame. We are going out."

"You have only just come in." She eyed him with obvious disapproval. "From the look of it, you spent the night in odd company, monsieur."

He looked at her with upraised brows. "I have no intention of telling you how I passed the night, madame. It is better you do not know." He sat down heavily at the table. "I beg you will not weep over this, for it is a contretemps I cannot control. *Mignonne* and I must depart this house. You will assume we will not return, madame, monsieur."

"*Que c'est amusant, Monsieur le Comte*," said Madame.

"*C'est bien drôle*," agreed Monsieur.

"*Mon Dieu*, if that were only so." The Comte passed a hand over weary eyes. "Madame, you will supply *Mignonne* with a scarf and shawl? We leave immediately. You know not where we go, monsieur, or why we go." His eyes were veiled for a moment before he turned the full force of his gaze on M. Tourell. "You will no doubt entertain a visit from— the police. You will undergo extensive questioning, I have no doubt. But you have nothing to fear, monsieur, for you have nothing to disclose." He passed a packet across the table. "Spend this wisely. Be sparing of laying out large sums. You will draw the eyes of the police, should you become careless."

"But the little one, Monsieur le Comte. Her condition—"

"*Oui.* I know, monsieur." He stood. "I think we leave now, *mignonne.*"

They went by hired coach to the Rue Montmartre, descending before the Coq d'Du. To Annette's surprise, they passed along before its door and continued on down the Rue Pasquelle. His hand beneath her elbow steadied her repeated stumbling in the clumsy sabots, though he seemed to have no difficulty with his own. She lost count of the number of times they rode from one area of the city to another, to descend and walk again before boarding another coach, to repeat the process over again. She vaguely realized they were confusing the route of their passing to ensure their safety, but ceased to care. She was too weary.

The street of his choice was exceedingly narrow and enclosed by closely huddled, tumbledown houses. Scarcely a dwelling had its windows intact; panes were cracked, or replaced with a bit of board, or missing entirely, with tattered curtains flapping listlessly against the openings. The air was foul, noisome with the odors of sewage running unhampered in the gutters.

They proceeded down the squalid street to the third house on the right. The door stood open, a circumstance which could not signify. It would scarcely be expected to swing on its sagging hinges, had one tried. Trash lay strewn in the hall and up the stairs, with the smell of boiling cabbage redolent on the air. Annette gagged and gratefully accepted the handkerchief held to her nose by the Comte. "Just a little way now, *mignonne,*" he murmured in her ear. "Only a few more steps," he encouraged, half carrying her upward to the topmost floor.

The room into which he led her was scrupulously clean, if sparsely furnished. Being situated above the surrounding roofs, the air was fresher and no eyes could peer in upon them through open windows. Additional rooms, three bedrooms, in fact, and a kitchen, completed the space. The Comte led Annette across to a chair. "Rest now, *mignonne*," he said gently.

"*Merci, Monsieur le Comte.*"

"No, *mignonne*. Arnaud. I fear it will always be just Arnaud. I have failed, you see."

"Failed?"

"It seems strange," he mused, "the role fate plays in one's life. In yours, *mignonne*, as in mine. One formulates a plan, *n'est-ce pas?* One stakes all, eh, *ma petite?*"

There was no mistaking her perplexity. "I—think I do not follow you, Ar-Arnaud."

He smiled at her first use of his name. "I will explain, *mignonne*. It cannot matter now. I will tell you that, but for the revolution, I would be the Comte de Ducienne. You realize, I am sure, that I would make a push to have my title and estates restored. Bonaparte agreed, with one stipulation: I was to deliver into his hands documents supplied by—I regret, *mignonne*—English traitors." He sighed. "One is often limited by the quality of one's tools."

"Lord Bodkin and Wadding!"

"You are acute, *ma fille*. To make short telling of it, they proved more inept than I would have thought possible. The information they supplied was false."

Her eyes were round. "So you flee for your life!"

"And yours, *mon ange*. Make no mistake about that. We will not deceive each other, *n'est-ce pas?* You will be advised," his smile flashed, "to obey in future. We will strive together to restore you to your husband, eh?"

"Oh, Arnaud!" Annette exclaimed, coming to her feet, her face radiant.

"Sit down!" he said sharply, his eyes never wavering from her face. He seemed to reflect. "I wonder if I am a fool," he murmured, and, turning on his heel, strode to the window, to stand with his back to her.

"Arnaud," Annette began, taking a tentative step toward him.

"Keep your distance," he growled without turning his head. "And speak French!"

She flushed and her eyes reflected her surprise. She made no attempt to speak, but her hands shook slightly as she reseated herself. She stayed still, her eyes on the back of his head, and waited, wishing she could understand his many moods.

"I told you we would not deceive one another, *mignonne*," he finally said, turning to face her. "I have told you a portion of the contretemps that has brought us to this pass. I will now tell you the rest. You may be proud of your husband, *ma petite*. He has suffered much in the service of his flag. I know you well, you see," he added with a rueful smile.

"Why—what do you mean, Arnaud? What has Drake to do with you?" She stared at him, struck. "You don't mean—you cannot mean—"

"He, and others, *mignonne*, sought to effect a capture of those who would betray their country. I would believe they have succeeded in that part of their plans, even though I escaped."

Tears glistened on her lashes. "He begged me to trust him. Yes, I know. You need not say it. I behaved abominably. I have always been headstrong and would not listen."

"As it turned out, it would have been wiser to have told you the truth, but one cannot foresee events. I venture to think that I might have acted differently had I been able to foretell the future."

Her lips tightened. She said with a touch of disdain: "By procuring the service of additional traitors? I think not, sir. Not many Englishmen are so despicable."

"You mistook my meaning." He was silent for a moment. "There is more I must tell you, *mignonne*. My past is not one in which I take pride. My treatment of you only followed my usual pattern." He crossed and sat down facing her. "I could say it was your fault. Beautiful women drive men mad, *n'est-ce pas?*"

"Don't judge others by yourself."

He leaned forward, speaking earnestly. "I have made a promise to myself, Annette."

"I have not given you permission to use my name."

For a breathtaking moment she thought she had gone too far. The silence grew between them as his eyes studied her. "We will be forced to linger here for weeks, *mignonne*. If I know ought of us, we will be more at ease as friends."

In spite of herself, she smiled. "It is a truce between the warring forces, then?"

"Doubtless we should not take Pierre unawares."

She stared, uncomprehending. "Pierre?"

"I think you will find him amusing," he answered placidly. "We will be his guests."

"You have some special reason?"

"Actually, *mignonne*, I have two reasons. It is impossible for you to remain here alone with me. You are of gentle birth. It would not do."

"Pray spare me virtuous posing. For weeks now, you have seen fit to ignore my plight."

"Ignore it? I believe not, *mignonne*."

"Then why have you done nothing about it?"

He shrugged his shoulders, wondering at her innocent outlook. "An appropriate time had not arrived," he offered neutrally. He crossed his legs, and idly swung one foot. "My expectations for returning you to England in the usual way have become dashed, along with my personal expectations. Do not look so worried, *ma fille*. It will not be simple, but we will yet accomplish it. It will just take a trifle longer, I think."

"How much longer?" Annette demanded grimly.

"I do not know, *ma petite*, but doubtless we will prove equal to the task. We will remain here until the hue and cry dies down. Pierre will supply our needs."

"I only hope you know what you are doing."

"Do try to have a little faith, *mon ange*. I was wrong about you, I admit. I am attempting to rectify my mistake."

Annette hated the tears that gathered in her eyes. Unsure of her voice, she kept her gaze resolutely on her hands.

He moved restlessly in his chair. "Your husband will by now have received the terms of your ransom, Annette. He will know that you are safe."

"I wish you will tell me how you can think that."

"It is the custom with an abduction."

She looked doubtfully at him. He seemed perfectly serious. "When did you send Drake word you were holding me for ransom?"

"Immediately we landed in France."

Her eyes widened. "Are you saying you have let me worry all these weeks when you could have eased my apprehensions?"

"I have not been certain all these weeks that I

could let you go. You see, *mignonne*, I would keep you for myself."

The room seemed to spin before her eyes. Unable to bear the sight of him, she shut them. "Please, Arnaud," she said faintly.

He stood and paced the length of the room. "I would keep you, *ma petite ange*, but I find myself putting your wishes before my own. This is a new thing for me, eh?" he added with a touch of bitter humor twisting his lips.

She opened her eyes and blinked at him. "You cannot know what you are saying," she said in disbelief.

"Ah, but I do."

"But you scarcely know me."

"I know you well enough. I told you we share Pierre's rooms for two reasons, *mignonne*. The second has to do with you. I would protect you from myself."

CHAPTER TWENTY-FOUR

The cart lumbered onward through Montluçon and entered upon the road to Brive. Annette moved her shoulders in a vain attempt to ease her back and gazed with uninterested eyes on the landscape. The flat country through which they were passing offered little to relieve the tedium. Distant mountains would perhaps have occasioned remark had they come close enough to see them clearly. The road, however, maintained its stubborn distance, curving always in a sort of blind devotion to the meandering course of a slow-moving stream. Annette withdrew her gaze from the landscape to stare fixedly through the ears of the animal pulling the cart.

At first glance one might write them down as the simple peasant couple they were striving to appear. Their clothing, already deliberately soiled, had been strewn with bits of straw from the bed of the cart, a touch of authenticity Arnaud considered wise. Regardless of her protests, Annette's cheeks and hands were smudged with dirt; she had rather have felt clean and only agreed when he permitted her to wash her hair. The curling locks were confined beneath a scarf, true, but at least (she scornfully told Arnaud) she felt less filthy. The shape of her body she could not disguise. Now seven months gone into her pregnancy, she could not admire the awkwardness of her every movement, though, happily, her face had not a swollen look, and her ankles, which had always been shapely, remained slender.

Arnaud, lounging beside her on the rough plank that was their seat, clicked his tongue at the plodding horse, and resumed his slumberous scrutiny of her face. He only hoped no one looked so closely as he. There was no disguising the intelligence in her eyes or the fine bone formation of her face. Beneath the dirt and grime and shapeless garments, she remained a remarkably beautiful woman.

The rooms they had occupied while Pierre's guests had at time seemed almost too confining. Under ordinary circumstances, the space would have been adequate to their needs, but their stay had become extended to five months. Annette had accepted this with a fair good grace, and though from time to time she became rather discouraged, this was no surprise. As for Arnaud, he remained grateful for Pierre's continued presence. He had been fully aware that his gaze rested broodingly on Annette at times, though he would never actually admit it, even to himself. Pierre had quickly sized up the situation and could be relied upon to remain on hand to deter matters from reaching a pass desired least of all by Arnaud himself. Since Annette never thought of him as other than her abductor, he felt it incumbent on him to act accordingly. But knowing she would soon pass forever from his life, however, he was not above permitting himself delightful indiscretions in his mind.

Arnaud had been surprised by the concerted efforts to ferret out his whereabouts. Only gradually had the police become convinced their efforts to entrap him had been evaded and Pierre could bring word the search had been abandoned. Now on their way to Bordeaux on France's western coast, he planned to purchase Annette's passage home aboard a smuggler's vessel, and owned the francs to carry out his scheme.

The only problem remaining, in all truth, involved restoring her to her husband prior to the birth of her child. Arnaud clicked his tongue yet again at the sorry beast pulling the cart, without results. Their plodding pace failed to increase very noticeably.

"I make no doubt the poor creature will drop in his tracks before the week is out," Annette remarked, interrupting his reverie.

"I do not think he will die within the week, but you are quite correct, *mignonne*. He cannot last much longer."

"I wish you will tell me why you saw fit to set forth with such a beast. He must be more than half dead."

"On the contrary, *ma petite*. A peasant would not likely own a thoroughbred, now would he?"

"No, of course he wouldn't," she admitted, looking so woebegone that he inquired if anything were the matter.

"Well, actually—I really do not think I shall be able to bear much more of this jolting."

He quickly turned to look at her. "Am I to understand that you must rest?"

She nodded. "Perhaps if we could break the journey—"

"I cannot think it wise," he began, but she looked so incapable of proceeding even a few more miles, he relented. "We will see if the next village boasts an inn."

The concierge, however, once they had arrived at his hostel, stood frowning at the rude equipage drawn to a creaking halt before his door. He had spent a trying morning and was in no mood for tomfoolery from the quality. The two who descended to request accommodation did not fool him in the least. His impassive gaze noted the solicitous way in which the man helped his companion to the ground—an action quite out of keeping with the peasant class itself.

Arnaud's glance took in the unencouraging look on the concierge's face. "You need not be concerned, monsieur. I can pay," he said, taking a purse from his pocket.

The concierge bowed, his countenance undergoing an immediate transformation. "If Madame, Monsieur will but come this way. You will wish a room? And perhaps some food, *n'est-ce pas?*"

"Two rooms, *monsieur*."

"Two rooms?" The concierge repeated, looking bewildered.

"*Oui.*" Arnaud turned to the plump, middle-aged woman coming bustling into the hall. "You will take Madame to her room," he said. "She will wish to rest."

The concierge motioned to his wife and stammered, "Will—do you wish—perhaps a bit of fish, monsieur? Or an omelet?"

"An omelet will do nicely. You will serve Madame in her room."

"As you wish, monsieur," said their host, now all obsequiousness and mentally tabulating the number of francs to be garnered from his very odd guests.

Arnaud dismissed him with a slight wave of his hand, a most aristocratic gesture, and strolled into the coffee room. Sitting down, he felt vaguely perturbed by Annette's exhaustion. They hadn't had much sleep these many nights, but stopping in this place for a good meal and rest should enable them to go on in the morning. He felt certain of it after tasting the food soon served him, finding it excellent.

Arnaud looked back over his past with the deepest misgivings. He had thought he held life in his hands, having for acquaintance a set of very good fellows, always ready to uncork a bottle or go seeking a wench to straddle. He had been content, only looking forward to the restoration of his title and estates. How fruitless it all had been. For reasons best known to himself, he found it as ashes in his mouth, and knew it must remain so. For upstairs, and forever beyond his touch, lay resting the one who had become, insensibly, so necessary to his comfort.

The concierge, managing to look worried and aggrieved at one and the same time, materialized at his elbow. "Madame—your wife, monsieur. Will you come along upstairs? Your wife's labor has begun, monsieur."

Arnaud swung around, thunderstruck. "What did you say?" he demanded, looking as if the ceiling had suddenly come crashing down upon his head.

"Your wife, monsieur," the concierge said again, speaking in the long-suffering tones of any innocent bystander caught up in unwanted affairs not his own. "The babe now comes, *n'est-ce pas?*"

"Are you sure?" came Arnaud's desperate reply.

"Indeed, monsieur." The concierge, a large person, regarded the smaller man before him, reproach written in every line of his bearing. "Had you no notion of the bustle going on around you?" An aggrieved note crept into his querulous voice. "Let me tell you, monsieur, I had no idea my house would be turned into a midwife's station when I admitted you to the premises."

"But the babe isn't due for two months!"

"Of a certainty, monsieur, I make no doubt you neglected to inform him of that. My good wife, bless her, says you are to come. The first room on the right, monsieur."

Seeing no help for it, Arnaud threw up his hands in a gesture of despair and went with reluctant step toward the stairs. Looking up—he felt inclined to disbelieve his eyes. Annette stood swaying at the top of the flight, her hands fluttering indecisively, stark terror staring from her eyes. "Arnaud," she sobbed. "Don't leave me. Please don't leave me. I c-can't have my b-baby alone."

"Here now, what does this mean?" exclaimed the concierge's wife, hurrying toward Annette along the upstairs hall, her arms piled high with clean linen. "What are you doing out of bed, madame? You come right along back to your chamber."

"*Mon Dieu,*" breathed Arnaud, taking the steps three at a time. "Don't move," he called as Annette, turning her head at the sound of the midwife's voice, lost her footing and tumbled forward.

Caught up in his arms, only vaguely aware of the crack of her head against the rail of the balustrade, she moaned once, and sank down, down into the dark—

CHAPTER TWENTY-FIVE

She woke slowly, conscious of pain, and of the strangest ringing in her ears. Why am I not at home? she wondered, gazing around in surprise before drifting back to sleep. When she again awoke, she lay for a time with her eyes still closed, feeling extremely weak. She could not recall how she came to be in this place, or even where it was, her memory was so blurred. If my head did not ache so, perhaps I could remember, she thought, and raised it from the pillow.

"Oh, my lady. You are awake at last," a voice spoke from beside the bed.

Her head swam unpleasantly and the room seemed to revolve—she sank back on the pillow and lay still. To move was to court disaster. The figure swam in and out of her vision: an elderly lady, plainly dressed, and looking at her with compassion.

The figure stood and leaned over her. "Drink this, my lady," she said, putting a glass to her lips. "There's a good love."

She tried to turn away, but pain shot through her head, and she cried out, "No, no. I want Papa."

"Come now, my lady. Just a sip."

Who was this person? And where was she? "I want my papa," she insisted.

"Oh, my," a voice spoke from across the room. "Her ladyship's out of her senses, poor dear."

Annette gazed about in mute alarm. Why was everything so strange? she wondered. This room in which she lay—the drapery seemed so fresh; it had been faded a short time ago. And the pattern of the fabric—odd that it had a stripe; she could remember roses. She could not puzzle it out. She was too weary.

She did not sleep well during the next days. She felt feverish at times, at times chilled. Voices vaguely penetrated her dreams, only to fade away again, their words a meaningless jumble of sound. Shadowy figures came and went throughout the days and nights, lacking substance, as insubstantial as memories half forming in her brain. She tossed and turned and cried out in pain, was quieted by a man's deep voice. Papa? She could not know. Any more than she could know whose hand forced liquids down her throat.

But the day came when she woke on a long sigh, and stared about her, realizing the room no longer swam before her eyes, but was, in fact, quite steady. She still felt extremely listless, but, blessedly, the pain had lessened. Her hand went to her by now only dully aching head; it was swathed in cloth. She struggled to raise up, but quickly subsided, suddenly enveloped in stabbing pain.

"You're to lie still, my lady," a vaguely remembered voice spoke from the door as its owner came hurrying into the room. "Your ladyship's feeling ever so much better."

"Who are you?" she asked puzzled.

"Why, I'm Josie, my lady. Now, you just lie still while I call Nurse."

"Nurse?"

"Mrs. Andrews, my grandmother. And a proper dragon she can be too, when her patients won't do as she says. Your ladyship had best do what she wants."

"No, wait," Annette began, but the girl had vanished through the door. *I suppose Papa has been hard-pressed, to engage the services of such a one,* she thought, and wondered where he found the funds to pay her wages. He must have moved us to new lodgings, she mused, and only hoped she would not find other changes so unaccountable as those already encountered.

The middle-aged woman entered the room, saying, "I am Mrs. Andrews, my lady. Everyone calls me Nurse."

Annette had reached the end of her endurance. "I do not in the least understand what is going forth here," she said, "but I have not the slightest intention of permitting it to continue. You will inform my papa I wish to speak to him."

"I am relieved you are feeling better, my lady."

"What did you call me?"

"Why, my lady, of course. You are the Countess of Ardley."

"I do not know what you are talking about. I am Annette Redding. You will inform my father that I am awake."

Nurse looked thunderstruck. "Your father?" she gasped.

Her patient turned deathly white, fear clutching at her heart. Was Papa ill? "Get him!" she ordered, her hands trembling.

Nurse needed no further urging. Nor did her granddaughter. Josie followed her elder from the room with a dispatch clearly indicative of fright.

Their return was heralded by their voices, clearly audible to their patient some little time before they themselves arrived outside her door. "I don't know, my lord," Nurse could be heard to say, "she is talking of being Annette Redding and asking for her father."

"Leave this to me, Mrs. Andrews," a man replied,

his voice vaguely familiar to Annette. "You say the fever has broken?"

"Yes, my lord, it has. She seemed so lucid, at first. Then she began to babble."

Josie's voice intervened, full of importance and excited talk. "She talks so queer, your lordship wouldn't believe. Right out of her head, she sounds."

"Josie!" reprimanded Nurse. "No one asked for your opinion."

"Wait outside, Mrs. Andrews," said the man. "I will call you when I need you." He stood on the threshold, looking toward the bed. "So you're awake," he murmured, and smiled.

Annette stared across at him, unsure, and feeling shy. He looked familiar. But did he? She wasn't sure. There was something; she felt confused, bewildered. "Who are you?" she asked, staring across at him.

His eyes widened. "I'm Drake, my dear. Your husband. May I come in?"

She shrank, terrified. "Dear God!" she moaned. "Where am I?"

"You are at Monkshaven," he answered, himself feeling shaken. "You asked for your father?"

"Where is he?" she asked, waiting for his answer, yet afraid of what he might say.

He crossed the room, to stand looking down at her. "Your father is dead, my dear," he said as gently as he could.

The tears started down her cheeks. Her brain reeled, agonized. Papa dead? Oh, dear God, she thought. What has happened?

"We will talk about it later," he was saying. "For now, just rest. You are much improved, my dear."

"Why does everyone keep putting me off? Why do

you say my father is dead? Please, sir, let me see my papa."

He didn't know what to reply to that. She had had a nasty rap on the head and needed humoring. Accordingly he said, "I am only teasing. He will be home shortly. You should not worry, Annette. He knows that you are better."

"But what has happened?"

"You have a head injury. You will remember, but you must rest. It will all come back to you."

She had much time for reflection during the ensuing days, and no one with whom to share her thoughts, once her fears became abated. The man called Drake appeared for periodic, though brief visits, but of her father she saw no sign. She was told he had been called away on business, or that she had been asleep when he stopped by.

Nurse's words continued to ring in her ears. What had she meant when she called her Lady and said she was the Countess of Ardley? Why, that was absurd. She wanted to shake them all. Though it seemed unlikely that she could forget what had occurred during the last days, that was apparently exactly what she had done. It made her feel very doleful indeed. She thought that she had better set herself to remembering, but having made up her mind to do so, found herself unable to do so. It might be better to say nothing further to these people around her. Those few questions she had put forward had, to say the least, met with but vague replies.

Having determined to keep her thoughts to herself, she found herself confronted by a fresh alarm. Could her mental stability be called in question? She at once perceived that it could. Nurse looked at her at times with questioning eyes, while Josie made no secret of the thoughts she harbored. At the same time, however, they did not venture to voice any doubts. But there was also Drake to be reckoned with, and upon reflection, she decided not to risk his doubting tongue further. Tears stung her eyelids; she blinked them away, casting a quick look at Nurse to see if she had noticed. Relieved to find she hadn't, Annette closed her eyes and thought of Papa.

She had not before considered what all this could mean to him. He loved her dearly—it seemed so long ago—but would he too question her sanity? She could not think that he would. Nor could she for an instant believe he would permit others to do so. But if whispers about her spread over the countryside, could she permit him to disassociate himself from those who looked askance at her? The very notion must be repugnant. Feeling as though drained of all emotion, she drew the covers more tightly to her chin and gave over to the exhaustion rapidly depleting her already lessening strength.

Only gradually during the following days did she become aware that Drake was skillfully asking questions. The prospect chilled her to the marrow, but judging by his heightened interest, she deemed it wiser not to demur. She answered his queries, one or two a day, as candidly as she was able, and tried not to plumb his motives too deeply, not even in the furthest recesses of her mind. She suffered this for some time, and presently became pushed to the limit. She determined to put forward a few questions of her own, only waiting to seize the first opportunity to do so when it arose.

Having progressed to a state of recovery approved by her doctor, a cot had been set up for her before the windows, that she might enjoy the view. She lay reclining upon it, propped up by pillows, and happier than she had been for many days. Her eyes might be a trifle feverish, and her cheeks slightly flushed, but the sun was shining and she felt quite gay.

Drake seated himself in a chair facing her and regarded her steadily. He was no longer smiling. "Now you are recovered sufficiently, shall we talk of our future?" he asked politely.

She looked at him in a startled way. "Our future?"

"I have been thinking of it," he explained carefully. "I have been wondering what is best for us to do."

Her heart jumped at his words. "What has your future to do with me?" she asked with scarcely a tremor.

He reached out his hand and clasped her fingers in his. "I have thought very deeply about this, my dear, and have decided there is only one thing for us to do that is sensible. We must continue on in our marriage as before."

She fairly gaped at him. "Good God!" she gasped, appalled.

A flush rose in his cheeks. "Is the thought so repugnant?"

"I did not mean that," she hastily assured him. "I'm sorry if you thought—"

"Don't apologize. I understand perfectly."

"But you don't. I have been telling you for days— how can I make it clear—"

"You are speaking of your loss of memory."

"It is not a loss of memory. I do not understand what has happened—" She shook her head and took a deep breath. "Drake, will you listen to what I have to say?"

"Have I a choice?" he asked with a touch of humor.

She smiled in response; it occurred to him she was very determined. "It is stupid of me not to have spoken before now," she admitted, and relapsed into profound thought. "It all started when I woke a few days ago," she began, and leaning back, became lost in her tale. On and on throughout the quiet, sun-drenched afternoon she spoke, her voice rising and falling, reflecting the happiness and joy, the pathos and sadness, of her life with her father. She had completely forgotten her life with him. There could be no other explanation, incredible though it was to him, difficult though it was to accept. She remembered nothing at all of being his wife. He became a believer during that long afternoon, chilled to the soul, but a believer nonetheless.

The cessation of her voice found him on his feet, pacing back and forth across the carpet. He had listened without interruption until her voice had died away. Almost without volition he now began to speak, the words flowing from his mouth, rushing to be spoken. But in French, the native tongue of his mother, the second language of his childhood. It was a memorable epic of a speech. Among other things, he consigned fate, graphically and without reservation, to hell, along with most of mankind, the world, and the universe, and wound up this diatribe with a further pungent delivering of the past, present, and future, individually and collectively described, to the devil.

She listened throughout this tirade with an admiring and appreciative understanding of his fluency, tinged with a certain demure regret that she could not have equaled it. A glint of amusement shone in her eyes. "You have left very little out," she remarked placidly.

He swung around to face her, startled. "Did you understand what I said?" he demanded.

"Every word."

"Then I abjectly beg your pardon."

"Please don't. I enjoyed it."

"You should never have listened."

She smiled. "You listened to me, after all."

"It appears we have certain shortcomings in common. I must, however, ask you to forgive me."

"Nonsense," she said matter-of-factly. "It is as well it happened. I've a notion we will deal better together because of it."

"You are full of surprises," he remarked, reseating himself in his chair. "I do not mean to suggest that I doubt your sincerity in what you have told me, but I think you will perhaps wish to hear what I have to say."

"But, of course."

"You have heard of—amnesia?"

Her cheeks became tinged with pink. "You are wrong in what you imply," she said icily.

"May I be presumptuous and beg you to hear me out? I promise not to plague you."

She hesitated, then said with a sigh, "Pray continue."

"Thank you. I will be brief." He leaned forward in his chair and inquired evenly, "What year of our Lord is this?"

She opened her mouth to speak severely, then closed it. "What a stupid creature you must think me," she said, eyeing him disdainfully.

"I think you remarkably courageous, my dear. But the fact remains, you are my wife."

"Don't be silly," she said crushingly.

"My dear, it is 1811. You left your father's home in 1809."

She raised a hand to shade her eyes. "Am I to understand you are back to saying Papa is dead?"

"Your father loved you dearly, but he was taken from you," he said gently. "You have had rather a tragic time of it, I'm afraid. You don't remember, but English traitors captured you and turned you over to a French spy. The ship carrying you to France sailed only hours prior to my arrival on the scene. I nearly went wild, Annette. You, and our child you were carrying, were all in the world I cared about."

The tears were running down her face. "I wish you wouldn't make up such a story."

He rose from his chair and crossed to sit beside her on the cot. Taking her hand in his, he said, "Perhaps we should terminate this conversation until you are feeling stronger."

She searched for her handkerchief, couldn't find it, and accepted the one he pressed into her hand. Wiping her eyes, she said: "I assure you I will not again resort to missish behavior. I don't know why I did. I don't, as a rule."

"Yes, I know you don't. Are you sure you feel up to this?"

"I wish you will continue."

"In the weeks following your disappearance, a virtual army of investigators became involved in the search for you. But France and England are at war, remember."

"I—I suppose if this were true, it would make things difficult."

"Extremely so. But it turned out to be more difficult than any of us could have had any reason to expect.

For it developed that even Napoleon's police were unable to locate Arnaud Ducienne."

Her soft chuckle took him by surprise. "He was a resourceful rogue," she commented almost inaudibly.

He stared at her and decided not to point out this brief glimpse of returning memory. "He must have been," he said, buoyed with returning hope. "He brought you and our son home to me."

She clutched at his hand, her face bleak. "And now you tell me I have a son. You baffle me, sir."

A smile flickered across his face. "I find that hard to believe, my dear."

"To that I can only reply, I admire your finesse."

Laughing, he rose to his feet and crossed to reseat himself in his chair. "I find it not difficult to understand Ducienne. He was bewitched. It could not have been easy, spiriting you and the child out of France. He must have taken deplorable risks."

She stared at him, stung by a sudden thought. "How old is he—the child—if this is true—"

"Three months."

"And you accepted him—"

"Completely, my darling. There can be no doubt. The child is an exact duplicate of me at that age," he added proudly. "Except for the color of his eyes. They are blue, you see. Just like yours, my dear. When you are able to be about, I will show you a portrait painted of me when I was that age, and sitting on my mother's lap. Aunt Agatha unearthed it; God only knows where."

A silence fell. Annette wondered who Aunt Agatha could be, but decided against asking. Conscious of his eyes on her, she averted her face. "And this—Arnaud? What of him?"

"My dearest, I felt only gratitude of the profoundest sort. Life would have been over for me, had I lost you. You can imagine my emotions at having you back. I forgave Ducienne completely."

"You haven't mentioned my injury."

"We had a bit of luck there, Annette. Ducienne told me the concierge of the inn where the boy was born reported him to the authorities shortly after you were up and about. He escaped with you in the nick of time. As it was, a local gendarme at Bordeaux was attempting to arrest him just before your ship was due to sail. In the brawl that followed, you were knocked down a flight of stairs. It was all Ducienne could do to get you aboard the vessel."

"Are you saying a French ship granted us passage knowing we were pursued by the police? Were they smugglers?"

"Ducienne beggared himself, but the ship did sail with the three of you aboard. I assure you financial problems no longer plague Arnaud."

Another silence fell, neither of them seeming inclined to break it. Annette thought of the tale he had just spun, and didn't know what to make of it, or him. Sighing, she cast a frightened glance around, and looked straight into his eyes. "Having heard me out," he said, "can you set some store in the truth of my words?"

"Since you have been so thoughtful, may I ask you to be more thoughtful still?"

"I can safely promise that."

"Then I will once again trespass upon your kindness. I find myself somewhat shaken and would remain a few days more under your roof."

He seemed to pause before saying, "I wouldn't hear of anything else."

"Thank you. I am more than grateful for your hospitality, and I have every intention of assisting your staff in the running of your household. From what I have seen of her, Josie cannot be depended upon to fulfill her duties with any degree of natural desire. She will need to be coached, if not actually pushed."

"She is here for a very brief time. She will depart with her grandmother when you no longer require their services."

"She will be here for as long as I will."

"May I suggest you wait until you are feeling more the thing? We will talk about it then."

She leaned toward him, her face serious. "Won't you see my side of it?" she asked with a hint of unrelenting and (he thought) stubborn pride. "Your generosity is most commendable, but I cannot, and will not, impinge upon it."

"You are certain this is what you wish?"

"Indeed I am. If you will instruct— Oh, dear. I'm much afraid I have not as yet had opportunity for intercourse with Mrs. Williams."

He smiled, secretly elated at her recalling the housekeeper's name. "She is most adaptable, I'm sure. She will follow any instructions you see fit to give her."

"I do not wish you to suppose that I will interfere with your staff in any way. If Mrs. Williams will but arrange to have the sheets and linens delivered to my chamber, I will set about the task of mending them."

He kept his gaze carefully on a ring he wore on his right hand, lest she see the amusement in his eyes. "And when you have exhausted this source of employment?"

"By then I should be away from Monkshaven."

"Am I to understand you prefer to journey about, alone and unprotected, rather than to remain here?

Without wishing to seem rude, I should like to hear your reasons. I am entitled to an explanation, won't you agree?"

"Actually, sir, there are several reasons. Nurse will now need to seek another position, and I could not remain if she were not with me. It would cause a most dreadful scandal."

"No scandal would attach to your being here, my dear. You are my wife, as I have told you many times."

"I find that impossible to believe."

He regarded her closely, all the while twisting the ring he wore. "Won't you give me a true explanation?" he asked quietly.

She seemed fascinated by the lights darting from the ruby turning in his fingers. "The truth is not so strange." She took a deep breath. "Could I remain in the house with a man not my husband?"

"I had wondered if it could be that."

"You are most acute."

"Your standards are admirable, my dear, but in this instance, they are sadly misplaced."

She threw him an incredulous look. "Well, sir, and what if they are not?"

"If you can convince me that I am not your husband, my standards will equal your own. But if you cannot—I mean to have you."

"Pray do not be vulgar."

"I beg your pardon once again, Annette," he said solemnly. "We have reached the point where I find myself compelled to speak. I have determined not to exercise my husbandly rights until you wish it."

She blushed furiously. "You cannot be serious!"

But it appeared he was. He said, "Now that you

know my intentions are honorable, you will forget your notion of leaving?"

Unaccountably, tears stung her eyelids. "Pray don't. I can bear no more. I—I am tired."

He immediately stood and walked to the door. "You should rest now, my dear. You will need your strength to oppose me at every turn."

She found that she was trembling, her nerves quite overpowered, and tried to marshal her thinking into order. She had never fully accepted the explanations so glibly falling from his tongue. How she came to be at Monkshaven, and his assurances that they were married, were things she had not understood, any more than she had fathomed dear Papa's continued absence from the scene. All the pleasure in her improving health was at an end, replaced instead with mortification at finding herself in so compromising a situation. She found to her dismay that tears were pouring down her cheeks, his words rising up to haunt her. For so long as she remained in his home, she would continue subject to his will. And what his will could be she dare not contemplate. She made a despairing gesture with her hand. Knowing the need to escape with a fear born of desperation, she crept quietly to the door.

The light in the corridor was dim and she stayed still until her eyes adjusted to the gloom. Moving silently, she descended the servants' stairs and went through the kitchens to the stableyard, pausing in the lee of a wall. Where to now? It scarcely mattered.

A stable boy gaped, but saddled a horse. "Will his lordship be wantin' the roan?" he asked around a straw protruding from his mouth.

"No, he is ill," she said, quickly improvising. "I shouldn't bother him if I were you."

The sky grew darker as she rode on, with a storm looming on the horizon. She perceived a cottage beyond a rise and momentarily considered seeking shelter. She had no idea whether it was occupied or not, having very little knowledge of the area, and decided not to risk it. The more distance she managed to put between herself and Drake, the safer she would be. Beyond this, she did not permit herself to think.

The blind fright that had seized her in its grip at the outset of her wild flight subsided to mere quivering alarm. She noted that her hands were much more steady, and felt uplifted. Wondering with a kind of detached interest whither she could go with no money about her person, she tried to formulate a plan. It wasn't long before the wisdom of forethought obtruded. She never should have come away without her reticule.

A sudden flash of lightning drew her attention to the angry sky. Black clouds boiled, shaken by thunder and rising wind. She tried to calculate how far she had journeyed, but gave it up, having no idea where she was. Presently rain began to fall, gently at first, and then in torrents, quickly obscuring her vision and soaking her to the skin. She had never been out in a storm before, nor been so conscious of acute discomfort. The afternoon grew much darker, and she lacked the sense of direction to know where to guide her horse. There seemed nothing left for her to do but droop in the saddle and let the animal go where it would.

She heard a shout and sat bolt upright, a scream tearing from her throat. Drake was galloping fast toward her, the huge stallion eating up the ground in long powerful strides. With a kind of numbed horror, she saw the massive bulk of Monkshaven looming up behind him. The mare had carried her back, headed for the stables and the warmth of her stall.

She whirled her horse, her heels digging into its flanks, and sent it crashing blindly through the dark. Sobbing now, the breath gasping in her throat, she clung to the mare's back, and galloped on, exerting no control over the direction of their wild flight. A hedge rose up out of the mist. They soared over it, and thundered on. Her mind, numb, torpid, without thought, failed to warn her to control the horse. The end came swiftly. A hoof unknowing and carelessly placed, a rattle of rock, and the mare came crashing down, sending her soaring over its head, to land in a heap in the wet and mud.

She lay without moving where she had fallen, in the cold and pouring rain.

She moaned once when someone lifted her, and vaguely knew that she was carried, but the veil of blackness closed in, easing her spirit while rendering her senseless.

When she regained consciousness, Drake was seated beside her bed. Her gaze focusing on his face, he rose to bend over her, and raise her fingers to his lips. "You frightened me half to death," he said, smiling tenderly into her eyes.

Her eyes opened wide, staring up at him. "Drake!" she cried joyously, flinging her arms around his neck. "I'm home!"

He understood immediately and gathered her close. "Yes, my darling, you are home. You are truly home at last."

Dell's Delightful
Candlelight Romances

Dell Bestsellers

- [ ] F.I.S.T. by Joe Eszterhas $2.25 (12650-9)
- [ ] ROOTS by Alex Haley $2.75 (17464-3)
- [ ] CLOSE ENCOUNTERS OF THE THIRD KIND
  by Steven Spielberg $1.95 (11433-0)
- [ ] THE TURNING by Justin Scott $1.95 (17472-4)
- [ ] THE CHOIRBOYS by Joseph Wambaugh ... $2.25 (11188-9)
- [ ] WITH A VENGEANCE by Gerald DiPego ... $1.95 (19517-9)
- [ ] THIN AIR by George E. Simpson
  and Neal R. Burger $1.95 (18709-5)
- [ ] BLOOD AND MONEY by Thomas Thompson . $2.50 (10679-6)
- [ ] STAR FIRE by Ingo Swann $1.95 (18219-0)
- [ ] PROUD BLOOD by Joy Carroll $1.95 (11562-0)
- [ ] NOW AND FOREVER by Danielle Steel $1.95 (11743-7)
- [ ] IT DIDN'T START WITH WATERGATE
  by Victor Lasky $2.25 (14400-0)
- [ ] DEATH SQUAD by Herbert Kastle $1.95 (13659-8)
- [ ] DR. FRANK'S NO-AGING DIET
  by Dr. Benjamin S. Frank with Philip Miele .. $1.95 (11908-1)
- [ ] SNOWMAN by Norman Bogner $1.95 (18152-6)
- [ ] RABID by David Anne $1.95 (17460-0)
- [ ] THE SECOND COMING OF LUCAS BROKAW
  by Matthew Braun $1.95 (18091-0)
- [ ] THE HIT TEAM by David B. Tinnin
  with Dag Christensen $1.95 (13644-X)
- [ ] EYES by Felice Picano $1.95 (12427-1)
- [ ] A GOD AGAINST THE GODS
  by Allen Drury $1.95 (12968-0)
- [ ] RETURN TO THEBES by Allen Drury $1.95 (17296-9)
- [ ] THE HITE REPORT by Shere Hite $2.75 (13690-3)
- [ ] THE OTHER SIDE OF MIDNIGHT
  by Sidney Sheldon $1.95 (16067-7)

At your local bookstore or use this handy coupon for ordering:

DELL BOOKS
P.O. BOX 1000, PINEBROOK, N.J. 07058

Please send me the books I have checked above. I am enclosing $_____
(please add 35¢ per copy to cover postage and handling). Send check or money
order—no cash or C.O.D.'s. Please allow up to 8 weeks for shipment.

Mr/Mrs/Miss_____

Address_____

City_____ State/Zip_____

IN 1918 AMERICA FACED AN ENERGY CRISIS

UNCLE SAM NEEDS THAT EXTRA SHOVELFUL

Help Uncle Sam to Win the War
by following these Directions

UNITED STATES FUEL ADMINISTRATION

An icy winter gripped the nation. Frozen harbors blocked the movement of coal. Businesses and factories closed. Homes went without heat. Prices skyrocketed. It was America's first energy crisis now long since forgotten, like the winter of '76-'77 and the oil embargo of '73-'74. Unfortunately, forgetting a crisis doesn't solve the problems that cause it. Today, the country is relying too heavily on foreign oil. That reliance is costing us over $40 billion dollars a year. Unless we conserve, the world will soon run out of oil, if we don't run out of money first. So the crises of the past may be forgotten, but the energy problems of today and tomorrow remain to be solved. The best solution is the simplest: conservation. It's something every American can do.

ENERGY CONSERVATION - IT'S YOUR CHANCE TO SAVE, AMERICA

Department of Energy, Washington, D.C